THE SKINNED MAN

DARREN BRUCE

First published in Great Britain as a softback original in 2022

Copyright © Darren Bruce

The moral right of this author has been asserted.

Design, typesetting and publishing by UK Book Publishing

www.ukbookpublishing.com

ISBN: 978-1-915338-36-5

For my wife and children, who may recognise some of the traits in the main character

THE
SKINNED
MAN

CHAPTER 1

T he woman read the text as it flashed up on her laptop screen, "So we are agreed on a price and killer?"

She swiftly typed her reply, "Yes, agreed. With the Bitcoin directed to the account as instructed."

The text reply in the chat room came back, "Excellent, then the process will begin tomorrow and the private live feed will only be accessible to you. It will start at the point of abduction when you will receive an alert so make sure to be ready. The feed will continue up to the point that the body is deposited and will then conclude. You will be able to access the footage via the encoded file path at any point to watch it again, just remember that any attempt to access the file without the correct code will automatically delete all the data and this is then not recoverable. If you try to access the file from any device other than the one linked via the coded access then again, it will automatically delete the data."

She typed back, "Understood, but I want to make sure that there are enough cameras to capture everything and the sound is good. I don't intend to make this kind of payment for some grainy footage and unintelligible voices."

The answer was curt, "We are a professional organisation, and I can assure you of 4K visual and the highest quality sound. You won't miss a thing."

TUESDAY 27TH OCTOBER

The body was found by a dog walker, out for some exercise in the foggy autumn daybreak. The light mist was rolling in off the sea, and it was only down to the dog not returning when called that the owner wandered down to the shoreline to reclaim the wayward hound. They saw the hand first, almost as if it was reaching to pull the body out of the water. The 999 call to police was breathless with the dog barking incessantly in the background.

The corpse was face down in the shallow surf as the tide was ebbing back out at Glyne Gap near Bexhill-on-Sea in East Sussex. The first uniformed officers to arrive at the scene were young and this was their first experience of death. The recent influx of recruits had meant that the pair had less than twenty months between them and the nearest they had been to seeing a murder was on television. With it being the lead-up to Halloween, they had expected it to be a mannequin or a prank. Even though they were both young in years and service, anyone who lived on the south-east coast, and especially the Hastings area, was familiar with the series of murders in the late 1990s. They had made the town more famous for its deaths than the Norman invasion as the bodies piled up. The local policing area had been called Senlac Division, but the unfortunate translation from the Norman term meaning 'Lake of Blood' resulted in it being changed to remove any link to the spate of killings.

What the police found was a naked male. The face was destroyed, leaving the officers in no doubt that this was not some suicide, and the manner of injury certainly didn't look like a boating accident. Sergeants and other officers soon arrived, and cordons were set to keep the public away and prevent the imminent media arrival from taking pictures. Crime Scene Investigation tents were erected and a steady flow of detectives working up through the ranks arrived one after another while frantic Gold Group meetings were held with the senior officers and the Chief Constable, fully aware of the frenzy the discovery could create with the press. The similarities to twenty years ago were immediately apparent: the location was the same as that of the first victim's body deposition, and the victim was also naked, raising the question of whether the murderer was intent on re-enacting the earlier serial killer.

There was one difference, though: the current victim was a yet-to-be-identified male, not a female.

CHAPTER 2

DS Annie Bryce sat in the mortuary looking at the report she had written to brief the pathologist and awaited the arrival of Tom Martin, the Crime Scene Manager, and one of his team of CSIs.

She was well aware of the pressure this case was already generating and, if she had been in any doubt, the comment from her boss, Detective Chief Inspector Matt Cornish rang loud and clear in her ears: "Do not miss anything and make any fuck-ups." Generally, a Detective Inspector should have been in attendance, but Annie had been covering for her DI, who had been off sick for several months, so had been sent in their absence. In fact, she had far more experience than both her DI and DCI, who had been swift risers through the ranks but lacked the practical knowledge in hands-on detection of major crime. The current fashion for fast-tracked promotion was great, in Annie's opinion, if you wanted someone to sort out finances and budgets. It was severely lacking, though, if they were expected to get a suspect convicted. Neither of her bosses had ever given evidence or been an officer in the case for a trial at Crown Court themselves, but this didn't seem to stop them being put in charge of the Major Investigation Team dealing with murders and kidnaps.

Annie was often referred to as "the safe pair of hands" senior officers deferred to. Years of working in various CID departments dealing with everything from rape to child abuse and murder meant she was well known and respected for her knowledge and investigation abilities. For the last ten years she had worked as the Enquiry Team Leader on the Major Investigation Team, watching a series of other detectives come and go in the ranks above her, occasionally riding on her coat-tails to get to the next rung on the promotional ladder.

Annie Bryce was 52, slim and fit, spending much of her time away from work either in the gym or walking her Labrador. As a female officer, she had always felt she needed to prove herself better than her male colleagues, whether it was when in uniform and being able to chase down larger male offenders, or just being able to outlast everyone else in the yearly physical they were all expected to pass. She took up boxing classes, then Krav Maga, and had passed her qualifications to be a police self-defence instructor just to prove a point to one of the trainers. But there was never any doubt of her abilities as a detective, running countless investigations successfully to court over the years and being respected by both prosecution and defence barristers, along with judges, who recognised her thoroughness and integrity to the point she was rarely challenged on her evidence at trial.

She looked down at the report again. It was a concise summary of the investigation so far, albeit only a few hours old, and gave details of the body, first account from the witness and attending officers and who was in charge of the investigation. Tom would be bringing a disc of images taken at the scene and she would take the pathologist down to the location following the post-mortem. There had been discussion about whether the pathologist wanted to see the body in situ before it was removed to the mortuary, but they had preferred to get on with the post-mortem as soon as possible, citing that little would be gained from a site visit first, and they would be content with the photos provided by the Crime Scene Manager.

The doors to the mortuary swung open as CSM Tom Martin walked in with Terry, one of the Crime Scene Investigators, who was there to take the photos of the examination. Both had their hands full, Terry with his camera equipment slung over one shoulder and carrying a clear bag full of pots and evidence bags. Tom was juggling his laptop and paperwork in his usual chaotic fashion. Despite being an excellent Crime Scene Manager with years in the job, he always gave the impression of a harassed academic about to explode like a party favour.

"Hi Annie, are we late?" Tom asked, grinning and trying to look at his watch while at the same time spilling sheets of paper onto the floor.

"No, you're fine," Annie replied. "Still waiting for Dr Ludstein, as usual. No doubt he will be another half an hour and then say he was stuck on the Dartford bridge."

"I've been hearing the same line for more years than I can remember. Some day he may arrive on time, but I think the shock would kill me and he'd end up with two bodies to examine for a cause of death," Tom joked back.

He sat in front of Annie and started to set up his laptop with the crime scene images as Terry went through into the next room where the post-mortem would be conducted to start arranging his equipment. Tom should really have retired, but couldn't bring himself to go. He still loved the job and his quirky nature made him a favourite of most officers. Thirty-plus years in the job and he prided himself he hadn't had a haircut the whole time, wearing it tied in a long ponytail at the back. He got away with it as a civilian member of police staff and had seen at least ten Chief Constables come and go in his time. Maybe they had just forgotten to pension him off? He was tall with a fast-developing paunch and, as far as Annie could ever recall, his whole wardrobe consisted of black work trousers, white short-sleeved shirts and heavy army surplus boots. Even if she had bumped into Tom socially at some police function, he seemed to be in the same clothes. Maybe he even slept in them? Add to that she had never seen him wear a tie in all her years working with him. His looks, however, belied his abilities.

"This one takes me back a bit," Tom said, looking up from his screen. "Can't believe here we are twenty-one years later, and someone thinks it's a fun idea to play guess whodunnit with Charlie Knights still serving his sentence in prison. He is still inside, isn't he?"

Annie nodded back at him, "Still there."

"Just checking. Wouldn't want him out and about and us being the last to be told he was on day release or something. I mean, they did it with Myra Hindley, didn't they?"

"I think so, Tom, but I can tell you that he's locked up and never coming out. Also, he's about 75 by now. So whoever did this is just following on from what Knights did and copying some of the same details. None of which are exactly difficult to find. I mean, you look him up on the internet and it will tell you everything about the murders, including the deposition sites."

Tom was looking at the images on his laptop, flicking through them. "Well, as long as whoever is responsible this time doesn't go on a spree and we end up with another bunch of bodies spread around the town …"

Their conversation was interrupted as Sally, the mortuary technician, walked in with Dr Jacob Ludstein, the Home Office pathologist.

"Sorry you two. Bloody bridge was a nightmare coming from Essex."

Annie and Tom exchanged a surreptitious smile as Dr Ludstein, or 'Ludders' as he was affectionately known, sat down. He was well into his late sixties and his hands had begun to take on a barely perceptible shake recently, but he was still the most respected pathologist in the country. He was a short, stocky man in his traditional three-piece check suit and tweed tie. He had a ruddy face, walrus moustache and head of unruly white hair. He looked the typical eccentric figure that would appear in dramas on television. Whenever he was called to give his evidence at court, there never seemed to be a challenge to it by a defence counsel. In fairness, to put yourself in the witness box and go against Ludders as an expert was akin to professional suicide. With his reputation, if you lost then that would effectively be career over and nobody would employ you again. Safer to have a professional discussion beforehand and agree whatever points needed addressing than lose a livelihood that took years to attain.

"So, here we go again. Bit late in the year if they wanted to do the whole copycat murder though, isn't it? Didn't they start in the summer with Knights?" Dr Ludstein asked.

"The last girl disappeared at the end of September; she just wasn't found until October," Tom replied. "So, we're in a similar timeframe, if you look at it in one way."

Annie looked at both of them, "This may just be coincidental. All of the girls that Knights killed were lone females that he picked up. This victim is a male, there's a lot of physical damage to the head and face, which is different. The similarity is the location and the way the body was disposed of: naked and at low tide. Saying that, anyone who watches Channel 5 and all their bloody crime shows know that putting a body in water, especially salt water, gets rid of a lot of the trace evidence. With television and the internet, you can pretty much find out all you need to know about how to commit a murder and what we look for."

"Well, I've read the report you kindly emailed to me Annie, so Tom, if I can have a quick look at the scene images then we can get on with the matter at hand," said Dr Ludstein.

CHAPTER 3

The post-mortem room at the Conquest Hospital had recently had a refurbish and was now all pastel shades as opposed to the old, cracked and faded magnolia paint. They had put in fresh air conditioning, which certainly helped with any odours, but had the unfortunate side effect of making it freezing.

"Sorry about the temperature," said Sally as she wheeled in the corpse, which was still inside its sealed body bag. "They can't seem to figure out why it won't go above 16 degrees in here, but just put on an extra scrub top if you're cold."

Sally was as jovial as ever and, that day, was sporting a shock of bright pink hair to go with her ensemble of colourful tattoos. She was nothing if not a stereotypical mortuary technician, and Annie often wondered if one of the prerequisites to get the job was to be as strange as possible. There are not a large number of people, at school, who have 'cutting up bodies and then learning to sew all the bits back together again afterwards' as a job aspiration.

"Classic FM or do you fancy a bit of thrash metal today, Doc?" Sally asked the pathologist as Ludders was finishing gowning up.

"Why don't we split the difference and go with some country music," Ludders replied.

Sally grimaced and went off to set the radio, which came on to play Tammy Wynette singing 'Stand By Your Man'. "That's apt then," Sally laughed. "Terry, do you want to get a picture of the tag seal before I open up the bag?"

Terry ambled over, adjusting his lens and flash. He took a quick snap of the numbered tag before it was snipped off and the green plastic bag holding the body unzipped.

"Are we going to try for any trace?" Dr Ludstein asked. "I mean, we can get the nail clippings and scrapings and try some hair-combing, but with the body having been in the sea there may be very little."

As Ludders helped Sally slide the body onto the mortuary table from the trolley, he paused. "Well that solves the question of nail samples, anyway. They've all been removed," he remarked, looking down at the right hand of the corpse.

Annie and Tom moved in closer to look at the victim's hands as Terry took more photos.

"That's different," remarked Tom as Ludders began to make his preliminary examination of the body from the front.

"So's this," said Ludders, inspecting the underside of the right hand further. "The killer appears to have taken a blowtorch to all of the fingerprints and palm, so you won't be getting any identification that way. Have to take a sample from the psoas muscle and some blood to get some DNA and check against the national database."

"Well let's hope that they're on it," said Annie, "otherwise we have an unidentified victim and suspect. Anything you can tell me from a first look?"

Ludders looked up from the body, "Well, there's no dentition due to the facial damage, so that's another route to ID gone. Minimal bruising or injury to the front of the body with the exception of the face. Once I've detailed these, I'll turn him over and check the back, but it will have to wait until I finish dissection before I can give you a possible cause of death and, even then, it may have to wait until the toxicology and brain come back, which will be at least eight weeks. If only these things were as quick as on the TV shows, we'd all know who he was by teatime and have the suspect arrested and down the pub before the day was out."

With no immediate identification of the victim, the lines of enquiry were going to be difficult. Start looking at missing persons reported in the last twenty-four hours or so, then a week, a month. Were they local or from further afield? *This is not what the boss is going to want to hear*, thought Annie.

The post-mortem continued for the next three hours as Ludders dissected the body, looking for obvious tissue trauma or injury from weapons before he stepped back and asked Sally to close the body for him.

Annie, Tom and Ludders were back in the little mortuary waiting room.

"Cause of death then?" Annie asked hopefully, if a little dejectedly.

"At the moment, unexplained pending further investigation is about all I can say," Ludders replied. "There's no obvious injury from a weapon and no sign of strangulation or asphyxiation as no petechial haemorrhaging and the hyoid bone is intact, although the latter doesn't always break. There's no water evident in the lungs to say the victim drowned, so they must have been placed where they were found after death. The damage to the face is all concentrated around the lower half and appears to have been caused with the intention of damaging the teeth. That, I can say, was conducted post-mortem, and therefore doesn't assist with the cause of death."

He stopped to look at Tom before continuing, "The brain is unremarkable but will need to go off to the neurologist for their opinion. The bloods and histology will need to go for tox, and I would recommend checking for the usual recreational drugs, sedatives, prescription medication, etc. Other than that, I'm afraid all I can say is that the deceased is a white male, small build, probably in his twenties or early thirties but physically fit with no obvious health issues. Other than being dead, obviously."

Tom didn't remark on the last comment but asked, "Any help with how long they've been dead?"

"They had been deposited at the tide's edge as opposed to having been brought in by it," Ludders replied. "There was no damage to the body to indicate that it had been rolled in the surf as it had been carried in, so I would suggest that someone or some people had carried the body down and left it there as the tide went out expecting it to be found before the tide came back in."

"Taking a hell of a risk carrying a naked dead male down to the beach isn't it?" said Tom. "The car park at Glyne Gap is a good few hundred yards away; surely you'd be seen?"

Annie looked at both of them, "Well, even though there was a body discovered there twenty-odd years ago, the council still haven't seen fit to put any CCTV cameras in, so you won't get caught that way. I suppose with the dark and fog they could hope that no one would be around at that time but still …"

"There's not going to be very much to help from the scene, I'm afraid Annie. We've got less than ten hours with the way the tide is coming back in and there's no footprints as the beach was all shingle and pebbles where the body was found. By the time the cordon was extended to cover the car park near the cafe, well, you saw on the first news reports how many looky Lous turned up to try and get a gawp," said Tom.

Annie sighed, "The search team will be going over the area for a fingertip search, but I can't imagine the suspect will have decided to have a fag and then conveniently dump the butt in the scene while he was dropping off the body. Seem a bit too savvy for that, don't they? Best we can hope for is that there were some cars parked there that might have seen something. I mean, it is a known dogging site, so you'd think there would be someone looking out their car windows. I think there's an ANPR camera on the main road as well but if the car used was on false plates then that's a dead end as well. I'm going to be as popular as a fart in a lift when I get back and tell the boss this."

She said her goodbyes as she left for her car parked near the back exit and told Tom she would be in touch later. As she got into her standard police silver Focus, Annie began thinking about the way forward. This was going to be a long-haul investigation if they didn't get a break on the victim's DNA. They had no suspect, no cause of death and no witnesses other than the dog walker who'd found the body. This was not going to sit well with the boss when he had to face the media for the next news bulletin.

CHAPTER 4

nnie stood at the back of the room as DCI Matt Cornish began the press briefing at the MIT office just outside Brighton. The Chief Constable had decided to try to downplay any similarities to the historic killings and deal with the death as a standard murder enquiry in the hope it stayed that way, so her boss had been put in front of the media. It was fairly low-key, with representatives from the local media, a couple of freelancers and the BBC reporter for the south-east. The murder clearly hadn't flagged any of the big networks yet, so he wasn't in for a hard time.

DCI Cornish started speaking, "Good evening and thank you all for coming. I'm going to keep this a concise briefing and then will take a couple of questions after. Richard, who you all know from our corporate comms team, has handed out a written draft of the briefing and this is being run as Operation Oaktree. Earlier this morning, a member of the public walking their dog at Glyne Gap made the sad discovery of a deceased male at low tide. Following a post-mortem conducted this afternoon, we have launched a murder investigation. Currently the identity of the victim is still to be established. We are asking the public to contact us if they were in the area of the beach or car park between 6 p.m. on Monday 26th to 8 a.m. on Tuesday 27th October. We are particularly interested in anyone who may have been in the vicinity in the early hours leading up to daylight. If you have any dashcam or mobile phone footage that you believe may be of assistance to the enquiry then please get in contact on either the numbers that will be on the bottom of the screen, dialling 101 or via the internet on the Major Investigation Police Portal using the operational name. If you wish to remain anonymous then you can also call Crimestoppers on the number provided. Thank you."

"DCI Cornish, James Carter from the *Hastings and St Leonards Observer.* Have you any leads as to the identity of a suspect yet and, secondly, is there a wider danger to the general public?"

Cornish looked composed as he answered, "This investigation is in its early stages, but I want to say that this kind of murder is extremely rare, and the public are to bear that in mind. Take normal precautions as you go about your daily business and if you are concerned at all or feel in danger then ring 999."

There were no further questions and Cornish excused himself, giving Annie a nod to follow him as he left the room heading to his office. She caught up with him in the corridor as they walked.

"Not exactly giving a lot away at the moment are we," she said.

"That's because at the moment we know the square root of fuck all," Cornish replied, "We have no suspect, motive, vehicle, witness, CCTV, victim ID and, unless you want to enlighten me any differently, nothing from the house-to-house of nearby properties either?"

"No boss."

"Well then," he continued, "I suggest we get a move on and find something as I don't intend to go into the next briefing and tell them we're still scratching our asses with nowhere to go. I'll make us a coffee and we can thrash through where we're going for the rest of the week. How many have we got on the team working this?"

Annie shrugged, "Oh, the whole team, boss, all eleven of them currently. With abstractions and leave we're begging cap in hand to Division to let us have some DCs for enquiries. We already have the uniform staff doing the house-to-house and PolSA doing the search of the scene. Trouble is, with what we have at the moment, unless we get a break from the CCTV scoping, then we've got nothing to go on. It's like the body dropped on that beach out of the sky because it definitely didn't get washed in from a boat."

"For fuck's sake Annie, this is a Cat A murder investigation. I've already gone to the Command team and told them we don't have enough staff for this. If this was a Met enquiry they'd have about fifty detectives on it, but just because we're a smaller Force I'm expected to run this investigation as the Senior Investigating Officer with the handful of DCs from our team and some direct-entry detectives likely just out of training school. I've asked top brass for a request to go out to Kent, Surrey and Hampshire for mutual aid and, if we have some budget, to go to private companies for ex-DCs. We cannot run this with what we have. Sorry, that wasn't directed at you, just frustrated," Cornish apologised.

Same old story, Annie thought, police numbers had kept being cut nationwide for the last few years and it was getting harder and harder to convince officers to go down the detective rout. When she had joined CID, it was seen as the glamour side of the job, with plain clothes allowances, beer in the bar after work, and sometimes during. Now, though, it was long hours with minimal staff, too often coming in for a day shift and still being in custody with prisoners and nobody to hand over to at 3 a.m., waiting for the Crown Prosecution Service to give a charging decision, cancelled rest days at a minute's notice, beaten up by the media over perceived figures and failings. No wonder most new officers wanted the relative security of the two earlies, two lates, two nights uniform pattern where you finished mostly on time and handed on to the next team. When you added the extra responsibility of high-profile cases, weeks at court with trials and the constant scrutiny of the media, it was no surprise officers weren't exactly beating a path to get into CID any more.

She looked at Cornish. *Christ, I remember him starting in the job*, she thought, *can't have been much more than ten years ago? Fresh-faced and keen, now look at him.* He can't have been 40 yet, but his bald head shone under the office strip lights. Having this offset with his wispy, blond beard, which he obviously thought of as some form of fashion statement, always looked like he had his head on the wrong way up. The wire-framed glasses and thick chalk-stripe suits he wore daily appeared to be more about trying to look grown-up and taken seriously. He was okay as far as bosses went, though, generally leaving most of the practical investigation side to her and the other DS on the team while he sat and wrote his endless line- of-policy decisions. They must have loved him on the Senior Investigators' Course when he took it; he followed the book to the letter, mainly because he didn't have the experience to fall back on.

After the meeting with Cornish, Annie returned to her office. She shared it with her colleague and friend, DS Tony Ali, who was poring over some statements on another investigation as she entered.

"Evening Annie. See the new job's going well," he smirked without looking up.

Annie could have happily slapped the grin off his face, but just sat down opposite him before picking up a foam stress ball and throwing it at his head. He ducked easily out the way and the ball hit the wall behind him.

"Your aim's getting better but, sadly, so are my reflexes," he laughed before picking up the ball and tossing it back.

Annie grinned back. She had known Tony most of her career and they had always got on well. He was the calm, happy yin to Annie's bad-tempered and grumpy yang, or so everyone else said.

"How is it you always get the jobs where the suspect is either caught committing the crime on a nice, clear CCTV camera or a full confession in interview and I get the ones where there's absolutely nothing?"

Tony took the time to look at her and replied, "It's because of my naturally amazing investigation skills and your shitty luck at picking up the wrong jobs. Can't be helped, must just be my charismatic personality makes people want to confess while they take one look at you and decide they never want to speak again!"

"You know you're not even slightly amusing, don't you?" Annie commented, considering throwing the stapler next as Tony got up from his desk and walked to the kettle to turn it on. A skinny frame and badly receding hairline made him look somewhat comical and it wasn't helped by his permanent smile. "Coffee or tea?" he asked.

Annie had no idea how Tony could drink cups of tea at thirty-minute intervals and not spend half his day going to and from the toilet. He just seemed to absorb the liquid and grazed constantly on his seemingly never-ending packed lunches made by his wife, Thalia. He couldn't be said to burn it all off with nervous energy as he never seemed to move anywhere quick enough. It was a fast metabolism, he often remarked. Annie fully expected to come in one morning and see he'd put on fifty stone overnight when it all suddenly caught up with him.

"I'll have a coffee," she said. "And have you been dicking about with my desk again?"

Tony carried on making the drinks and replied, "Might have. Like to keep you on your toes and see if you notice."

Annie was often thought of as being a bit OCD. In her mind this wasn't the case; it was just that she preferred everything in its proper place and Tony liked to make little adjustments to her desk when she wasn't in the office to wind her up. Generally successfully. "It's not funny Tony," she said as she moved her mug coaster from the left to the right side of her desk. "I just so happen to like things in a certain way, and it gives me one less thing to have to think about."

"Oh yes, of course. Nothing weird at all about having to leave your desk the same way every night with its set-square precision," he laughed as he put her coffee down on the coaster – on the right side. "Makes you the Annie I know and love." he blew her a kiss as he walked away.

She pulled a face at him, and considered throwing something even heavier than the stapler. "Let's tidy up this paperwork and call it quits for tonight. Been a long day and you can treat me to some of Thalia's samosas on the ride home. If there's any left."

Tony had the decency to at least look sheepish as he lifted the lid on the empty lunch box to show Annie she was going to be disappointed. "Been a long day," he shrugged.

CHAPTER 5

As she put the key in the lock to open the front door, Annie could already hear the tip tap of nails on the wood flooring and the expectant whine awaiting her.

"Hey Bella, how's your day been?"

The yellow Labrador answered by bouncing excitedly from foot to foot before dashing off to find some toy from the front room. There was a note on the kitchen table from Kevin, her dog walker, to say he'd been round a couple of times in the day and had fed Bella earlier in the evening. Annie would be lost without Kevin, never knowing when she went to work in the morning what time she'd be back. Bella was her company, and it was only right that she had someone to look after her in the day so she didn't get lonely. Some colleagues had criticised her for getting a dog when she lived alone, saying it wasn't fair, but Bella was well cared for and went everywhere with Annie when she wasn't working. The dog came back with a soggy piece of rag in her mouth and sat down, looking at Annie with large, soulful brown eyes.

"That thing really needs to be replaced," Annie said to the dog as she took the tatty piece of cloth to throw for Bella to chase. "You've had that from a puppy and it smells as bad as your breath."

Annie was happy on her own with Bella. She had never seemed to want a long-term relationship, fearing that another person would just get in the way. The dog reappeared and Annie threw the rag toy once more before heading upstairs. She undid her trousers and dropped them to the floor after kicking off her left shoe. She slid down the sleeve from over the liner on her right leg and breathed her usual sigh of relief as she took off her false lower right leg. She rubbed the stump below the knee with some cream after taking off the pad she used to protect it. *It's like finally getting to scratch an annoying itch*, she thought, *just bliss.*

She had lost the lower part of her leg as a passenger in a car accident when off-duty but had never let the small matter of having one fewer limb hold her back. There had been no question of her not passing every medical and fitness test when she wanted to return to duty. The Force medical advisor had found out her determination when he made an ill-informed comment when he came to assess her. After challenging him to run against her in the bleep test, to which he hastily and politely declined, she had not only gone past the paltry qualification standard but had to be told to stop running when she got to level 14 and showed no signs of quitting, having run all her colleagues and instructors into submission. Most of the people she met would never have even known about her disability, but there were those such as Tony who had occasionally seen her take her leg off and prop it by the side of her desk when it had been a particularly long day. Obviously Tony, being Tony, had once used it as a paper weight when she wasn't looking. He'd got bored in the end when she didn't look up from the files in front of her and he'd had to cough repeatedly to get her attention to show off the joke. She hadn't laughed, even though he thought he was being hilarious. She recalled it was whiteboard marker she'd aimed at his head on that occasion, missing as normal.

Her home was equipped with rails along the walls in all the rooms and in the bathroom to help her move around the house without her prosthetic. She rarely used the crutch she had for support when she took it off.

She used the rails to assist her as she headed downstairs to the kitchen, made a sandwich and coffee, and sat at the table with Bella lying at her feet as she ate it thinking about the unknown male. Maybe this was just a coincidence of location.

WEDNESDAY 28TH OCTOBER

CHAPTER 6

Annie rose early to walk Bella in the dark morning before driving into the office, where she found Tony already on his second cup of tea and eating a sausage roll.

"Morning happiness," he greeted her. "Can't beat a Greggs to get the day off to a good start."

"Not every day though. What does Thalia say about it?"

"You think I tell her? I'll eat the fruit and what can only be described as scrapings from a bird food factory floor after. don't worry. Any update yet?"

"Only that they loaded the victim's DNA profile onto the database and it's come back with no hits. Not exactly helpful, is it?"

"Maybe he's a misper that next of kin just haven't got around to reporting yet."

"Or maybe he's an asylum seeker that came into this country illegally and will never get reported?"

She sat at her desk, putting in the password to log on to her computer. As her emails pinged up, Annie started to think about where they would go with the next press release. They could try a reconstruction of the victim's face but that would only be accurate to a degree with the damage that had been inflicted, and they could end up with a composite image of someone who looked completely different to the male they were trying to identify.

Her phone rang and she answered it on speaker, recognising the number as DCI Cornish.

"Morning boss. Did you get the email regarding the DNA?"

"Yes, and we'll need to start looking at other opportunities for identification." He sounded particularly miserable that morning.

Tony paused halfway through his sausage roll to hold up a note which said "Good Luck in your new job", to which Annie flipped him the middle finger and mouthed "Twat".

"Even with the damage to the victim's face and jaw can we get some kind of image to put out in the media?" Cornish continued. "Although I suppose if it's not accurate it may put the right people off if it looks too different."

Well, maybe he was learning then. "It's better than nothing, and if you're missing a loved one and there's a picture on the news of a person who even looks vaguely similar, then surely you're gonna take the time to at least call in and check, aren't you? If the caller's not related we can still use them to locate nearest family members to get familial DNA and compare it to the victim's," Annie replied.

"Fine, get a digital facial image created that we can release later today. It'll keep the public interest going because we've got nothing else to tell them at the minute," Cornish answered, cutting off the call without any further pleasantries.

"He really is a bit of a dick, isn't he?" Tony said with his mouth full of pastry, and then looked up. "The phone definitely isn't still on speaker, is it?"

"No, he's gone. Must be some briefing with brass that he's got to go to; far more important than talking to the likes of us."

CHAPTER 7

The message appeared in the inbox, "Is there any limit with regards to historical timescales?"

He sent the reply back, "None. You can choose whoever you want at any time in history. Obviously, there can be cost implications with regards to complexity and the obtaining of certain historically factual items and these can also impact on the time it takes to arrange the assignment. Once we are provided with the specifics and a deposit has been paid then a date for completion can be provided. The balance payment is expected prior to the actual assignment being completed."

The inbox flashed again, "Understood. I will send through my request in full and will await your reply as to the cost and means of payment."

He sat looking at the laptop screen. He had no concerns about being traced; there were so many filters and false IP address pathways that it would be virtually impossible to trace back to him. He made sure that he used a fresh laptop for every client and destroyed it immediately after the job had been completed. Those working for him had never met him or even spoken to him in person and he, in turn, had no idea who they were. It was all dealt with by covert messaging from chat room conversations. No person could identify any of the others concerned unless they arranged to do so and the other party agreed. It appeared to be serving them well and the media coverage for the first killing showed the police were already at an impasse with no information to go on whatsoever.

He had considered spreading the latest assignments around the country, recognising that overworked police forces still seldom communicated sufficiently. Even with the national databases, by the time they had researched cases and the information passed back to the relevant department investigating the murder, it would be weeks later and all it would say was a vague link to a previous murder. The only risk he could foresee was if they were to undertake murders that copied those from decades back, then it could clearly not be the same killer. If there were too many copycat murders, eventually some clever officer might pick up on it and make a link, but the likelihood of that was slim. The databases for the research would only go back so far and certainly not pick up on any crimes before the 1950s, so he felt confident to proceed. He looked forward to the proposal, wondering how far back it would be. *Let's keep this in Sussex for now,* he thought, *and see how busy we can make them.*

CHAPTER 8

It was mid-afternoon before Cornish made a personal appearance in Annie's office, striding in through the door and dropping into the chair in front of her desk.

"Progress?" he said without any pleasantries. *Tony's right, he really is a dick*, thought Annie.

"Absolutely none. We still have no ID of the victim, nothing relevant from a national search request on missing person systems, nothing from the house-to-house or any new witnesses coming forwards. We have the ANPR data back for the relevant timeframes you set out but, unless there's a link to go on, all we have are hundreds of vehicles passing the nearest camera which is a mile away on the A259 junction with Harley Shute Road. In the other direction it's this side of the roundabout as you get to Little Common. You can bypass both of those in countless directions to get to the scene, and the chances of our suspect sticking solely to the main coast road to come and deposit the body are remote at best. It's going to be weeks before we get the tox results back from the lab, even if we push it, being a Cat A murder. We need to catch a break somewhere because at the moment we are properly fucked."

Cornish sighed, taking his glasses off and rubbing his eyes. "The chief wants something to give to the media so that we can reassure the public. Not helping me much Annie and I have the media briefing to catch the evening news to go out in an hour."

"What do you want me to say? This isn't going to be a nice, quick, that's-our-suspect-let's-get-him-charged-and-remanded job. This is going to be one for the long haul and hope that it's a one-off. Maybe drug patch-related and they've just decided to dump the body on Rother area," Annie said hopefully.

"What's the next step then?" Cornish asked.

"Familial DNA checks on the victim is going to be our best chance for an ID going forwards, and you know how long that's going to take. We've got to hope that there's a similar pattern on the database to compare to the victim that we can then look at any possible relation, but there could be hundreds to work from or there could be none."

"That kind of work needs a lot of staff and can take months, if not years." Tony had decided to chip in helpfully from behind his desk.

"Thank you for that extremely useful input DS Ali. Maybe you could try and come up with a positive suggestion to help the investigation as opposed to stating the bloody obvious." Cornish muttered without bothering to look round. "Okay, I'll sort out a vague briefing with Tim from the press office and give the usual public advice. We should have some new staff landing from area tomorrow, so make sure they're gainfully employed."

Annie looked directly at Cornish, "What with? At the moment the best we can do is staff up an anniversary stop check in the area for vehicles and pedestrians in the hope of a witness being identified, but that needs to be in the early hours of the morning around the time the body was discovered, and we can only cover the main road and beach area. I'll start looking at it now and see who we can pull in. Think the overtime budget's gonna take a spanking on this for the next couple of weeks at least."

Cornish was already out of his chair and heading for the door before Annie had finished. "Budgets are the least of our problems on this," he said as he continued out.

"Lovely guy isn't he?" said Tony after the boss had gone. "It's almost like he's got no people skills at all. So supportive as well. Why don't you take a couple of days sick and then see how he copes without you telling him what he should be doing?"

"I don't do this job for the likes of our illustrious leader," Annie replied. "Seen too many bosses come and go to their next job to care. Just do our usual and try and connect the dots and hopefully something will drop into place to give us a head start. I'm going to debrief the team from today, which will take about five minutes from what we know, then I'm going to go over everything we have again to make sure nothing's been missed."

Tony got up from his desk and took his jacket from the back of his chair. "I can tell you what you've got now: bugger all. Sorry. Don't be too late here; another happy day tomorrow to look forward to. Luv ya."

Annie looked at her screen as Tony left the office, then picked up her phone and called the intel unit. *Maybe they had some new information*, she thought wishfully.

CHAPTER 9

The young male walked along the road only vaguely aware of his surroundings as the music pumped through his earphones. The streetlights cast an incandescent yellow glow, giving areas of light and shadow as he passed between them. Fairlight Road was deserted at that late hour, but working in the late-night convenience store meant that getting a taxi at 1 a.m. was the equivalent of an hour's pay, so it was worth the thirty-minute walk home instead. He couldn't believe that some jerk had slashed both his bike tyres behind the shop while he was working. If his boss had bothered to fix the CCTV after it went on the fritz the day before, at least he could have seen who'd done it. It was too much effort to push the bike home with it on the rims so he'd just have to walk until he could get into town tomorrow and get some new inner tubes.

He never heard the car approach from behind him or the doors open before the strong hand was clasped over his mouth and he felt a sharp scratch on the side of his neck. Instantly, he began to feel dizzy and weak as he tried to struggle and kick back at the person holding him, but the grip was vice-like, and he quickly felt his head spinning before everything went black.

The car pulled away silently, its electric engine humming softly as it headed past the country park.

***

He awoke slowly, eyes adjusting to the faint light coming from the corner of the room. There was a damp, earthy smell mixed with a pervading acrid stench of vomit. He could see small red lights blinking around him as a figure moved slightly into his field of vision, which he realised was restricted from the sides by some kind of blinkers attached to his head, as you would fit on a horse.

"I apologise for the aroma; you didn't take well to the anaesthetic."

The voice sounded muffled, but he couldn't tell if that was his hearing or if the figure was speaking though a mask or filter. "Can I suggest that you don't try and speak; once we were sure that you weren't going to be sick any more, we took the opportunity to glue your lips together. I find it so much more convenient than worrying about a gag and it ensures that you won't be a biter. I don't like biters."

He could feel the adhesive on his lips, and the pain as he made an attempt to open them to speak meant he quickly stopped. A small murmur was the only sound to emanate from him as he tried to take in what was happening.

The figure moved directly in front of him. They were dressed in dark coveralls which rustled like paper as the figure moved, and he could make out they had on blue latex gloves and a hood covering their head. A medical mask covered most of what he could see of their face and a pair of heavily tinted glasses obscured the rest.

The figure spoke again, "You are here for a specific reason. This is nothing personal. I will not give you any false hopes, however, as your sole purpose now is to die in the fashion requested by the client."

He struggled against the bonds holding his arms flat against the armrests of the chair and panic caused him to try to scream. The searing pain this caused to his mouth was nothing compared with the panic and terror rising from the matter-of-fact comments about his impending death.

"Shall we begin?" the figure calmly spoke as they moved towards him, and he could finally see what they had been holding in his hands.

THURSDAY 29TH OCTOBER

CHAPTER 10

Zoe Ball was chatting to Ed Sheeran about his latest song on the radio as Annie drove from the MIT office across to Hastings police station, where she would be briefing the local officers and meeting DCI Cornish later to conduct a scene visit. Although the scene itself had been stood down the day before, the ebb and flow of the tide having taken anything of use away, Cornish wanted to have a look to 'get the feel' of the place. It was a beach, what more did he want to know?

She kept coming back to the lack of any information, which was unusual. The majority of murders were domestic-related between partners or family members. The number of motiveless, random attacks was tiny in comparison and this latest made it even more so as it showed prior planning to dispose of the body and awareness of forensics. It was apparent to her that the suspect had a good knowledge of the area, and most significantly the deposition site. So, they must have been down and identified that there was no CCTV. Surely that wasn't just a lucky happenstance? They had to have checked it to make sure, nearer the time, nothing had been installed. There was little point running the ANPR for comparisons with the thousands of cars that went along the main road between Eastbourne and Hastings every day and, anyway, she still felt it likely that the suspects hadn't used the coast road. There was a far greater chance of getting pulled over by a bored officer in a patrol car in the early hours hoping for a drink-driver. Did that make the suspect local, or maybe have a previous connection to the area?

There were so many guesses, with nothing firm to go on. She had the intel team checking the family and associates of Charlie Knights to establish any potential links. The information from the prison check yesterday had shown nothing in his recent phone calls, in or out, other than a couple of supervised calls made to the nursing home of his ailing mother. His only sibling had nothing to do with him since the trial and all his post was checked, in and out. The latter was limited to people wanting to interview him for either a book or, the current trend, a podcast, and he refused them all. Even his internet usage showed nothing other than the news and some searches on his own name. Clearly his ego was still alive and kicking, despite his age.

The ring of her mobile phone cutting across the radio nearly made Annie drive into the car that had stopped ahead of her at the roundabout, and she was inches from their bumper as they pulled away. "DS Bryce," she answered sharply. With the number showing as withheld, it was either the office or a call centre wanting to know if she'd had an accident that wasn't her fault.

"Annie, it's Tony. Do you want the bad news or the really fucking bad news that's got Cornish shaking like a shitting dog?"

"Lovely turn of phrase, Tony. I suppose you'll tell me anyway, so go on."

"They've just found a body hanging up on the Fairlight cliffs outside Hastings."

"And? They're always having suicides up there."

"Unlikely this is a suicide. This fella's hanging upside down by his feet and it looks like whoever did it decided to show that they have top knife skills and have cut all the skin off the body. Member of public who found him decided to take a picture and post it on social media before they called it in to us as well. Bet that's gonna get their follower numbers up."

Annie sighed, "Tell me you are kidding me and this is just your idea of a bad joke."

"Sadly not, although I am generally hilarious. We've had images being sent in from all over where people have seen it on social media feeds and reported it in. By all accounts there's been several drones up and around the scene so it may be the press or just nosey Joe public getting some additional pictures. Either way, it's going to be a complete circus up there if you don't pull your finger out. The media office is being swamped and you're to go straight there and meet the local Superintendent, a Jessica Clarke. I'll send you the what3words reference, so you know where to go. Good news, though: I've now been taken off of everything else and am riding over the hills to rescue you. Cornish has been dropped down to deputy and Temporary ACC Livingston is going to be the SIO." Tony laughed, "You know, the bloke you said couldn't find his arse with both hands taped behind his back."

"Fuck my life, the day gets better and better. Okay Tony, I'll see you later if you're coming over here. Give me a call when you land at Hastings and tell me where you've set up."

Annie cut the phone off and heard it instantly beep as she received the message from Tony with the scene location. It would take her about thirty minutes to get there, by which time it would be all over the news. Hastings was about to become a very popular place.

CHAPTER 11

Annie parked her car at the outer cordon rendezvous point and wished she'd put some boots or at least her trainers in the back of the car before she left the office. She hadn't been expecting to go tramping over the hills to see another corpse and her kitten heel patent leather shoes were not going to recover from the mud along the path she had been directed to take. It had been marked out with blue and white police tape to give a common approach path so that any evidence in the surrounding area wasn't disturbed before they conducted the PolSA search. A young female officer stood at the entry to the inner cordon, which had again been marked off with more tape.

"DS Bryce," Annie announced as she approached the officer and pulled out her warrant card on its lanyard from inside her jacket.

"Morning Sarge. I'll just sign you into the scene log and then you can go through. Mr Martin has said that he wants everyone to put on a scene suit, boots and gloves before they enter. He left a pile here."

Annie could see a group of four white-clad figures about fifty feet ahead of her and the body suspended from the lower branches of a tree as she put the Tyvek suit on, pulling up the hood to cover her hair and then slipping on the plastic overshoes. There wasn't much cover on top of the cliffs and she could hear a buzzing in the distance. She looked up into the grey sky and saw a white drone hovering above the group. *I hope that's one of ours and not one of the media's with sound capability*, she thought as she walked to the group, pulling on a pair of blue latex gloves.

They stood in a huddle, concentrating on the body in front of them, so she walked to the end of the group and looked across.

"Ahh, the illustrious DS Bryce. Lovely to see you again so very soon," chuckled Tom Martin, his forensic suit straining heroically across his midriff.

"Don't take this wrong, Tom, but I was sort of hoping it would have been a little bit longer," Annie replied as she looked at the dead male hanging from the tree. The arms were hanging vertically down with the fingers just above the grass as the body swung ever so gently in the slight breeze. All the skin appeared to have been expertly removed, leaving the body looking like an exhibit at a museum. The figure's genitalia hung limply, pointing towards the face, where the eyes stared out, unlidded and blank.

"Have we not got something to at least put a cover over?" Annie asked.

"Afraid not until we cut the poor chap down," Tom said. "As soon as we finish all the 360-degree photography and drone footage then we can look to get the body down and to the morgue. The Conquest will be thrilled to have Home Office post-mortems so close to each other. I've already put a call into Ludders, before you ask, to make sure he can attend for this unfortunate chap. I appreciate that it's completely different circumstances to the one on the beach the other day, but I don't think it's too far a stretch to link the pair, do you?"

Before Annie could answer, a female at the other end of the group spoke, "DS Bryce, I'm Superintendent Clarke, the Area Commander for Rother Division. I appreciate you coming directly here. That's our drone in the air that one of the Technical Support Unit lads is operating from his car outside the cordon. We were waiting to see if Dr Ludstein wanted to come to the scene but he said he'll look at the footage and photos later. As you can imagine, this is not what we wanted with the other murder only a couple of days ago. I gather the Temporary ACC is on his way over here as well?"

"Ma'am?" Annie replied, momentarily confused. "If he is then he'll probably go straight to Hastings nick. I wasn't told that he would be coming here at all."

Jess Clarke shrugged her shoulders and made a veiled attempt to cover a look of contempt, but failed badly. "I do hope you're not relying on Livingston to move this investigation forward, are you?"

Annie was taken aback, "Sorry Ma'am?"

Clarke looked straight at her, "I don't know you Annie, but Tom does, and speaks of you very highly. He also tells me you are the one who's actually going to do the investigation work and advise those above you as to what they should be doing so they don't fuck it up too monumentally. Isn't that correct?"

Annie felt like she was caught in a set of very powerful headlights as all eyes in the group looked at her for a response.

"It's fine," Clarke continued. "You know Tom and his CSI and the other person standing next to you is one of my Detective Inspectors, Ged Lake, who I have known and trusted for many years. Nothing you say in this little clique is going any further. I've had plenty of experience of Mr Livingston and his decision-making. He's only in the Temporary ACC post because he's part of the white, middle-aged, good old boys' club and spending his last year over-promoted to that rank by his mates to get a nice, fat lump sum and boosted pension."

The bitterness dripped from her comments like battery acid as she spoke.

Fantastic, thought Annie, *not only do I now have two Cat A murders to deal with, there's also the small matter of open hatred between the Area Commander and my new SIO.* As far as she was concerned, Clarke was on the button with what she was saying, but it was somewhat surprising to hear the frank comments said not only openly in front of a group, but also to her from someone she'd never met. She decided to try to take a diplomatic stance under the circumstances. It didn't sound like it was just Livingston's promotion that Clarke wasn't happy about, and she'd wait until she could have a word with Tom on the quiet to find out what else there was.

"Notice anything immediately, Annie, other than a dead body in a tree, obviously?" chipped in the CSM.

"Such as?" Annie replied, looking slightly puzzled.

Tom Martin made a theatrical show of sniffing the air as if he was savouring the bouquet of a fine wine.

Annie sniffed and a gust of breeze blew a sharp smell towards her that she hadn't paid any attention to until that point.

"Is that bleach?"

"Excellent, either bleach or similar. I will hazard a guess that the body has been washed down with chemicals to attempt to remove any trace evidence before being brought to the scene. Whoever is responsible is clearly trying to cover all the bases, aren't they?" Tom seemed quite impressed as he spoke, "As soon as we cut him down we'll do some trace recovery here under a forensic tent before we bag the body to go to the morgue for the PM. I'll get the rope fast-tracked to the lab but, from what I've seen so far, I doubt the perpetrator will have been careless enough to have handled it with their bare hands. Worth a try though."

Superintendent Clarke stepped towards Annie, crossing behind the group, "I've called Mrs Millar, the county Coroner, and informed her of this second murder and she's authorised the post-mortem to go ahead as soon as we can arrange it. She's looking at doing the inquest opening for both murders at the beginning of next week and is happy to just have a brief note from the SIO at this time which she will read out on their behalf. Think she understands we're going to be a bit busy to attend the formality of an opening and adjournment."

Annie shivered involuntarily, again wishing she had put some warmer clothes on when she left home. The Tyvek suit didn't give a lot of protection from the elements with just her blouse and trousers underneath. Up until that point, the officer introduced by the Superintendent as DI Lake hadn't even looked in her direction. Under his forensic suit he appeared thickset. His face was fixed on looking at the body hanging in front of him. There was a puckered white scar on the left of his face running from his short-cropped grey hair, across his eyebrow, down his cheek and ending in a fork near the corner of his mouth and chin. Lake looked round just as this point and Annie felt guiltily aware she had been caught staring at the disfigurement.

"You can't see it as long as I stand with you on my right side and don't turn round," Lake said trying to break the brief tension. "Had a disagreement with a bottle a few years ago that some lad thought would be a clever idea to hit someone with. I got my head in the way as he swung, and the next thing half my face was hanging off. Completely ruined my potential modelling career," he joked.

"Sorry, I didn't mean to stare."

Lake had turned to face Annie head-on, and she could see he was good-looking in a rugged, Tom Hardy kind of way. The scar made his face more interesting, if anything. He extended a hand and Annie noticed the tattoo that was showing at the cuff of the forensic suit.

"I gather you've got your own small matter to cope with," Lake said, nodding down to Annie's right leg.

"Has it been mentioned to you before that you're a bit blunt?" she asked stiffly.

"Thought I'd get it out of the way now so that you don't have to wonder if I'm going to ask about it. Same as my face; always feel that it's easier to just bring it up first and then there isn't any awkwardness. Makes no difference to the way I work and neither does yours."

"If you two have finished flirting, can we get on?" Tom asked. "Beth's finished the initial photography and 360, so we can get the body down." He turned to the DI, "Ged, dear, can you get a couple of uniform lads and a stepladder to assist us. I want him lowered down onto a fresh tarpaulin, so they'll need to be gloved, suited, and booted and wearing face masks as well. If you can get someone to nip to B&Q and buy us a wood saw, that would be useful as well."

Lake looked puzzled, "You're not looking to take the tree as well are you, Tom?"

"No, just the branch he's hanging from. We can cut the rope above the knot around the ankles and leave the other part still attached to the branch for now. I want the branch and rope bagged and it can go on a second submission to the lab if we get nothing from the first one we fast-track. I don't want the whole branch but I'll have a look before they go up to cut it to see if there's any indentations on the bark from a ladder or other tool marks. There must have either been two of them to put the rope over and lift the body up or they'll have put the rope over and pulled, which will have left marks from the friction on the bark."

Tom was thinking aloud now, working it over in his mind, "Nope, there had to be at least two of them as they would need one to hold the body in position as they tied the other end off on the branch. It couldn't be done with just one," he pondered.

"What's the chance of one holding the body up as opposed to pulling up on the rope?" Lake asked.

"Two reasons spring to mind. One, I wouldn't want to get face to balls or arse with a skinned corpse to then transfer its DNA all over me, and two, it's far easier to put the rope over the branch and then use that to pull the body up. With the fingers being only just off the ground, it points to that being the far more likely scenario out of the two."

Annie looked at the branch, "Do you think they may have tested it out first to see if it would hold the weight? You wouldn't want to be pulling a body up and then the branch snap and you have to run around with a naked dead body looking for another suitable tree, would you?"

"Good point," Tom acknowledged, seemingly finding her comment amusing. "And even more reason to recover the branch."

Lake stepped away and cupped his hand over his mobile phone as he made a call to the control room. It would have been easier to have used a radio, but most of CID used their phones so frequently that they barely remembered to take their radios from their chargers, let alone out of the station.

Superintendent Clarke moved into the gap next to Annie vacated by Lake, "Two in a couple of days. Is your team going to be able to cope with both investigations?"

"I doubt it. We've got nothing to go on at the minute from the one on Tuesday and still haven't identified the victim. This one," Annie said glancing at the suspended body, "is going to really set the media on fire. The witness who found him stuck pictures on their Snapchat account and they've since been posted on Instagram and dozens of other platforms. As soon as they're taken down, someone else who it's been sent to posts it again. The way he's been skinned and left means we'll have every broadcaster camped out here by tonight."

Clarke's face was drawn tight, "I've been told BBC, Sky and ITV already have their main news correspondents at the back of Hastings nick and are broadcasting live now."

She was taller than Annie and slim to the point of gaunt, the Tyvek suit hanging off her like a white paper sack. Annie couldn't tell if the striking green eyes were natural or enhanced with coloured contacts. What she could see of her face was attractive and olive-toned.

"Ma'am, I don't want to be presumptuous, but is there anything I should know about you and Mr Livingston?" Annie thought it best to get it out of the way when there were limited people around and those that were present Clarke seemed to trust. "He's going to be basing himself over here for the next few days, I'd imagine, so that he can cover the media briefings, and with you being the Area Commander ..."

"Nothing I want to discuss at the moment, but let's just say that he's likely to be less than thrilled to have to be seen working with me."

Annie could guess the most likely reason. She'd been in the job long enough to see many officers have affairs. Long hours spent in the company of a colleague, late nights and it almost became a cliché. Still, she'd never heard any rumours about Livingston, and he seemed happily in a long-term marriage with a couple of teenage kids from what she knew on his Force 'Get to know the Command team' profile. If there was any scandal in his past, it had been well and truly hushed up or he wouldn't be in his current position. It obviously helped that he was an old friend of the Chief. Still, things like that normally leaked. She'd have to wait and see if Clarke wanted to let her know what the animosity was about.

It was another twenty minutes before two uniform officers arrived, one carrying a metal stepladder and some rope and the other had several large sheets of rolled plastic and a new metal wood saw still in its packaging. Both stopped abruptly when they were close enough to see the corpse and the damage inflicted on it.

"Chop chop, haven't got all day. Time to test your lumberjack skills," Tom said jovially.

Neither officer looked that keen to get any closer, so Annie helped Beth lay out the plastic sheet on top of a body bag to catch any debris when the corpse was cut down. The two officers and Lake helped lower the body onto the bag as Tom cut the rope holding it up just above the knot. No sooner was it down than one of the officers rushed over to some bushes and the sound of copious vomiting could be heard from his direction as he bent over. Beth wrapped the plastic sheeting around the body and then zipped up the bag, putting a numbered evidential seal at the end of the zipper when it was closed.

"At least he had the decency to wait and do it out of the inner cordon," Lake said dryly after they had moved the body bag away from the tree. "You okay up there, Tom? Don't fall and break a hip at your age."

"Absolutely fine, thank you Ged." Tom was busy sawing at the branch, having had another piece of sheeting placed underneath. He paused to catch his breath, "I think if we wrap the branch in the plastic and then tape it up and then repeat the process it should be forensically secure."

He had already tied another rope around the branch which he'd looped over a larger branch above it. Beth and Lake were taking the weight at the other end so it could be lowered to the ground instead of just dropping.

"You sure we shouldn't have just got Trumpton up here with some of their kit to cut it down, Tom?" Clarke asked, standing well away from any potential drop zone.

"We don't need a bunch of fire officers in full kit and boots tramping around all over the scene before we've conducted a PolSA search. They'd want half a ton of scaffolding up for health and safety and cut half the sodding tree down."

Tom was still out of breath and Annie wondered if he was going to give himself a coronary. He loved to do everything himself, the more bizarre the better, so the opportunity to take a saw to a branch actually ranked way down on the list of things she knew he'd done previously.

He continued working with the saw and the only warning he was nearly through was when he gave an abrupt "Timbeeeeer" and she saw Beth and Lake suddenly pulled forwards by the unexpected weight. They managed to slowly lower the branch, and Beth took a series of photos of it and rope before she proceeded to package the exhibit up. As she was doing this, two well-dressed Coroner's ambulance staff arrived with a trolley to put the body bag on. Annie recognised one of them as a retired police officer, and he gave her a brief nod as the pair rolled the body away to the black ambulance parked a short distance away near to where she had left her car.

Lake, Clarke and Annie left Tom and Beth to finish up and headed to their respective cars to leave.

CHAPTER 12

He sat back watching the various screens and laptops showing news broadcasts from the different corporations. All covering the body now being referred to as 'The Flayed Man'. He alternated between them, catching their repeated broadcasts on the 24-hour channels every twenty minutes or so with little change. Every channel seemed to have some pseudo-academic or retired cop giving their views and opinions which, he had to assume, were based on pure speculation as the police hadn't released any details publicly yet. What there was, however, was a photo of the body hanging inverted from the branch which had circulated first on social media and was now on the prime-time bulletins. Not the sort of thing that would normally come out from a murder scene but, oh, the wonders of the internet and everybody able to connect at the press of a button. They did have the decency to pixelate much of the body before the watershed.

Every time the channels put the image up it was preceded by the newsreader giving a grave warning to the viewers about the graphic content of the image and to ensure that children were not present. As if they hadn't seen it already! He knew what kids were like; this would have done the rounds amongst groups before being posted on every available app out there. The benefit for him was that it would be known in the right circles who had been responsible, well, if not him personally, then at least his pseudonym. How wonderful for future business. His last client was in raptures about the killing and the media it was now generating. The money they were prepared to pay for such work meant little to him. He would happily dole it out to the people he employed to get the assignments completed, and they were more than happy to take it. He paid exceptionally well, and this engendered a kind of loyalty. He imagined that if the deposits into their hidden accounts were to suddenly dry up then that loyalty may rapidly disappear, but he wasn't worried. There was no way to connect anything back to him; he never met anyone in person and had so many buffers and filters on the dark web that it would take the police years, if ever, to trace anything back to him in person. It was a simple matter of locating the right people for each assignment and for those selected to follow his instructions to the letter.

He planned meticulously, with some of the preparations conducted months before. The actual murders were simple in comparison: select the killer and manner you wanted to see the victim die and, voila!

All live and in high-definition clarity. It was the prep work and the post murder clean-up that took the real effort. When many of the original murders had been conducted, there were no such things as mass CCTV coverage, dashcams, video doorbells and mobile phone cameras to capture their every movement. Even DNA profiling for suspects didn't figure until the early 1980s. Now the slightest touch could transfer cells onto the victim or an object that the scientist could use to not only identify a suspect but show that the chances of the perpetrator being someone else could be as high as one in a billion. For most juries, that evidence alone was enough to convict someone, so you had to be far more careful in how you conducted yourself.

It was the knowledge of what the police were looking for at a scene and what the scientists could do with the evidence to extract data from blood, saliva or even sweat that benefitted in knowing how to combat it. From early DNA identification, when they needed a significant amount of blood to conduct tests on, to now, with modern processes where a DNA profile could be obtained from a droplet of blood, science had made massive advances. This was not only on victims, but also if a suspect was identified and the clothing worn to commit the crime was recovered and examined. Microscopic airborne blood particles, referred to as aerosol spray, invisible to the naked eye, could be found and that would be the end of you. Care and planning, that was the only way. Detectives were also forever quoting Locard's Exchange Principle, that whenever there is contact between two items, there will be an exchange of material, whether it be fibres, hair or microscopic materials such as pollen or soil.

He took off his glasses and placed them on the desk in front of him and absently rubbed the bridge of his nose; one of life's little hardships as a spectacle wearer. He had always struggled with contacts, only being able to wear them for short periods when necessary. There were other rules that he lived by: no pets, for one. He was not going to be linked to a crime or a contact just because Fido had left hairs on his trousers or Tibbles had curled up on top of his jacket for a nap. Petty things, but they could be the difference between his current happy life and spending the rest of it being moved from one Cat A prison to the next. He did not by definition class himself as a serial killer, and neither did the people he used to actually commit the crimes. He never used the same people on another job so, by definition, they could not be serial killers. Obviously if they decided to branch out themselves and carry on then, well, there was little he could do about it, but he was careful with his selections and the large sums of cash that were deposited in their bank accounts would most likely mean that they would be happy to fade into the background and far away from any connection to the crimes.

He never used anybody local to the area, bringing people in from far and wide with no connection to each other. No standard mobile phones were allowed to be used so no links via call or cell site data. All communication was over encrypted satellite phones or via web-based chat rooms which changed regularly. He sometimes felt he should be surprised at the number of people that were out there willing to conduct themselves in the ways he directed. There were even a few who he had found that would have been happy to have paid him for the privilege. Those were the ones to definitely avoid. Choose only those that were in it for the money, not the glory or some need to test themselves against the police. They were the ones apt to get caught as they challenged detectives with clues to gain their fifteen minutes of notoriety. No, he chose only those that did exactly as he instructed without deviating. That was the only way to conduct his business.

He turned up the volume as a psychologist voiced his opinions on Sky News. It was the usual prattle he had heard hundreds of times. The faces and names may change but the rent-a-psych willing to appear on these programmes could have been reading off of the same notes. It was always the suspect was likely to be a white male, mid-twenties to early forties, a loner or having few friends and working in some clerical or computing job. Throw in living with their mother and tortured small animals as a child and you pretty much had the description of every killer given out since criminal profiling had gained popularity with the FBI Behavioural Science Unit in America and gone on to be the subject of dozens of TV shows and documentaries. However, the chances were that, in most cases of serial murder, this description, vague as it was, would cover the suspect if they were identified. Oh, there were always anomalies, but the fact remained that the percentage of serial killers around the world being white and male was well in excess of fifty per cent, so they had a one in two chance of it appearing to be a correct description. They would certainly struggle with him.

As he leant back in the chair, he felt his back crack several times and then stood and walked to the large picture window. The view was spectacular from his apartment and worth the exorbitant monthly rent he paid under an assumed name. There were scant furnishings: just the desk and screens in front of it. No coffee machine, no plates or cutlery. The less that he had the less he could touch. He only had to wipe down a couple of surfaces every time before he left. He could hardly be seen walking in wearing a mask and latex gloves, could he? The clothes he wore were generic, off-the-peg but fashionable enough to not make him stand out to the other residents. Look as if you fit in and that is what people will think. Never enter or leave wearing glasses, minimal but polite conversation to others and be aware of the CCTV camera locations. He had a tried and tested stride pattern he used when he was near the premises and moving around; gait analysis was another identification method that could trip you up – no pun intended.

He walked back to the desk and prepared to leave, picking up and fastening his false stomach and padded pants inserts which gave him a far bulkier frame than his usual proportions. The last items were the wig and eyebrows. These, along with the clothing inserts, he ensured were thoroughly and chemically cleaned after each use and left at another, unconnected location ready for collection when next required.

Be clean and be careful, that was the ethos he lived by.

CHAPTER 13

O n her return to the station, Clarke found that T/ACC Mark Livingston had set himself up in her office, much to her annoyance. She shut the door behind her.

"Morning Jess. Do hope you don't mind sharing. I noticed that you have the conference table in here so we can both work." He was immaculately turned out, and was that the hint of a spray tan?

"Mark," Clarke acknowledged curtly, pulling her loose black hair back and securing it in a tight pony tail. "More than happy for you to share my office, but it would be nice if I could sit behind my own desk. And it's the afternoon now, if you hadn't noticed."

He stood and walked towards her with his right hand extended. Clarke brushed past him and sat down.

"Time flies. It's not going to be a problem me working with you on this, is it? We are both professional officers, after all." He pulled a chair out and sat down at the table, indicating for her to join him.

"Not when there's anyone else around, certainly. But don't expect me to be all sweetness and roses in private; we're a long way from that. How's the wife and kids?"

Livingston was sure the temperature in the room was actually getting icier as she spoke.

"Come on Jess, you knew what you were getting into. I never said that I was ever going to leave Sonia. You didn't seem to be complaining at the time."

"No Mark, what you said was that it wasn't the right time to leave. It was never going to be the right time though, was it? Not with your career going so well and you being so far up the arse of the Chief."

Her voice rose as she spoke, and she tried to control her emotions. "I'm well aware that my career is as good as it's ever going to get all the time Ash is the Chief and he's got your back. You're the only officer I've ever heard of who's gone from Superintendent to a Temp Chief Super and then bounced up again to Acting Chief, especially when there's other people qualified to do the job. They must be a big part of your fan club."

"Look Jess, he asked me to do the job. I wasn't going to start questioning why he wasn't offering it to others, and certainly not turn it down. It's a fantastic opportunity and ..."

"It's going to be a nice lump added to your pension?" she cut in. "Got to pay the mortgage off on that big house of yours somehow, and the cars. I suppose he's also arranged some nice, cushy civvy job for you to come back to as well."

Livingston sighed and put his hands up in the air in an attempt to stem the flow of words being thrown at him, "Okay, okay. Can we just leave this for now and try and focus on the small matter of some skinned male left hanging on the cliffs in your division?" He placed the emphasis on 'your'.

Clarke took a moment to compose herself, "Yes, fine. Thanks for pointing that out, in case I hadn't noticed. What do you know so far?"

Livingston pulled out a small bundle of papers from a manilla folder. "I've read through the current situation report and obviously I had a provisional briefing with the rest of the Command team early this morning from your DI Lake. What did you get from the scene?"

Clarke reached for the conference phone in the middle of the table, "Before we start, we might as well get Ged and Annie in here so we don't waste time repeating the same thing. Tom's still finishing at the site."

She dialled a number, "Ged, is Annie with you?" A pause. "Okay, can you find her and both of you come up to my office in about ten minutes?" She wanted time to make sure she had calmed down and maybe try to diffuse some of the tension in the room before they walked in. Livingston heard a muffled reply as she put the handset back into the phone cradle.

"Will you be going to the PM?" she asked. "Tom said they can't get it arranged until tomorrow morning."

"As the SIO, I wasn't planning to. I thought I'd let Annie go and she can report back to the both of us. I feel it's more important that I'm here so that I can make any immediate decisions as opposed to being out of contact for half the day in the mortuary."

The pompous manner in which he spoke was not helping Clarke's composure, and it didn't come as any surprise to her, knowing full well that the ACC had more than a little issue with dead bodies. He avoided attending a post-mortem when he could send someone in his place, always citing that he was needed elsewhere. She knew for a fact that even when he had no alternative but to attend, he stayed well back in the viewing gallery and not on the mortuary floor with the pathologist, preferring only to get the report after. She was disappointed, though, having hoped to have him out of her hair for most of the following day.

"I'm leaving DCI Cornish to continue with the press briefings for the moment. He can cover that side while I concentrate on the crime itself."

You absolute shit, Clarke thought. So the face the public would associate with the current crimes would be Cornish and not Livingston. Talk about hanging someone out to dry. She was confident, however, that if there was a break in the case or a suspect was arrested, then Livingston would trample all over Cornish to be in front of the media to report it. *The arrogance of the man. What did I ever see in him?*

She looked up from her desk: Livingston had the face of a film star and the patter to match. He was always impressively turned out and she was sure his uniform was tailor-made at the same places he bought his suits. Everything about him, from the expensive leather valise he liked to carry down to his Mont Blanc pen screamed confidence and power. He had literally charmed the pants off her, and she had fallen for every word he'd said. She hated herself for it and wanted to hate him as well, but she was well aware they kept repeating the same cycle of on and off affair. *This time it's different*, she thought. *you've got far more pressing matters to attend to and she had someone who was interested in her; and not just as a bit on the side.* Livingston could save all the fancy talk for his next conquest.

There was a knock on the door, and it swung open without waiting for Clarke to reply.

"All right to come in, Ma'am?" said Annie, acknowledging the ACC with a nod and "Sir" as she entered with Lake.

Clarke waved them both over, "Yes, come in and take a seat both of you. Sir, this is Ged Lake, one of the DIs over here. He conducted the online Teams briefing for you this morning."

Livingston stuck out his hand, which Lake shook before both men sat down at the table, with Annie taking the seat in front of Clarke's desk.

"Yes, thank you Jess. Nice to meet you, Ged, and thanks for the brief earlier." Livingston absent-mindedly smoothed the front of his shirt down.

Lake shrugged his shoulders, "Sorry there wasn't much of it. We hadn't really had a chance to do much from the point that the witness located the body other than put up some cordons and make an initial assessment. We've gone through the current mispers and none of them seem to match on a quick-time review. Same as the other day from the beach, we're fast-tracking the swab that Tom's taken with a traffic bike, who's on his way on a blue light to the lab to try and get a DNA profile and compare to the database."

"What have you got staffing wise?" asked Livingston.

Clarke looked across at the ACC, "I've had Force Planning put out a rant-and-rave text to all Eastern Division officers to ask them to come in on rest day or from leave and they've carried this across to Central as well. I'm going to put the response teams on twelve-hour shifts for the next couple of days so that we can have an overlap of staff to use and take out one whole shift to just work on this latest job. PCSOs have been paired up with detectives from CID to be on foot up on Fairlight Country Park to pick up any potential witnesses. We'll get the mobile pod up there later. They're using the media release at the moment, but we'll need to draw up a proper questionnaire for tomorrow. If we can get a house-to-house coordinator then they can take that side away and concentrate on the one task."

"Agreed. Annie, I asked for DS Ali to come over and lend a hand. Can he pick up on the body from Tuesday and leave you to move this one forward? I take it from a quick chat with DCI Cornish before I left that it's likely to be more protracted enquiries unless something fresh comes in from a witness. This latest has to be the priority. As far as the public's concerned, the male from Glyne Gap could have been a suicide. A skinned body hanging on the country park is likely to cause far more panic. Jess, I need a full breakdown of the staff that's available for the next seven days. We can't be seen to be dropping in staff just because it's the weekend coming up, so I want maximum numbers across the board, understood?"

Annie could see that he was following the Murder Investigation Manual playbook on this. He probably had a laminated sheet of the areas he needed to cover for his main lines of enquiry in that flash bag at his feet.

She was also wondering about the tension when she and Lake had walked into the room. It had been palpable. There was also the interesting dynamic of Clarke referring – correctly as she was in company with other officers – to the ACC as "Sir", but he seemed to have no qualms about calling Clarke by her first name. A little unprofessional, or was he just trying to prove he was the big dog in the room?

A mobile phone began ringing on the desk and Clarke snatched it up, answering it quickly, "Superintendent Clarke, I'm in a meeting at the moment, can you ..." She paused, listening, "Get a couple of detectives round to the address now and make sure they get her phone. Give her one of ours so that we can keep in contact, but I want hers downloaded immediately." She listened again, "I don't care. Tell them to go and buy one on the way there if we haven't got any."

She hung up and looked at the other three in the room, "The control room have just passed on a female who says her boyfriend hasn't been seen since he left work late last night. He normally bikes home to his flat, lives on his own, and was meant to meet her this morning. When he didn't turn up, she called his work and they said that his pushbike was still locked up out the back of the premises with two flat tyres, so he must have walked home after he finished. He lives just past the country park."

CHAPTER 14

By mid-afternoon, the identification of the skinned male was almost narrowed down. Samples had been recovered from his flat after they had forced entry, and were being rushed to the lab to compare against the samples sent earlier in the day by Tom Martin.

The victim's name, if the comparison proved positive, was Jack Piper, a 24-year-old white male who was a life resident in the town, having been born there. His girlfriend, Katie, had given a description of him, along with a photo, to the two detectives who went to see her. The intel room were working up a subject profile and had already identified a Facebook and Instagram account. A pair of officers had been dispatched to his parents, who now lived in nearby Kent, to prepare them for the agony message that would inevitably have to be given, and family liaison officers, often referred to as FLO's, were being allocated to attend later.

Annie looked at the computer screen and flicked through the information that had been sent to her. Not a great deal was known about Piper. He had a community resolution for shoplifting as a juvenile and had been a witness to an assault a couple of years ago, so there was no DNA held for him on the database. Never mind, because they had a toothbrush and comb recovered from his bathroom for a direct comparison and the results were expected by Friday morning at the latest. All the evidence pointed to Piper being the victim: his disappearance for no reason, his height and weight seemed to be similar, and the location where the body was deposited, near his home address.

She mused over the other details. Piper's bicycle, removed from the back of the shop and now being examined by Tom and his team, had been found to have both the front and back tyres cut with a sharp implement. Hardly an accident, and would have meant that Piper had no alternative other than to walk home when he finished his shift. They had the CCTV from inside the premises so knew when he had left. The SIO could set the relevant times around that for his briefing and give the press something to focus on. At least they would be able to give the media a name on this one. They had two murders with no identification of victim or suspect, but if this was proved to be Piper then they at last had a starting point for one of them. She began noting down lines of enquiry to explore: family, associates, phone, work. They could conduct house-to-house along the route Piper would most probably have taken, scope for CCTV, and ask the public for any dashcam footage they may have if they were in the area.

Lake walked in, "Enjoying my office?"

"Thanks for the space and letting me share. Anything else on our victim yet?"

Lake took a seat to the side of the desk. "Well, the girlfriend says he has full sleeves tattooed on each arm, although until we find the skin, that isn't going to help us at all. One of my DCs thinks he's got Piper's dentist and is on his way there now to see if they have any dental X-rays and paperwork from his last visit that can be used to do a comparative analysis with the victim. I've got a forensic odontologist heading over from one of the army bases in Kent. She should be up at the morgue to meet Tom by 5 p.m. and if we have some decent records from Piper's dentist then she says she should be able to give a yes or no pretty much straight away."

Lake had rolled his sleeves up to the elbows and Annie could see an array of grey and black patterns inked onto both forearms. He looked down, following her gaze, "I'd like to say it was down to a misspent youth, but it was more a mid-life crisis."

"I suppose it's cheaper than getting a divorce and buying a sports car," Annie said dryly.

"Actually, you got the divorce part right."

She flushed. "Shit, sorry Ged. Didn't mean to drop a bollock there."

He laughed, the smile creasing the scar on his cheek. "You're fine, but just to make you feel even less comfortable, she left me for a younger model and not the other way round. We always used to go to the same timeshare near Marbella, had it for about ten years. I must have been too concerned with topping up my tan and having a beer to notice that she was so pally with one of the lads who came to do the pool every day. Wonders of Facebook meant they could keep in touch, and then one day she up and announced she was going to Spain to set up home with him. Not a cliché at all, is it? He's all of 27 and she's 42, so I'm sure it's a love that will last forever. She did say it wasn't anything to do with my boat race though, like that made a difference."

He didn't appear overly upset at the situation.

"Well, changing the subject, and to try and make me feel less like I stuck my one good foot in it, if this is Piper, I can't see anything at the minute to indicate that he's linked to drugs or anybody that would want to make him a statement killing. He's not just been plucked off the street though, has he? I mean, look, he had both tyres slashed on his bike; it isn't a coincidence, is it? Someone has done that so he would be on foot going home and be an easier target than if he was cycling. Also, if they'd grabbed him from his bike and then left it there, we would have had a specific point to start from, wouldn't we? This is looking more like a planned abduction and murder."

She answered her mobile as it started ringing, "Yes boss, be right there," she said and cut the call. "ACC wants to see us both up in the Super's office now."

CHAPTER 15

He wondered how long it would take for them to identify the victim? He'd already researched those involved in the investigations; the internet was such a useful source. He had no concerns over ACC Livingston as the senior officer; he was just a figurehead so the Force could show the importance they were placing on the crimes. He had found nothing on Livingston to show he had been involved in any high-profile cases, or in fact any cases at court at all. Cornish was of minor concern currently as well. Now, Bryce on the other hand, was very interesting. It seemed that every case that Sussex had for the past decade had her name stamped all over it on the media releases and press coverage of the trials. She seemed to know what she was doing and would be worth more than his cursory attention. Let's see how quickly she begins to join the dots, he wondered. Will she need a few breadcrumbs to push her off the right track or would he need to take a more proactive approach? He had obtained a copy of her police file as well, detailing a number of interesting facts along with her home address, bank details and phone numbers. Her social media footprint was minimal. This pleased him; she clearly didn't want too much of her personal life out on public display. She lived alone as well. Sad. He hoped she wasn't married to the job. There was so much more to enjoy, and all work and no play would be a waste of such a talent. *We're going to have such fun, you and I, Annie Bryce*, he thought. You look like a lady who likes to be busy, busy, busy. He would make sure that was what she got.

CHAPTER 16

When Annie and Lake entered the Superintendent's office, the ACC, Clarke, DCI Cornish, Tony Ali, and another female who Annie recognised as Zoe Tims, one of the press office team, were all seated round the oval table.

"Sit down. I'd like your input around the media statement that Zoe's prepared. I want to give the briefing to the press as soon as we have a confirmed ID on the latest victim. Matt, have we got the FLO's on their way to his mum and dad?"

"Yes Sir, they should be with them by around 18.00 hours so they can feed in the confirmation, if we get it from Tom at the morgue."

"What's the accuracy of the odontology?" Livingston said, looking at Lake.

"From what she said to me on the phone, Sir, if we have the dental records and any X-rays, then she can be 100 per cent. Pretty confident when I spoke to her. She's used to going out to war zones to do this on bits of bodies, so having one intact is a bit of a novelty."

"Lovely jubbly." remarked Tony.

He looked like he'd slept in his suit for the last week and Annie could see the remains of the last attack he'd made on his lunch box marking his right lapel. It looked like mango chutney, but she thought maybe now wasn't the time to mention it.

Cornish threw Tony a look that could have withered sheet metal, "If DS Ali has finished? Good. I've read through the release Sir and I'm happy with it. Annie, Ged, is there anything you want to add?"

Lake shook his head. Having finished reading the press note, he couldn't see much that would impact the investigation or give their hand away. It was a standard brief with the added details of the victim, passing on the Force's condolences to his family and friends and assuring the public they were working full-time to identify and arrest the persons responsible. Officers would be out on foot on Friday making enquiries and there would be high-visibility patrols in the area for the coming days.

"I'd like to see a part included that we believe it to be a targeted attack, Sir," Annie commented, looking up to the top of the oval where the ACC had seated himself.

Livingston frowned, "Do we want to give that kind of information out at this stage, Annie? I was of the opinion that we should keep the details around the damage to the bike quiet for now. Not wanting to show what we know."

Jesus wept, Annie thought. *And this is the best we've got as an SIO?*

"With respect, Sir," the phrase was generally taken to mean no real respect was meant and the other party knew fuck all, "the suspect knows full well that they slashed the bike tyres. It's too obvious to have just been a random, unrelated incident. They also will know that even basic enquiries, once we have a possible name for the victim, would have taken us to his place of work. We then would have had the bike and put two and two together to make four. Piper wasn't grabbed at random off the street just as he walked past; this was planned. They knew when he'd be leaving and where he'd be walking, meaning they must have had some surveillance on him in the days or weeks leading up to the abduction to know where and when the best time would be. There's no calls in from last night with people worried because they heard a scream or saw a male being dragged into a car or van. That tells me that unless we pick up a witness or CCTV locally on the route, we will have to have to work back to preceding days for any suspicious persons or vehicles in the area. It's no different than the murder from Tuesday, other than we look like we know who the victim is now for this one. By saying that we believe it to be a targeted abduction, then we can show that we are moving forwards to the public and hopefully try and make some connection to a suspect."

The ACC looked around the table for any further comment. None was forthcoming until Lake raised a hand. "Actually Sir, I tend to agree with Annie, taking her perspective. Bit of public reassurance that we don't have people just being plucked off the street. Might even flush out a bit of information. I can tell you now that having spoken to the source unit, there's nothing coming back from any of their usual informants."

"Okay, agreed. Zoe, can you add a line in and just run it by Annie. I think we're all happy with the content of the rest of the brief. Matt, can you come and see me once you've met the press and give me a feel for how it's gone."

Livingston closed his folder as a signal the meeting was over as far as he was concerned.

CHAPTER 17

The confirmation that the flayed victim was Jack Piper came through from Tom at the mortuary by five-thirty and no sooner had the FLOs delivered the news to the parents and let them see the media release, than Cornish was giving the agreed details to the assembled press.

Annie had checked the teams all had work to complete for the night, given them a 10 p.m. stand down and told them to be ready for an 8.30 a.m. briefing on Friday. She was just putting her laptop in her bag with a view to heading back to the office to get some peace and quiet when Superintendent Clarke walked into the office, shutting the door behind her.

"You off home?" she asked quizzically.

"No Ma'am, just back to the MIT office. Don't think there's much else I can organise over here for tonight and I want a bit of headspace on my own to gather my thoughts. Tony's going to be here until the stand down for the night and will call me if anything of relevance comes to light tonight. Was there something you wanted in particular?"

She sat back down.

"Firstly, please call me Jess when there's only the two of us." Clarke put a fresh Costa coffee down on the desk in front of Annie. "Thought we could have a chat over a couple of things before you go, just so that we start on the right foot, so to speak."

"Sure, and thanks for the coffee." Annie was running low on caffeine, and it would help with the drive back to Brighton.

Clarke sat down, unclipped her tie and unfastened her top button. Annie noticed the clear nail polish and small gold stud earrings the Super wore as she sipped her coffee and waited to hear what was coming next.

"I take it that we can speak in confidence?" Clarke raised an eyebrow and waited for Annie to answer.

"Yes Ma'am, sorry, Jess. What's this about?"

"As you may have gathered from earlier, I'm not exactly a fan of our new ACC. We have some history which remains unresolved. It won't get in the way of work as far as I'm concerned and he's far too conscious of his promotion to let it affect him. Saying that, I'm the Area Commander over here and, as such, have a responsibility for the officers and staff and also the members of the public on this division. As far as the investigative side goes, I know I'm only being invited to the briefings out of courtesy, but I would like you to make sure that I'm kept up to date with any matters that become relevant. I don't want my arse handed to me on a plate by a member of the press buttonholing me with details that I haven't been told and left looking stupid on my own patch."

Annie was getting the feeling she was going to be caught in the firing line between Clarke and Livingston and wasn't looking forward to it. She had more than enough to concentrate on.

"I'm not asking you to tell me any details that are confidential and case-sensitive. I've signed a disclosure agreement like everybody else on the job and I just want to be kept fully in the loop. It's been a tough time recently and two Cat A murders on my area within a couple of days of each other mean that the top table are looking at my management of the situation very critically. If this is fucked up in any way, I have no doubt that it will be on my shoulders."

Paranoid as well. This is going splendidly, Annie thought. "I can assure you that you will know all of the information that I can give, but if it is case-sensitive ..." She left the last comment hanging.

"I completely understand, and your position on the enquiry. Did you notice the ACC brought the press officer over with him? Zoe, isn't it?"

And another tick; add jealous to the mix. "I wasn't here when they came over. Maybe just saving cars and time?" Clarke nearly snorted her coffee out of her nose as she tried to stifle a laugh, "C'mon, Annie, you're not that naïve or that good an actor. Did you look at her? Her skirt barely covers her arse and every time she speaks to him, she does that little twizzle thing with her hair. You're meant to be one of our best. If you try and tell me you don't see it then maybe we have the wrong person on the enquiry." The bitterness dripped from every word as Clarke spoke.

"Look, I'm not interested in what other people get up to as long as it doesn't compromise my investigation. And, if I can speak bluntly, if I see the working relationship between you and Livingston becoming an issue then I will be the first one to pull you aside."

Clarke put the coffee down and raised a hand in a placatory manner. "Sorry, I can assure you there won't be a problem. I just wanted to let you know that you have my full support and confidence. I want us to work well together, Annie. The spotlight will be on us all, some more than others."

"Okay Jess, but don't let whatever has gone on in the past side-track from the job in hand. It's not only those at the top that are going to be watching the progress carefully; this job's likely to be played out in the press as well and I don't want there to be any issues to derail it."

Clarke left the office shortly after, as Annie pondered what had been intimated. Office affairs were as standard in the police as they were in every walk of life. The difference being that if it came down to point-scoring, she wasn't prepared to let others' sexual habits get in the way of finding her suspect.

CHAPTER 18

By the time Annie arrived home it was almost midnight, and she was nearly bowled over by Bella as she walked in the door.

"Hi sweetheart. Sorry, been a long day. I'll make sure Kevin gives you an extra-long walk tomorrow and maybe you can go and spend a couple of days at his."

She'd already called him in preparation. The next few days were going to be long and intense, and it would at least make her feel a bit better if she knew Bella wasn't home alone for the whole time. She was used to going to the sitters and some time spent there would mean Annie didn't have the added stress of worrying about leaving her dog with no company.

She walked into the kitchen, flicking on the lights as she went from room to room. Annie kept meaning to get a security light outside her house for when she got home late; the streetlights seeming to be turned off earlier and earlier. She could barely see to get her key into the lock sometimes and had to use the torch on her phone. Kevin normally left a small lamp on in the living room for Bella, but that was no help with the curtains drawn. She had never liked coming home to darkness; it was one of the downsides of living alone for many years. Occasionally she did envy her colleagues who had partners and families waiting for them, but the whole permanent relationship thing had seemed to pass her by. She'd had various partners over the years, but they always ended up wanting to settle down and couldn't understand why she didn't. She had her routine and had never wanted to change it. Work, Bella and the gym, that was pretty much it. She didn't smoke and only drank a glass of red wine or gin and tonic to relax.

She checked the fridge and found little in there to inspire her. She needed to go shopping but that was going to be off the agenda for a few days at least. Oh well, at least there was an M&S at the garage on the way to Hastings; she could pick up some salads and bread there tomorrow, first thing.

Her mobile phone sounded a tone, indicating a WhatsApp message, and she took it from her bag to look and see who it was from at that hour. Just Tony checking that she had actually gone home and wasn't still in the office. He'd taken the job car and gone straight home after finishing.

"Message me that you're home. Not that I don't trust you but share your location as well. Give Bella a pat for me x", she read.

If ever she had a work husband, it was him. "Yes, I'm home and no, I'm not sharing my location like a small child. Have this instead", she answered, sending a picture of Bella sitting looking up at her.

A reply came back instantly. *He must sit on his phone,* she thought, "Put the telly on so that I can see that's not an old photo".

Annie laughed, "FFS Tony, this isn't a ransom request for a kidnap victim. See you tomorrow x".

There was a laughing emoji followed by "I bet you're having toast cos you've got nothing else. I've just had a lovely pie and chips Thalia lovingly left for me. You need looking after. See ya tomoz x".

Annie put her phone on the counter, smiling to herself. Toast? Now there was an idea.

She took a cup of tea and two slices of toast upstairs, with Bella following behind her expectantly. Taking a bite, she sat on the bed and began the process of taking off her trousers and her prosthetic leg before going to the bathroom to wash and moisturise the stump. When she came back into the bedroom, Annie was surprised to still see the toast on the bedside table with Bella sat next to it staring, as if willing it into her mouth.

"Good girl," she said, giving the dog half of the toast as she ate the rest. She stripped off the remainder of her clothes and slid into bed, the sheets and duvet cold on her body. With a nod, Bella jumped up onto the foot of the bed and stretched out, soon to start snoring contentedly as Annie drank the last of her tea.

"Let's see what fresh joy tomorrow brings," she said to the sleeping dog as she flicked off the light.

Neither of them stirred when the figure in dark clothing slid into the house after slipping the lock on the patio doors.

FRIDAY 30TH OCTOBER

CHAPTER 19

Annie came awake slowly. She could hear a faint ringing and vibrating and then realised she'd left her phone in the kitchen before going to bed. She pulled on a towelling dressing gown and made her way downstairs just as the caller rang off. Manoeuvring herself around the house on one leg wasn't a problem; she was well adapted to her disability. The caller ID showed it was Ged Lake, and she rang him back instantly.

"Morning. Am I late for something?" She looked at the digital readout on the oven and saw it displayed 06.25am. No wonder it was still dark outside.

Lake's voice sounded like he'd just woken as well, "No, just a quick heads-up that the DNA has come back and it's a 100 per cent match for Piper, so there's no doubt as to the identity. You had much sleep?"

"About six hours. I was going to be getting up in about ten minutes anyway. I'll head straight over to you, use my own car today, save going into the MIT office. We still briefing at eight-thirty?"

"I haven't had anything to the contrary." He paused, and she could hear him yawning in the background. "Sorry, not really a morning person until I've had a coffee. See you when you get here." The line went dead before Annie said goodbye.

Clearly not one for long meaningful conversations in the morning, she mused before heading back upstairs to take a shower. Bella was still flat out on the foot of the bed. *Oh for the life of a Labrador,* she thought as she dropped the dressing gown onto the floor.

***

He looked at the four cameras on the split screen of the monitor. Good, they all worked, and the sound was clear as well. He figured the battery life was up to four weeks, dependent on live usage. Plenty of time for his purposes. He was glad that he had told the contact to clone her mobile phone as well. It was very helpful that she had left it on the counter and not taken it upstairs with her when she went to bed. He'd noted the stump of her right leg, having seen reports regarding it in her file, and was pleased to see how agile she was even without the prosthetic. He spent no time watching as she came back into the bedroom from the shower with only a towel wrapped around her. He wasn't a voyeur or peeping Tom after all, and turned off the camera to allow her to change in private. The cloned mobile would allow him to listen into all her calls and view any emails or messages that she sent and received, and he was already noting her frequent contacts. Annie eventually appeared on the kitchen camera dressed, and he watched as she made a coffee in a Thermos mug and fed the dog. That had been a surprise to him, and he had been pleased that it hadn't woken or moved from her bed when the contact had been moving around the house in the night. Obviously a heavy sleeper and not a guard dog. Something to note for the future. He continued watching the screens as Annie bent and hugged the Labrador before grabbing her coat and keys and headed out the front door. The camera for the drive also picked up her car, a silver Audi RS3Sport, the index plate reading AY20EXB. I wonder if she will park in the police yard today? Be ever so useful to have a device inside that as well. He could always track her from the phone but wouldn't want her to go astray after all.

CHAPTER 20

Annie managed to eventually find a space and parked on Church Road, walking the few hundred yards to the police station. There were vans with satellite dishes parked all along Bohemia Road, completely ignoring the double yellow markings, but she didn't think the local bosses were going to want to get caught arguing about that in the current climate. There were several reporters wrapped up against the cold giving live reports from the front of the police station and more at the rear entrance to the back yard car park. A PCSO was stationed outside to make sure the camera crews didn't decide to just wander in through the open gates and to ensure they also didn't get run over by any cars leaving on blue lights to attend an emergency.

A microphone was shoved in her face as she walked by. She brushed it away with a polite "No comment" and continued to the rear doors. When she got to Lake's office, he was already sat at his desk on a call and nodded a greeting as she sat down, pointing to the coffee that was on her desk. She mouthed her thanks to him and gratefully took a sip. Black coffee, no sugar; everyone could get that right.

Lake came off the phone. "Morning, thought I'd time it about right. The ACC is already in with the Super and said he'd see us at the briefing. I think Tom's attending in person along with some of the troops, but the rest is going to be via video link. I haven't had any information passed to me that's earth-shattering this morning, so hopefully it'll be a quick run through and update around the main lines of enquiry and then get everyone out and boots on the ground so we can make the most of the day."

Annie looked at her watch, "We've got half an hour. Have you seen Tony? I want to know if there's any progress on the other murder."

"He's using a desk along the corridor in the main CID office. Do you want me to take you down?"

"You're fine," Annie said, getting up. "I'm a detective, reckon I can find him."

Tony was eating what looked like half a large cake when Annie saw him. "Hi," he said through a mouthful of yellow sponge and rainbow-coloured fondant icing. "It was Tara's birthday yesterday and she ended up with two cakes, so I thought I'd help out with one as I missed her party last night."

"Shit, sorry Tony. I completely forgot. There's a card and present sitting at home for her; I'll bring it in tomorrow. How's she feel being a teenager now?"

"On the basis that she spends most of her time either on TikTok or YouTube watching some shite about people being paid to take things out of boxes, I'm not really sure. She's decided to go through a Goth phase, so the Hello Kitty cake I bought maybe wasn't the best choice. Hence why I'm having it for breakfast. Thalia got her one with black icing. Go figure."

He shrugged his shoulders as he took another massive bite of cake.

"Seriously, I don't know where you put it or why you haven't got diabetes. Any movement on the beach body?"

"No movement. It's dead." He noted Annie's look, "Erm, yeah, I'm working on it, but this cake's not helping much." Tony laughed, spitting bits of cake across the desk.

"Disgusting and not amusing. You know what I meant."

He wiped his mouth with the back of his hand, "Still no ID for the vic, no witnesses and no suspect. Brief and to the point. On the basis that your one from yesterday went missing from the night before, I've got the intel scoping through missing person reports from the whole of the south of the country and the Met going back forty-eight hours, so round about last Sunday morning. If we get any possibles then I'll get local units to the reporting persons and see if we can get hairbrushes and toothbrushes, etc. for DNA recovery. Might get lucky. Other than that, we're now scoping back within a five-mile parameter for CCTV. Once that's identified and recovered, it's a long haul to watch it. The DCI wants a relevant time of twenty-four hours prior to the body being located, so this is gonna be a massive ask. We could have hundreds of hours to view, so I'm going to get a CCTV coordinator arranged to cover that and I'll set some parameters about how we want it done."

Annie could already envisage the problems that was going to bring with having to find an area with viewing monitors so a team could work in peace in one location. "How's the incident room taking all this?"

"I spoke to Jenny earlier. She's thrilled as you can imagine, already talking about what the boss wants as parameters and if he wants to set criteria on nominals."

Jenny was the office manager of the HOLMES team based back at the MIT office and her team would be responsible for inputting all the information that came in on both murders. "She said she doesn't have enough receivers or readers with new jobs going to be fully indexed. I said I'd speak to the DCI and he would need to sort it out. With both jobs currently being run as separate crimes, we really need two full HOLMES teams, one on each. They're Cat A jobs, so Cornish will need to get some more staff in from somewhere, or maybe outsource to Red Snapper to get some ex-staff in?"

HOLMES, an acronym of Home Office Large Major Enquiry System, had been essential on major crimes for nearly forty years. The Major Incident Room processed all the statements, reports, CCTV and data that came with a major investigation and allowed for this to be cross-referenced with the hope that small, vital clues weren't overlooked. The problem that came with it, though, was that you needed to feed the beast. If the data didn't go on fast enough then a key witness could be missed for several days and a whole line of enquiry wasted. Annie was always being told by Jenny that she ignored the process and did her own thing. Annie's view was that if the MIR couldn't keep up then that was their problem, not hers. Jenny seemed content to let her carry on as she wanted and managed to work around her, knowing that if Annie had a lead that needed fast-time development, then the information would get into the room one way or another. The pair had a lot of time for each other, and Annie knew the time Jenny put in outside of normal office hours to make sure the MIR kept afloat.

She left Tony to raise his blood sugar to astronomically new levels and headed to the second floor and Clarke's office. She was the last to arrive and the ACC was just confirming who they had online. Livingston was seated at the top of the oval table again with Zoe to his left and the Superintendent to his right. The press officer looked like she had just stepped out of some salon and Annie was conscious that she looked like a scruffy second-hand Ford next to a shiny new Ferrari beside Zoe. *Doubt it's for my benefit*, she thought. Ged Lake was sat on one side with Tom Martin with DCI Cornish opposite. Annie took the seat next to him. A large screen on the wall showed the various people that were connected online, and Annie recognised most of them, including Jenny. She placed her phone in front of her face down after checking it was on silent and waited for the ACC to begin.

"Right, morning all. For any that don't know me, I'm Temporary Assistant Chief Constable Mark Livingston and I am the Senior Investigating Officer. The operational name we'll be working under is Op Magenta, to differentiate from the previous body on Tuesday which is now Op Senna. DCI Matt Cornish will be my deputy SIO and DS Annie Bryce," he indicated across the desk, "will be the enquiry team leader. Any issues then please direct them to her in the first instance. We will be in for some long days over the weekend and into next week but that's essential to progress this investigation as quickly as possible. The national media are watching us very closely and we need to provide public reassurance by identifying and arresting those responsible."

Jesus, Annie thought, *is he reading this from page one of the SIO handbook?*

Livingston continued, giving an overview of the enquiry to date and details around the victim that were known. According to family and friends, Jack Piper had no money or drug problems, nor owed money to any of Hastings less salubrious individuals. At present, there was no reason why he had been abducted and murdered in such a high-profile manner and, as such, that was where the enquiry needed to be progressed. It was clear to Livingston that Piper had been selected and targeted, but they had to find out why and by whom. Annie would set the teams of DCs to follow up any relevant information that came from the house-to-house coordinators' teams or called into the MIR. He discussed the scoping and collection of CCTV with the Technical Support Unit manager before handing over to the CSM to give an update on the forensics.

Tom Martin was as ebullient and effusive as ever. "Hello all. Well, if you want to see the photos of the body in situ, they're on the CSI web pages. I've got Dr Ludstein attending the mortuary at the Conquest this afternoon at four for the PM but, other than that, it'll be a few days on the lab submissions to see if they have any DNA residue they recover which is different to our victim. Will you be coming to the PM boss?" he asked, pointedly looking at the ACC.

"Unfortunately not Tom; I have a press conference around five so I'll get either Matt or Annie to attend in my absence and then we can have a debrief later this evening?"

There's about as much chance of Cornish attending as me shaking hands with a ghost, thought Annie, knowing where she would be heading later.

There was some further discussion around call data for the victim's phone, as they hadn't located the actual device. That was probably in the same place as his clothing and skin. Annie hoped this had been dumped somewhere by the offenders, but they seemed to have been too careful so far to do anything remotely sloppy such as just hiding the clothes and phone in a bag and chucking it in the woods. Livingston wrapped up the meeting online and then asked those around the table to stay for a management discussion to go over his priorities for the day which, to Annie, seemed to be him sitting in an office with young Zoe and waiting for his next appearance in front of the cameras while everybody else ran around doing all the work.

***

The benefits of modern technology. To be able to sit miles away from a room and listen in to all the conversation just by opening the microphone on Annie's cloned phone. So, they had nothing other than the victim's identity, which was good and showed that those he directed had been following instructions. He had no worries with this Livingston running the investigation. From the interviews the ACC had undertaken the day before, he was confident that he would be leading from behind a desk. The way Cornish had quickly distanced himself from attending the post-mortem had interested him though. A bit squeamish, perhaps? Might be something to work with there. Well at least if Annie went then he could have a front-row seat to hear what the pathologist said and also if there had been anything left on the body to help them. He thought he would maybe give them the weekend to think it had calmed down a bit before he arranged the next murder. His clients were queueing up now having seen all of the news coverage, and he could pick and choose who to select next. It was time to really set the cat amongst the pigeons. The press will be thrilled.

CHAPTER 21

"Déjà vu, Detective Sergeant," quipped Dr Ludstein when he entered the mortuary. "Seems like only yesterday that we were here."

I'm so glad you find this amusing, thought Annie while maintaining a smile for the pleasantries. The thing about Home Office pathologists was they went from hospital to hospital, body to body, and then onto the next one. They rarely, if ever, met the families of the bereaved and, other than at the post-mortem, didn't often have a face-to-face with any of those involved in the investigation until the time of the trial. Even then, it was normally only in passing as they went in and out of court. They may have some phone conversations with the Crime Scene Manager, lead investigator and the barristers for the prosecution and defence. In the main, though, their role was to provide a cause of death, give an opinion on how it had occurred, and provide a report with all the details. They were seen as independent for the purpose of the crown court and to give an expert opinion. As a Home Office pathologist, they would conduct the initial PM for the police. This would then be passed to Her Majesty's Coroner for the area, and they would decide whether they would allow the defence team to conduct a second post-mortem using their own experts. This second PM used to be a regular occurrence, but sympathies for the victims' families around burial had changed processes in recent years so that now, unless the defence could give a substantive reason why they wanted one conducted, it would be denied. Generally, a tabletop exercise would be undertaken by the pathologist engaged by the defence, who would use the photos taken during the examination, with any other reasonable requests for such things as crime scene photos also considered.

It was the same personnel at the afternoon PM as a couple of days prior and, once the briefing had been given, it was straight to work. Tom had set up for the forensic exhibits on the bench beside the autopsy table and, once the body had been removed from the sealed bag and Sally had selected the music for the afternoon – 80s pop today – Dr Ludstein began.

"Well, at least I won't take so long as they've kindly already removed all of the skin for me. Very professionally too, by the looks of it."

He was poring over the body of Jack Piper as it lay on its back. "I would say that there is certainly a competent level of either medical training or very skilful butchery in evidence here. Look," he said as he pointed to the sternum of the victim, "you can see where a large, sharp scalpel has been used to make the Y incision, much as I would normally do."

Annie and Tom were either side of Dr Ludstein. He moved across to take up the right hand, "This, however, is much less precise. There is deep tissue bruising around the wrists which I would say was pre-mortem due to the damage indicating the victim was struggling against restraints at some point."

"Well, his hands weren't tied when we found him, so that makes sense that it happened when he was alive. Doubtful that he would have had them free when they were ripping his skin off," remarked Tom, smiling broadly. Terry, who was the attending CSI again, moved in to take a series of photos under the pathologist's instructions, using a scale measure.

"There are no fibres embedded. I would imagine they are still on the epidermis, wherever that is. The bruising has gone deeply into the dermis but whatever he was restrained with was very tight. I would not imagine he would have been able to move at all."

He lifted the right hand to look at the wrist underneath. "You can see here is a different pattern of bruising which suggests that the arm was secured onto a narrow, padded surface, perhaps the arm of a chair. There is also some significant tissue damage back towards the elbow under the forearm. This assists with the hypothesis as it indicates the victim was trying to lift their arm and straining against a flat surface."

Annie could see the areas he was talking about. This had to have been undertaken inside somewhere and, wherever that was, there had to be some evidence to help.

Dr Ludstein was still talking, "This is very interesting. I would say by the way that the skin has been removed it would have been taken first from the joint of the wrist down, removing it off of the hand like you would a glove, hence the term degloving, when the skin is pulled away from the fingers or such in an accident. Additionally, by the difference in the precision of the scalpel marks here as opposed to the main dissection on the chest, I would propose the victim was alive and conscious when it happened.

"What?" Annie was shaken from her reverie. "They skinned his hand while he was awake?"

Dr Ludstein gave her a curt look, "My dear Annie, that's exactly what I'm saying."

Tom had leant in closer to get a better look at the hand, "Well that's a new one. I'd imagine this was a torture or retribution then. Maybe they wanted some information from him? I mean, if they wanted to send a message out to others and put the frighteners out there surely there would be some reason for it, and from what Annie's said so far, he's got no links to any criminality that we know of."

Dr Ludstein had moved across to the left hand, "This one shows the same hallmarks as the right." He continued down the body to the feet. "And here. It appears that whoever was responsible removed the skin from both hands and feet in a similar manner."

"Could a person remain conscious for all of that?" asked Annie, a little incredulously. She couldn't imagine the pain Piper must have gone through.

Dr Ludstein paused and stepped back. "I would expect that a person, dependent on their level of pain threshold, would lapse in and out of consciousness. Once the pain levels became too intense, they may well black out for a period, only to come around in extreme agony. Depending on your perpetrators here, they may have continued while the poor victim was unconscious, or they may have wanted to wait to inflict fresh pain when they are awake again."

"And at what point would they die?" asked Tom.

"Oh, not from these wounds, I'm afraid to say for this young man. There would not be extensive blood loss and a person could very much survive, albeit they would require extensive skin grafts. No, I'd say that it was when the skin was removed from the head that they would have died from the trauma, probably from heart failure, but that may be more evident when I open the body and examine the internal organs. Whatever, it would be an excruciating death up to that point."

He moved up to examine the head, looking closely around the mouth and jaw to begin with. "That is odd. I can't see any deep tissue damage around the mouth area?"

Annie waited, "And?"

"It says to me that he wasn't gagged at all. Ergo, he would have been screaming his head off the whole time this was going on. I would estimate very, very loudly, too." Dr Ludstein stepped back to look at Annie, "Wherever this was done had to have been somewhere out of the way or incredibly well soundproofed, or you would have had people calling in from all around."

He began a closer inspection of the head. "I can see the dissection cuts. They're fairly tidy. I don't think our man here was conscious at the time his face was removed."

"That's a comfort," remarked Tom, with no small amount of sarcasm in his voice. "Maybe he'd had enough by that point."

Annie looked at the corpse in front of her, trying to imagine the pain Piper must have been in up to that point, strapped to a chair while another slowly cut through layers of your skin, removing them like gloves and socks, nerves screaming in extreme agony. She hoped fervently that Piper was either unconscious or dead by the time whoever was responsible had got to his head. Dr Ludstein went on to explain how the skin from the skull had first been removed from behind the ears and over the top of the scalp to peel it towards the back of the neck. The front section had then been eased down, pulling it over the face and onto the neck.

"I would say that this was undertaken in two sections; you're not going to be finding a complete skin like you would from a rabbit. This has been done with a level of ability and would have taken some time," the doctor commented.

All Annie could think of was how long this would have taken through the night. It had to have been completed in time for them to transfer the body to the country park and then hang it in the tree while it was still dark. There had been no calls about lights being seen moving around, but it had been pitch-black on Wednesday night, and there were no lights up in the park other than a few in the car park.

The pathologist continued with the post-mortem, cutting open the body once he had finished a visual examination of the front and back and noted anything of interest. He opined that Piper had died sitting up in the chair, the livor mortis showing the blood had pooled in the back of the thighs and buttocks. He continued, removing the various internal organs, weighing and cutting them as he went and dissecting small sections for further examination in the lab. The last thing he did was to take the vitreous fluid from the eyeballs – a procedure which Annie had never been able to watch as the needle was inserted – and then they left Sally to close the body.

"Cause of death then doc?" asked Annie.

"At the moment it will be pending further examination. I'll need the brain to go off separately and that will take about six to eight weeks to look for any microscopic damage indicative of lack of oxygen, small haemorrhages and the like. I'll also want further examination of the heart and toxicology completed to see if the victim was injected with anything. I couldn't see any obvious needle marks, but there's a distinct possibility that they could have used some chemical or toxin when he was abducted. Tom, just ask them to check for recreational drugs and any sedatives on the form when it's submitted, please. Specifically check for Rohypnol, GHB and ketamine; they're the ones most often used. Unofficially I would suggest that the victim died of heart failure induced by the shock from the pain. He has no other blunt force trauma injuries, no wounds that would indicate he was stabbed and, most interestingly, no defensive injuries to show that he put up any fight. Hence why I believe he may have been subdued using an incapacitant from the outset."

They finished up and headed in their different directions, with Annie left to wonder what kind of individual would torture another human being in such a manner, and for what purpose.

CHAPTER 22

He sat going over the post-abduction checklist he had provided. The location where the victim had been taken had been covered in plastic around where he had been sat prior to his arrival. The victim's skin and clothing had been incinerated straight after the body had been left in the tree. He was not one for trophies; they just helped the police to find you or proved your connection to the crime. Everything else, including the body, had been washed down with chlorine and hydrogen peroxide bleach, all thoroughly cleaned to remove any trace of those who'd worn or handled the items. The night vision goggles used had been replaced in the storage area where they would never show as having left and those involved had gone their separate ways with large sums of cash in their bank accounts. Even the car, once it had the plates changed back, had been returned to the second-hand lot in Surrey and the CCTV camera reconnected, the vehicle now waiting for an unsuspecting member of the public to buy. Oh, if only they knew what it was connected to, they might not want to transport their family around in it. He laughed to himself as he looked at the choices for the next assignment in front of him.

There were some interesting choices, and his clients were clearly getting more inventive in their desires. The benefit of this was the more complex the request, the higher the fee. He always planned ahead for most eventualities, structures and personnel in place should they be needed, so it was never a matter that he would need to start from scratch. The quicker he could provide his client's request, the better they liked it and the more business it generated. He looked again at the three requests in front of him, selecting one which appealed to him more than the other two. He hoped that the police would begin to make a connection after this, or he would have to give them a little nudge. It wasn't as much fun if they spent all their time blundering about without a clue.

Monday, he thought, *give them the weekend to be busy with Piper and fumble about trying to find a why and who, then I can give them a little bit more to concentrate their minds.* It would also allow for his latest client to have more time watching their requests being carried out. That, after all, was what they were paying for.

CHAPTER 23

The ACC sat with Clarke and Lake in the Superintendent's office as Annie gave them an update from the PM.

"And we still have nothing as to any motive for this?" Livingston asked Annie questioningly.

"No Sir. All of the information we have on Piper indicates that he was a decent lad with a low-paid job living a pretty average life. There's nothing at all from any of the source units' informants. As a matter of fact, they've never heard of him, and nobody is talking about anyone who might have been responsible. I know Hastings has had its fair share of violent crime and murders over the years, but this is a bit of a stretch even if it was in the Met."

"What the hell is wrong with these people? Who skins someone while they're alive for no reason other than the fun of it?" The ACC sat shaking his head.

Clarke looked across the table at Annie and Lake, "We need to get some traction on this fast. We can't have some maniac grabbing innocents off the street so they can get their kicks cutting them up. What else can we fast-track on the forensics?"

"We've drawn a blank on all the items Tom's sent up so far, boss. Whoever did this knew what they were up to. No fibres, other than from the rope around the victim's ankles, and that's just a generic kind you can buy in any DIY store. We are getting CCTV from the main stores and any small establishments in the vicinity though, just in case." Lake paused, "This can't have just been a snatch-and-grab, though: this was planned as they had to have a location to take him and know the area. It's the same as the unknown male from Tuesday; no borough CCTV and still nothing from the scoping of the private cameras on people's houses."

"That's ridiculous," Livingston was clearly frustrated, "the amount of the public that have their own CCTV set-ups or doorbell cameras, surely we must have something?" The annoyance was evident in the ACC's voice, and Annie expected he was already getting pressure from above.

"The local council have no cameras along Fairlight towards the country park. It's a fairly elderly area and so tech isn't very common. Even where there are doorbell cameras that TSU have found, these have been set so they only cover people's driveways, not the area outside or the road. Everybody is worried about intruding on their neighbours' privacy nowadays, so they just have it covering their own house. Not a single bit of footage we've got so far has shown anything of use."

Lake sounded as frustrated as Annie felt.

"House-to-house update?" asked the ACC.

Annie looked down at the notes written in her daybook, "Similar story to the CCTV recovery, I'm afraid Sir. We know that Piper left the shop shortly after 1 a.m. Thursday morning by the CCTV inside showing him locking up and turning off the lights. The alarm company confirm that the code was input, and the alarm set at 01.12 a.m. The problem is that at that time of night there's no streetlighting on the way up to Fairlight as soon as you get off the Old London Road. So, unless you're out walking yourself or have security lighting that's tripped by a person on the path, all we can hope for is somebody who's got up for a piss or to let the dog out and happened to glance out the window into the street. So far nothing, though."

Clarke leant forwards, "This seems impossible; we have two murders in less than seventy-two hours and neither one has any CCTV or witnesses at all? How often does that happen?" She ignored the ACC, looking at Annie for an answer.

"In my career, never. There's always something to go on. This can't be a coincidence. There's got to be a link somewhere between the two, but until we can get an ID on the Glyne Gap body then we can't say why. The only thing that stands out to me is that whoever is doing this has planned it out carefully and, if we don't get something come up soon, then I'm expecting another body. A killer like this, they won't stop at two. They won't stop until we catch them."

The silence in the room was broken by Annie's phone signalling she had an email. She quickly checked to see if it was important, stopped and then re-read the contents. Lake and the others were all looking at her when she raised her head. "I've just had an email from SCAS; they think they've got something that might help us. Problem is the crime took place nearly seventy years ago and the murderer is dead and buried across the other side of the country."

She frowned as she read the email to the rest of the group.

SCAS, the Serious Crime Analysis Section, were routinely sent details of all murders and stranger rapes which were then put through their data systems to see if there were any crimes held with a similar M.O. that might help to identify the offender. Generally, the result came back several weeks after the data had been sent to them, often when the offender had already been identified and caught, but it meant that other offences could be reviewed against the then-known suspect and investigated further. By chance, the details of Op Magenta had been given to an analyst who had a specific interest in the more bizarre cases and had taken interest enough to start conducting research around specific parameters. This had flagged up a series of murders committed in Devon in the 1950s. The offender, a James Whittaker, had been caught after committing the last of his three murders in 1955. The first two had been found hung in woods naked with their hands tied behind them and slash marks across their bodies. The third and final murder had been the one to give him his fifteen minutes of fame. The victim, a young female, had been found suspended upside down from a tree and Whittaker had removed parts of her skin. When he was arrested, several bits of flesh were found in jars in his garage, along with a number of animals he had evidently practised his skills on. He ended up being sectioned and managed to kill himself in 1974 while in Rampton Secure Hospital by cutting his own throat, but not before stabbing and seriously injuring another inmate and several hospital staff.

"Choice fella," said Lake, "but unlikely to be our suspect based on the small matter he's been dead for fifty years."

Annie was thinking aloud, "He's not, but what if somebody was copying serial killers? We have a naked body at Glyne Gap where we know Charlie Knights dumped one of his victims. We now have Piper left in a tree in the same manner this Whittaker left one of his."

Livingston scoffed, "That's a bit of a bloody stretch isn't it, sergeant? We don't even know how the Glyne Gap victim died yet. Could even be misadventure. Hardly the basis for what you're suggesting and certainly not a line of enquiry I intend to proceed with at this point in time. Leave DS Ali to concentrate on the first one; with any luck we can write it off as a suicide or accident at sea in a couple of weeks. You concentrate on getting me a suspect for Op Magenta, that's your priority."

Annie looked at him, stunned. *So, he was intent on just looking at the one murder and was already trying to write off the other as a drowning? Despite the fact the victim had somebody take a blowtorch to his hands and then kicked his face in! Some bloody accident.* "Well, I best get on then, don't want to waste any more of your time, do I?" she said curtly. She stood up and left the room.

Lake caught her up back in his office, "Didn't fancy waiting for the SIO to say off you go then?" he smirked as he sat down.

"What a prick. Why the fuck have they put him in charge if he's not open to look at all possibilities, especially those staring him in the face? If it seems to be too good a coincidence, then it generally means it isn't and there's a reason for it."

"Calm down, Annie. I'm on your side remember. We can siphon off a couple of DCs to have a look at these murders in Devon and get some more information around them. We know it's not Whittaker, but if the offender is using old crimes as his M.O. then there may be something there to help us. They can go over the ones of Charlie Knights at the same time. You never know, there may be something connecting the two."

CHAPTER 24

Well, *that was a surprise,* he thought. Frankly, he was astonished that a connection had been drawn to Whittaker in the 50s; he'd felt sure that they wouldn't pick up on it for several weeks. The benefits of modern technology and an analyst who's actually doing their job well. Wonders would never cease. He was pleased that he had continued to monitor Annie's phone in the meeting and was now reading through her emails, especially the latest one from SCAS. He wondered if this analyst had just stumbled on the details or had also made some 'interesting' searches on the internet and Wikipedia. You didn't have to look too hard if you typed in the right questions. Still, he supposed that an analyst working for the police wouldn't trip the authorities' interest as much as a member of the public making the same searches on their home computer. GCHQ would never admit to snooping around on the public's electronic devices without a warrant, but what government agency would? That didn't mean it didn't happen. Certain trigger words would create a flag and off they would go with a remote search of the contents of your hard drive. You'd never even know they'd been there until they turned up at your door holding a warrant. It was far harder for them to try to do the same with Tor or I2P, peer-to-peer networks on the darknet using encrypted software to allow users' anonymity, which is what made the deep net the regular domain for criminal enterprise.

He decided that this would now hasten the next murder. The victim had already been picked up and the personnel arranged. The only issues to slow matters down would be around travel, but this could all be accomplished in less than twenty-four hours. Let them have tomorrow; Sunday would be perfect for what he was now thinking. In fact, with a bit of an adjustment for dramatic effect, it would lead to a great deal of entertainment. He would have to charge more, as there was a greater risk involved to the personnel. You couldn't always select locations that were so out of the way as to be free of cameras but, with a careful selection, he could avoid those that were monitored by paid staff. If anything was picked up on private cameras then so be it. If the owners were sharp then it may even get onto social media before it made its way to the police.

He made the call using an encrypted satellite phone, bouncing the signal via his computer from various locations so that it couldn't be cell sited back to his current whereabouts. He had ensured that all his key personnel were issued with similar encrypted devices and under strict instruction to destroy the equipment as soon as it had been used and then move on to the next one. This in itself had not been a simple task: the obtaining of the mobiles was not the issue, it was the delicate matter of getting them to a number of different areas with no paper trail back to him that had made it a somewhat more complex affair. It wasn't like you could just get them delivered by Amazon. The key was to have filters at each point so that his direct contact was limited to only a handful of individuals. None had ever met him, nor could they identify him from his voice, with each call being made via different voice software, always changing on a random basis so that he could sound male or female, English, South African, Dutch, whatever took his fancy. He didn't ever speak himself, using the software to type out his comments and replies. Even if the calls were recorded on the receiver's side, it would be impossible for any voice analysis to link the speaker back to him.

He dialled the number and waited as the phone on the other end rang twice before it was answered. He had a series of pre-selected phrases he could utilise to save time and he clicked on his keyboard to start the conversation, "You have been selected for the next assignment. The instructions as to how the murder is to be conducted, including the placement of the body and clean-up process, will be obtained from the usual sites as previously arranged. All funds will be held in abeyance until the assignment has been completed and then paid into the account details you have provided. This is apart from the finances necessary to undertake the work, which you will receive at the end of this conversation. In the event that directions are not followed explicitly then a percentage of the payment will be deducted for every deviation. Do you agree to undertake this request?"

A female voice with a strong north-east accent answered, "Yes, we are in full agreement. The only question is around the travel. Where are we going?"

He typed in his answer and heard the electronic voice say, "The details are all in the usual location which can be accessed with the designated keywords. The element of travel has been factored into payment. Can I confirm that the subject has already been obtained? There is a specific time element here which I have factored into the additional payment."

The woman with the Geordie accent replied, "Yes, they were picked up a couple of days ago. It was only a small amount of work to identify a regular runaway. They've been reported to the police but that was just a formality; there won't be any real effort to try and trace them. They disappear for days at a time and the last contact they will have had will be with one of the local drug runners, so if there is any comeback then they will be the first person that's looked at. I have the right people for whatever you require, and all of the equipment has been obtained in advance from different sources, non-traceable back to me."

He typed a brief reply, "Thank you for your time and assistance. We will have no further personal contact from this point onwards." He cancelled the call.

He then began the process of advising the client and confirming full payment, giving them the details of how they could watch the feed in live time as the murder was conducted.

CHAPTER 25

Connor Reece sat on the mattress with his knees pulled up tight to his chest and the thin blanket wrapped around his narrow shoulders. His straggly hair hung limply in his eyes as he shivered from the cold, his breath coming out in pale mists in front of his face. He had lost his broken glasses, making his surroundings a fuzzy blur in the light of the lamp next to him. His coat and trainers had been stripped from him, leaving him in just torn jeans and an old T-shirt with a faded cannabis motif printed on the front. His toes poked through his filthy socks, once possibly white. An empty plastic water bottle and the remains of a Pot Noodle sat congealing in front of him. He hadn't been allowed a fork or a spoon to eat it with so he had resorted to slurping the contents straight from the plastic container. He burnt his mouth when given the first one and had been careful to let the next cool down before trying to eat it. This was all they had fed him, and he had been given five as far as he could remember. If he'd known what was going to happen, he'd have kept a better count. Connor had no watch and there were no windows in the small room, which meant he had no real idea of how long it had been since he had been taken off the street.

He remembered he had gone to pick up a deal, his next fix. Just a ten pound baggie, but when he walked over to the beaten-up Transit van in the far corner of the car park, he knew immediately it wasn't his normal dealer: the man was too large. Connor had kept his head down as he approached, and it was only when he was a few feet in front of the man that he looked up and noticed that he had some kind of latex mask over his face. Connor was about to back away when the side door of the van opened and he was dragged inside and thrown, face down, onto a bundle of foul-smelling wet rags on the floor. A strong hand had held the back of his neck, forcing his face down into the material, and he could feel the warm breath in his ear as a voice said calmly, "Listen carefully, little man. If you struggle or make a noise, the hammer I'm holding in my other hand is going to come down hard on the back of your head. Give me a happy thumbs-up, so I know we're clear."

Connor had felt the hard plastic frames of his glasses pressing into his forehead and cheeks until the pressure had caused them to split in the middle. Between the cloths smothering his face and the petrol fumes exuding from them, he had struggled to breath.

The voice asked again, harsher this time, "Did you hear me, little man? This hammer will go right through the back of your fucking skull if I don't get a thumbs-up right fucking now."

Connor managed to raise the thumb on his left hand, hoping the man behind him could see it.

"Good, that's good. Now don't fucking move," the voice said and the pressure on the back of Connor's neck eased. "Oh you dirty little bastard. He's fucking pissed himself, the cunt."

Connor was close to shitting in his pants as well if the truth be known, and it was all he could do to hold his bowels together. The acrid smell of urine mixed with the petrol fumes in the van as the voice continued, "This is how it's gonna go, smackhead. You're going to lay very still with your arms stretched out so I can see them both. You don't speak, you don't move, you don't try and look around, you don't even fart, cos if you do, that hammer will come bouncing down and smash what little brains you've got left in that head all over the floor. We're going for a nice drive now, so be a good boy."

A meaty hand had slapped Connor on the back of the head, and he lay rigid as he heard the vehicle engine start up and the van move off.

Connor had no idea how far they had driven, but the sound of other traffic slowly diminished, the van turning off the tarmac roads onto a rougher track, bumping Connor up and down as it went. When the van stopped and the engine was turned off, the voice behind Connor said, "I want you to lift your head back but keep your eyes shut. Same rules apply as before."

Connor had raised his head back as far as he could, his glasses falling off in the process, and a thick hessian bag had been placed over his head, completely obscuring any vision. He had been dragged out of the van and half-walked, half-carried into a building and then pushed down onto a stone floor.

"These are the rules, so listen up, smackhead. You put the bag on your head as soon as you're told and don't remove it until instructed. That's rule one. Rule two, and we need to be very clear on this, you don't speak or make a sound unless I ask you a question. Then you just answer it and shut up again. If you deviate from this rule, I will pull out one tooth for every word I hear you utter. Now, I'm no dentist, so don't be thinking there's gonna be any anaesthetic, either. Rule three, you stay in the room where we put you and don't make any attempts to get out. If you so much as touch the door I'll use the hammer on your fingers one at a time until they look like burgers, and when I run out of fingers, I'll have a go at ya toes. That's it, just the three rules to keep it nice and simple for a fucked-up little junkie."

Connor was shaking uncontrollably and managed to utter, "Why?" before a fist hit him in the side of his head like a truck, throwing him down onto the hard floor.

"Did you not listen to what I just said or are you fucking stupid, junkie?" the voice raged and a heavy foot kicked him in the stomach, forcing all the air out of him in a rush. He began sobbing as the voice repeated, "Rule two. Have you got it now or do I need to get the pliers?"

Connor didn't know what to do. If he spoke, he was likely to be beaten even worse, so just raised his hands in front of him, trying to fend off any further attack and hoping the attacker would take this as a sign of understanding.

"Now you're getting it. I'm going to step out for a bit now. When you hear the door shut, and you will, leave it to a count of fifty and then you can take the bag off. When you hear a bang on the door then put the bag back on and make sure you do it quick because if I come in here and see you not wearing it then that's gonna be the last time those eyes see anything."

The malice sounded in every word the male said. Connor lay motionless as they took his watch, coat and shoes from him, checked his jeans pockets and found them unsurprisingly empty, after which Connor heard footsteps moving away before the door slammed shut and he heard a key turning in the lock.

He had counted to a hundred to be on the safe side and, even then, had only slowly lifted the coarse material off his head, fearing a trick and that the male, or perhaps the van driver, was still in the room with him, waiting to hurt him again.

Once he was sure he was alone, he had looked at his surroundings. His room was no more than a ten-feet-by-ten-feet box. No window, just the heavy wooden door that he had been dragged through. A thin, stained single mattress was against the wall opposite the door and an olive green blanket was folded on top of it. A lamp was to the foot of the mattress, bolted under a cage fixed to the wall. He could see a cable for the lamp disappearing into the wall behind it. There was a bucket covered with a lid with a small heap of tissues on top beside the lamp but, other than that, the room was empty. The walls were large stone blocks and he had the feeling this may be part of an old farmhouse. His mobile phone had been in his jacket with his wallet, which had contained only the ten pound note he'd had to pay for the heroin. It had only been an old, cheap, pay-as-you-go phone, but his sole means of contact with the outside world had been taken from him. He had sat on the mattress trying to figure out what his abductors wanted with him. He had no money and neither did his family; those that he had contact with, anyway. If someone tried to get a ransom from his parents, they were apt to tell his captors they could keep him for all the trouble he'd caused over the years, stealing from them and having the house regularly invaded by police looking to arrest him for one reason or another. What the fuck was he doing there?

CHAPTER 26

The first time he'd heard the banging on the door, Connor had flung himself face down on the mattress as he struggled to pull the hessian bag back over his head. He heard the sound of a single person's footsteps entering the room, but nobody spoke to him before he heard the door slam shut again. He'd counted slowly to fifty before gingerly lifting the bag up, still lying flat, to check if he was alone. He was alone again, but a steaming plastic container was set on the floor in the centre of the room with a bottle of water next to it. Connor had drained the contents of the bottle in several large gulps before hungrily starting on the noodles in the tub. He'd stopped as quickly as he'd started when the boiling contents hit his mouth and he began to cough wildly, wishing he still had some water left. He sat back on the mattress, allowing the rest of the sparse food to get cold before finishing it, using his fingers to get every last morsel out. This same routine of food and water was followed the next time, and Connor had figured that he was probably getting three such deliveries a day, although he had no actual way to confirm this. Whenever he took off the bag after the door had shut, the same water and noodles were left on the floor and the empty containers had been removed. He knew that the bucket was being changed, as it alternated from red to blue. He hoped that he was never in the process of using the bucket when the knock came on the door and so made sure that he used it before he ate the meagre portions they left.

He thought he must have been in the room for a couple of days. He was constantly cold and hungry and in desperate need of a fix. He didn't know if it was because he hadn't had any heroin or his surroundings that was making him feel so bad; he couldn't think clearly, the stomach cramps were happening more and he had the shits to contend with.

A hand hammered on the door and Connor dropped flat onto the mattress, groping for the hessian covering, as he heard two sets of footsteps enter the room.

"I think it's time we dispensed with rule one. Let's get a look at you," a muffled voice said cheerfully.

Connor kept his face pressed into the mattress and held tightly to the bag. *I don't want to see you*, he thought. *If I see you then I know I'm dead. They'll never let me go if they know I can identify them.*

Rough hands lifted him up by the shoulders and forced him onto his knees as the bag was pulled from his head. He kept his eyes tightly shut, turning his head away from his assailants.

"C'mon, shithead, now's not the time to be shy."

A hand gripped him by the hair and pulled his head back and around so that he was facing where the voice was coming from, and a sharp slap stinging his face from the front.

"Open up those peepers or I'll get my knife out and cut your eyelids off."

The male's voice made him sound like he was enjoying himself, and Connor looked up into the masked faces of his captors.

The two males wore tight-fitting latex masks down to their necks, which was why the voice had sounded so odd to Connor. The one holding him by the hair had a mask that looked like a werewolf, and the other resembled Frankenstein. They were dressed in matching black from head to foot with leather-gloved hands. Terrified, tears ran down Connor's face and snot began to trickle from his nose in two glistening streams.

Werewolf said, "We've just taken a call from a friend, and you'll be pleased to know this nasty ordeal of yours is almost over."

The voice was mocking, almost laughing. Connor felt relief surging through him. He didn't know who they were or why he was there, but it was done. They'd likely just dump him somewhere, but that was okay, he didn't care. The reason they were keeping their faces covered could only be that they were worried he could recognise them again after – and there was going to be an after.

Words stumbled out of him in a flood, "Thank you. I promise, I won't say anything to anyone. I don't even know what this is all about."

"Oh, we know that." It was the first time the male with the Frankenstein mask had spoken, "But you will. We think it's necessary you see. We are firm believers that when a decision has been made, the other party always has a right to know. Only fair."

There was no menace in this voice. In fact, it sounded calm, as if discussing an issue with a friend to pass the time.

"No, please. I don't want to know anything." Connor sobbed, understanding that the less he knew the better his chances of surviving were.

CHAPTER 27

onnor was dragged, screaming, by the hair, scrabbling on hands and knees out of his small cell and down a short corridor before being thrown on the floor in a much larger room. "Strip," commanded Frankenstein.

Connor lay curled in a ball on the floor. "I won't fucking tell you again. Strip, or we'll cut your clothes off and maybe bits of you with it."

The voice carried enough menace to leave Connor with no doubt the threat would be followed through, and he quickly struggled out of his clothes, leaving them in a pile on the cold floor and covering his genitals with his hands. The room was an old farm kitchen with an Aga on one side and a large sink on the other. Wood beams crossed the ceiling, and a single window allowed the light to enter. There was a large crossbeam of wood on the stone floor and a sports bag, which lay by the sink. The room was warm, the heat coming from the Aga, where a pot bubbled away on top of the stove. At the far end were two cameras set on tripods with a large photographer's lamp behind.

"Down on the floor, on ya back," commanded Werewolf.

Terrified, Connor did as instructed, kneeling first then lying flat, still with his hands covering himself. Frankenstein kicked Connor in the shoulder. "Put the arms out to the sides. Do it now, or I will."

Connor moved his arms away from his body and, as he did so, he noticed another camera directly above, him pointing down. A red light flashed rhythmically. Whatever was going to happen was being filmed. He began to shake uncontrollably. This was bad. Very bad.

He heard Frankenstein dragging the wooden beam from behind him and it hit the back of his head. "Lift up, sweet cheeks."

There was humour in the voice, as if they found the situation funny.

Werewolf bent down over Connor and again took hold of his hair, pulling him forwards so that the beam could be pushed under his shoulders. Connor tried to move his arms up to protect himself and a fist smashed into his face, blood immediately mixing with the snot coming from his nose.

"Move again when you're not meant to …"

The sentence ended without further information, leaving him rigid with fear as Frankenstein cable-tied his arms outstretched along the beam, so he lay supplicated on the floor.

Werewolf stood over Connor, positioning himself so he could be seen. "Now, little man, this is the time when we can forget all about rule two. In fact, I think you'd really struggle to keep to it. Make as much noise as you want; there's nobody around to hear you and it all makes for better viewing." He indicated the camera above with his thumb before he stepped back out of view.

Connor heard the two males move to the end of the room; he couldn't lift his head enough to see them but heard a whirring sound begin. Both males reappeared into view, with Werewolf holding the nozzle of what looked to Connor like the end of a vacuum cleaner. Werewolf leant down so that Connor could see the implement in his hands more clearly and pressed a button on the side. There was a hiss, and a blast of steam was emitted from the end of the nozzle, the hot damp air hitting Connor in the face and causing him to thrash his head from side to side even though it was still several feet from him.

"Shall we begin?" Werewolf asked, and Connor screamed with all his lungs as searing pain burst in his armpits, where the nozzle pressed onto his skin, instantly causing the soft flesh to bubble and blister under the intense heat.

SATURDAY 31ST OCTOBER – ALL HALLOWS' EVE

CHAPTER 28

Wagner's 'Ride of the Valkyries' began to blare out from Annie's phone on her bedside table, waking her from a deep sleep. She had only arrived home in the early hours after another long day. She fumbled for the phone but only managed to knock it onto the floor in the darkness. Swearing to herself, she hit the bedside light as the phone stopped ringing.

She reached down and picked up her mobile, opening it with the Face ID, and checking her recent calls. Last caller showed as a withheld number at 4.05 a.m. *Terrific*, she thought as she slumped back onto her pillows fully awake, *all of about three good hours of sleep and now I have to try and do it all over again before I get up at six-fifteen.*

As she reached over to turn the light off, the phone rang again, startling her. She picked it up quickly and pressed the screen to answer the call, "Hello?" There was no reply. Annie looked at the screen and saw it was a withheld number again. "Who is this?" When she only received silence as an answer, she instantly disconnected the call. When it didn't ring again, Annie placed it back on the nightstand and lay back into the pillows. The house had been silent when she got home with no Bella to welcome her at the door, although Kevin had brought over a timer so that there was a light on in the hallway. He'd left a note on the kitchen counter, "Hi Annie, picked up Bella and will drop her back on Monday late afternoon. Have plenty of food. Any probs give me a ring. Kevin".

As much as Annie missed Bella being around, she didn't want her spending the whole of the weekend alone in the house, only getting company for a walk. Her stump had been sore when she took off the prosthetic; too much time wearing it and, even after all this time, it sometimes began to chafe. She'd poured a glass of red wine and taken it upstairs before showering and putting some cream on the slightly tender flesh. She then lay in bed trying to read a book as she drank her wine, thinking she would struggle to get to sleep with the last few days buzzing around in her head. Yet her eyelids had soon begun to droop, so she finished her glass, switched off the lights and closed her eyes, quickly falling asleep. The last thing she wanted was to be woken by two crappy calls with nobody on the other end. She rolled onto her side and tried to get comfortable again, pulling the duvet around her. It was strange not having Bella at the end of the bed fighting to see who could get the most space. Annie slowly fell back asleep, wondering what the weekend would throw at her.

***

He debated if he should make a third call now that she was settled back down. The small camera set in the corner of the bedroom had a night vision option which gave him a clear view of Annie, although in a green spectrum. She had looked so peaceful it had been almost a shame to wake her. Still, he'd wanted to see her awake. He'd kept the camera on earlier when she had changed to have a shower, averting his eyes only briefly as she removed her underwear, before putting a towel around her. He'd watched intently when she returned and began to massage cream into the stump of her right leg before letting the towel slip to the floor and pulling on an oversized grey T-shirt.

He'd seen Annie pull the bedcovers down and lay back, sipping her wine as she read her novel, her hair still damp from the shower. She was attractive, a bit older than his normal preference, but he admired her lithe physique. She obviously worked hard to keep it that way and there was a muscular tone to her arms and shoulders. He thought she could perhaps try a little harder and get her hair cut in a more fashionable style but, overall, she was very pleasing to the eye. He wondered what it would be like to get to know Annie personally and share that bottle of wine with her. That was something to ponder on.

CHAPTER 29

The alarm on Annie's Alexa device sounded at quarter past six and she stretched, her back and shoulders cracking pleasantly, before heading downstairs and filling the kettle. She made a mug of coffee and poured granola into a bowl, adding milk, and then sitting at the kitchen counter to eat with the radio playing in the background. When the six-thirty news came on, she paid more attention, listening to the latest national news and noting that the murders only featured at the end of the bulletin and, even then, only in passing. It would be more prominent later in the day, and the television bulletins would no doubt come from either Fairlight cliffs or outside Hastings police station.

She rinsed the bowl in the sink and took the mug back upstairs to the bedroom to get dressed for the day. Sitting on her bed, she massaged her stump before putting on some powder and pulling on the nylon sock to cover it. She placed the lining in the cup of the prosthetic, easing out the wrinkles, and then fixed the leg in place before pulled on a pair of black trousers.

Anticipating the cold of the day, Annie put a thin thermal vest on under a grey jumper and headed back down to get her shoes and coat, finally grabbing her keys and the present for Tony's daughter before leaving. All the time, she was oblivious to the eyes watching her, following her every movement around the house.

Annie arrived in the MIT office to find Tony making a tea, a Danish pastry hanging out of his mouth. He held up a cup and Annie nodded, "Coffee thanks."

Tony took the pastry from his mouth, "Want one? I've got a spare. Well, I say a spare, but if you don't have it, I'll be eating it as soon as I finish this one."

"You know I'd hate to deprive you of breakfast, Tony."

"Don't worry about that; I had a sausage roll when I picked them up. How's today looking?"

Annie sat down at her desk as Tony put a coffee in front of her in a faded Brighton & Hove Albion mug, "The small matter that nobody else has been murdered overnight means I think we're onto a winner."

"Winner, winner, chicken dinner." Tony smiled. "On that note, Thalia asked if you want to come for something to eat when we finish tonight. She said you've probably been surviving on rabbit food and sarnies. I obviously told her I'd been looking after you but for some reason she doesn't believe me." He shrugged his shoulders as he took a sip of his tea.

"Let's see what time we get off shall we."

Annie knew she'd be going back to the Ali household later. Failing that, she'd get a stream of calls from Thalia checking up on her and, anyway, it would be nice to have a proper meal with some company. With no fresh murders reported, they could look to progress some of the other tasks around the Piper killing. With any luck, they'd get the draft statements from the boy's parents and the girlfriend, Katie.

The ACC conducted an online briefing from his office at police headquarters in Lewes looking the epitome of white middle-class casual in his pale pink Ralph Lauren polo shirt. She guessed this was paired with a pair of beige chinos and some expensive loafers. There was nothing of high priority to come from the briefing, and he called Annie on her landline when it had finished.

"Morning Sir," she answered, seeing his details appear on the phone's screen.

"Annie," he said curtly, "I've got a prior commitment that I need to attend this morning. I'll be available on my mobile if you need me for anything, but if I don't answer then just leave me a message and I'll get back to you as soon as I can."

Marvellous, thought Annie, *we have two murders in a week and the lead SIO is going to spend Saturday at the golf course with his buddies.* She was more than confident this was his 'prior commitment' and wondered if it was with the Chief and the rest of the boys' club. She answered simply, "If we get anything from the lab then I'll contact you, other than that I think it's all in order for today. We have sufficient staff for the weekend at any rate."

"Good, we can speak later, around four. I have a press briefing at five this evening for the TV media and then a couple of radio interviews but I'm going to do them all over at HQ. Zoe's coming in later to help me out."

Annie smiled to herself. *I'm sure she is.* "I'm going to head over to Hastings in an hour or so and just be present for the troops. I can have a scrumdown with the Superintendent and DI Lake while I'm there."

She could hear the tension rise in Livingston's clipped tones as he spoke, "I don't think it's necessary for you to speak further with Superintendent Clarke. I've already spoken to her, and she's not directly involved in the investigation. If there is anything that crops up that I feel she needs to be aware of, then I'll tell her."

Annie hesitated before replying, "Er, fine Sir. I won't bother then." *Well,* she thought, *not so far as telling you anyway.* She wasn't prepared to leave Clarke swinging in the breeze just because Livingston had an issue with her.

"Good. Call me if needed," Livingston said, and hung up.

"That is beginning to seriously piss me off," said Annie aloud, looking at the phone.

"What's that then?" asked Tony, having now moved on to the second Danish.

"The ACC's lovely habit of just cutting you off as soon as he's decided the conversation is over. He's a misogynistic twat. Bet he wouldn't do that with you."

"Oh he does, if he can be bothered to even speak to me. I might be a bloke, but I'm not sure I'm his favourite colour."

"I guarantee, if he thought it would benefit him, then he'd have you running around behind him as his bag man."

"Well, I'm used to that then, all the running around I do for you." Tony laughed, pastry crumbs flying from his mouth as he ducked behind his computer screen to prevent Annie throwing anything at him.

"You're such a dick, Tony. I never understand how you get that beautiful wife of yours to put up with you."

"Simple Annie: I'm the best husband and father she could have, plus I'm hung like a baby elephant."

"Now you are talking bullshit." Annie laughed, for seemingly the first time in days.

CHAPTER 30

DCI Cornish arrived in the office mid-morning, breezing in with a Costa in hand, clearly no thought given to if either Annie or Tony would like one. "Any progress at all on Op Senna, Tony?"

Tony was busy working his way through the contents of a large sandwich box. "Sorry guv, still nothing. It's as if the body dropped from the sky."

Cornish leant against the doorframe, indicating he had no intention of hanging around. "I know what the ACC has said about it could be a drowning, but with Dr Ludstein finding no water in the lungs, that's never going to work as a cause of death. It may be an accident somewhere, burnt his hands on an engine, fell and smashed his face and was dead before he hit the water and washed up on the beach?"

Annie looked at the DCI incredulously, "You're not serious, are you? I mean, there's stretching the facts but that's going into the realms of fantasy."

Tony spoke with a mouth still full of food, "I wouldn't want to run that past the family or the cameras."

Cornish shrugged, "You're right. Especially as it would be me doing it. I think Mr Livingston would just like the first one to go away so we can concentrate on the second."

Annie was surprised at the frankness of the DCI, talking in this manner openly in front of Tony and herself. He was normally so corporate that he would never be heard saying anything that might get back to a senior officer as undermining. Maybe there was hope for him yet.

After Cornish had left the office, Annie cleared some emails then got in her unmarked Focus and headed across to Hastings. Despite it being the weekend, there was still a significant media presence at the police station and Annie gave her standard "No comment" as she passed into the rear yard and headed straight to Lake's office on the first floor. She found him sat at his desk looking at his computer screen.

He looked up with a smile as she entered, the puckered scar on his left cheek pulling the lip up slightly higher on that side. "One of the perks of the job, working weekends when you could be off. Never gets old, does it?"

"Never." Annie answered as she put her laptop bag on the floor and slumped into the seat opposite him.

"I've been through most of the updates and statements before I came over. Still nothing to say who the offenders might be."

Lake looked at some notes in front of him, "We have caught a bit of a break this morning. Had a call about twenty minutes ago from one of the TSU lads out collecting the CCTV. They've got a house up towards the country park with a Ring doorbell camera that they never set the privacy parameters on, so it covers the footpath outside their frontage and a bit of the road."

At last, thought Annie.

Lake held up both hands in front of him, "Before you get excited, there's no exterior lighting, so it's all just light and dark shadows. The camera flicks from colour to black and white in the dark, but they think they have a figure walking along and then a car pulls up beside him. A couple of shapes get out and when the car drives away there's nobody left in the road. Camera timer puts it at one-twenty in the morning. Must be Piper; there's no other figures passing around that timeframe and, before you ask, yes, they have checked the timer is correct."

"So what have they said about the quality? Does it capture anything to ID the people who grabbed him?" This was progress, and Annie was already thinking ahead with options as to what could be done with it. If there was enough resolution, then they could at least identify the type of car and have something to run against the ANPR data.

"It's just light and dark greys, like I said. It was a first-generation camera, so the quality isn't terrific. All TSU can say is there is a figure and a car plus two possible figures that briefly get out of the vehicle, nothing more."

"Okay, okay. Can they get a still from the footage? Best possible showing Piper, the car and the other two males? I'll get Tom to send a CSI up to the location. Is there a wall or a fence outside the property?"

Lake looked puzzled, "Didn't ask. Why?"

"Get that measured and then do a comparison estimate to get the height of the other two figures and the roof of the car. We know how tall Piper was, so we can use that for confirmation that the first figure is him. If we can get heights for the other two and the car then we can work that into the data."

She was excited. It was decent evidence giving the investigation the time Piper was abducted and where from, so they could concentrate on an area. They now knew he was put into a car and there were two assailants, both likely to be males. Even with poor footage they could at least get height and build. They could also rule out any vans or larger vehicles in the town. *There's always something, no matter how small, just a case of looking for it.*

Having called Tom Martin and made the arrangements for a CSI to attend where the footage had come from and take some measurements and daylight stills, Annie wandered up to the second floor and found the Superintendent's door closed. She knocked and waited for a reply. A few seconds later she heard Jess Clarke shout, "Come in. Just finishing a Teams call."

Annie went in and sat at the desk as Clarke ended the online call. Despite the comments from the ACC, Annie had no intention of leaving Clarke in the dark and told her the latest update.

"I haven't called the ACC yet. Was going to do it from your office, if that's okay?"

"Sure. As long as you think he'll be happy with me being present."

Annie could not have cared less about internal politics and egos, but she wasn't going to let Livingston use his position to keep Clarke out of the picture. "I'm sure it'll be fine. I'll put it on speaker," she said as she dialled the ACC's mobile number.

He picked up on the second ring, "Assistant Chief Constable Mark Livingston."

That's how he answers his phone? Annie pondered. *Just in case you don't know he's an ACC or what the letters stand for? He must love the sound of it.*

"Sir, it's DS Bryce. We've got some progress on Piper's abduction. Are you free to speak?" His voice went muffled, asking whoever he was with to carry on without him for a few minutes before telling her to continue. She informed him of the TSU discovery and the work going on around it.

He sounded disappointed and less than impressed. "Is that it? I'm in the middle of something; this could have waited until later. It's hardly earth-shattering or likely to get us anywhere today, is it?"

"With all due respect Sir," that phrase again, and Annie did her best to keep the contempt from her tone, "it's a damn sight more than we had a few hours ago, and I thought as the SIO you'd want to know."

Livingston had the decency to at least sound a little contrite, "Yes, I guess so. Well, unless there's anything else, I do need to get on."

"No Sir, I won't bother you again until this afternoon, unless it's earth-shattering, obviously." The last part of the sentence wasn't exactly respectful, but Annie imagined he wouldn't notice the sarcasm in any event, as the call was ended.

Clarke, who had been silent for the call, now spoke, "So, what is our illustrious leader up to that's so important that he doesn't want to be bothered with updates on the crime he's meant to be leading?"

"I think he's off playing golf."

Clarke stood up from her desk and walked round to the table to sit by Annie, "You are shitting me? So, he thinks it's okay two days into a major murder investigation to swan off and play a few holes with his buddies and then doesn't even want to be disturbed." She shook her head, "I do wonder what the fuck I ever saw in the man."

"Good looks and a fit body?" Annie asked.

Clarke looked at her for a minute before she laughed. "Probably. Does that make me shallow?"

"At least it wasn't to get the next promotion. Now that would be shallow." Annie was surprised that Clarke was so open with her; they'd only met for the first time on the Thursday.

"What about you then, DS Bryce? Who's your significant other? Don't see a wedding ring." Clarke was looking at Annie's hands resting on her lap.

"My significant other has four legs, drops hair all over my house and is currently lounging around at a friend's house, no doubt being thoroughly spoilt." Annie was surprised how relaxed this felt, just two women chatting. Not a scenario she was usually in, especially at work.

"I had heard you were married to the job; just took it you were private and didn't want people to know your business. Sorry, I don't mean to intrude or make you feel uncomfortable."

Annie sat back in her chair, "It's not an issue. There's been a couple of long-term relationships but both with people outside the job. It ended up the same on each occasion: you miss a birthday or a night out because something's come up at work, it happens too often, and you find that they want more than you're prepared to give. End of relationship. Don't get me wrong, I'm happy with just me and the dog; means the most I have to worry about is getting the sitter to take Bella for a few days. Can't exactly do that with a husband or kids, can you?"

Clarke looked down at her own hands with sadness in her face, "No you can't, and that was my mistake. Put the job first and just drifted apart from my husband. Didn't even notice until it was too late and there was no turning back. Now I get to pick the kids up every other weekend if I'm not working and have the bonus of seeing them happy and content with their new stepmother. Doesn't help that she's so nice. I can't even bring myself to dislike her, as much as I try."

She went on to tell Annie about the failed relationship with Livingston, the promises that never came to pass and the acrimony with which he had split from her. It had all been secret meetings, Livingston lying easily on overheard phone calls that he was stuck in some meeting or had to attend a conference. She should have realised she was only ever going to be his exotic little bit on the side, but he had convinced her otherwise until he'd discarded her.

"I think I better get down and have a chat with Ged. Are you heading back to the MIT office?" Clarke asked as she walked to the door.

Annie looked at the time and noticed it was nearly two. It would take her an hour, depending on the weekend traffic, to get back to the outskirts of Brighton. "Yes, I better be leaving soon. I was just going to speak to a few of the DCs that are working this weekend and head out to see where this camera is on the Fairlight Road then will head back along The Ridge. I'm hoping for a day in the office tomorrow, so I won't be back over here until Monday."

They said their goodbyes as they headed down the corridor to the stairs.

CHAPTER 31

It was nearly eight in the evening when Annie arrived at Tony and Thalia's in Stanmer Heights, just off the main A27 to the north of Brighton. As usual, the house was a bustle of noise and activity as Thalia opened the front door and ushered Annie inside. The couple had three children: Sonny, 5, Yasmin, 11, and Tara, the new teenager at 13. Annie at least had remembered to put the birthday present – a handbag which had been on Tara's wish list – in her car this morning, expecting to just give it to Tony, but he'd insisted on her bringing it round herself and staying for dinner.

"Hi Annie. How've you been?" Thalia asked, shutting the front door as the pair headed straight down the corridor to the kitchen. Thalia was as stunning as ever; slim in her tight-fitting leggings and navy silk blouse. Her dark hair, tied back in a plait on top of her head, still hung well past her shoulders. Tony, who had changed from his usual suit and trousers office attire into jeans and a Madness concert T-shirt which had seen better days, was seated at the kitchen table with a mug of tea in front of him the size of a small bucket and eating from a large packet of crisps. "I won't get up," he said between shovelling in handfuls of crisps.

"Doesn't change, does he? About as much use as a chocolate teapot," said Thalia, walking past Tony and checking on whatever was cooking in the oven, creating a wonderful aroma.

"Just pacing myself, my sun and moon. Don't want to peak too soon."

Annie sat down at the table, "Tony, we've known each other for years and I have yet to see this peak you so often refer to."

Thalia placed a glass of red wine on the table, "You're more than welcome to stay the night if you want, Annie. Tony can sort the sofa bed out for you in the living room. He said Bella's at the sitter, so you've got nothing to rush home for tonight."

"Thanks Thalia, but I didn't bring an overnight bag with me. I'll just have the one glass." This wasn't exactly true, as Annie always kept a bag in the boot of her car with a change of clothes, toothbrush, and other items in the event she was called away when at work and had to stay in a hotel. She was more than grateful for the offer of dinner and spending some time with Tony's family, but she wanted to sleep in her own bed that night.

There was a charging of footsteps in the hallway and Sonny came bursting in, shouting at full volume, followed at a more sedate pace by his older sisters.

"Hi you three. There's a present for you on the table by the front door, Tara. Hope it's the right one."

The eldest girl did a sharp about-face and Annie heard the ripping of paper followed by a squeal of delight, "Thanks Annie, it's great." The girl rushed back in, flinging her arms around Annie's shoulders, and planting a kiss on her cheek.

"You're very welcome, and sorry it's late."

Thalia was leaning against the kitchen unit, a gin and tonic in her hands, "They know you've been working. It's very kind of you. Dinner will be about fifteen minutes. It's salmon en croute with roast potatoes and veg. Hope you're hungry. Kids, let Annie have some peace." She waved the three children out of the room as she turned to Tony, "Any possibility you can at least lay the table and get Sonny into bed?"

"Anything for you, my precious," he said, brushing the crisp remains from the front of his T-shirt as he stood up and gave his wife an affectionate squeeze.

I could have had this. Annie sat, watching the family dynamics in front of her. *But no, I decided to live for the job. Always another investigation to deal with, another case to get to court. Having the respect of other officers is great, but that doesn't put a nice meal on the table or give me a back rub when I got home from another long day.*

She could retire at 55 in three years or hang on for another eighteen months and get her thirty years in.

It would no doubt be the latter: she had no reason to retire early; what else would she do? She didn't want to hang around after or come back as a civilian. The idea of not running her own investigations and just taking statements or sorting out exhibits horrified her. Rather leave and find something new to do. The last thing she wanted was to have officers looking at her and saying, "Didn't she used to be a DS?"

The three adults ate dinner together in the kitchen while the two oldest girls were allowed to watch a movie on the huge television in the front room. Tony loved his films and had somehow persuaded Thalia that a seventy-inch flat-screen with surround sound was absolutely necessary. Annie felt like she was in the cinema whenever she sat in front of it.

It was nearly eleven when she left, her stomach full of Thalia's excellent cooking, the salmon followed by a huge slice of banoffee pie. *God*, she thought as she started the drive back home to Ditchling, *I won't need to eat for a week*.

The difference between the lights and noise of the house she had recently left and the darkness as Annie pulled up on the drive outside the front of her own home could not have been more apparent. She used the torch on her phone to get her key into the lock and switched on the hallway light as she entered, double locking the door as she closed it. She walked into the kitchen, poured a large glass of wine from the previous night's open bottle, and took it to the living room, turning on lights as she went before dropping down onto the sofa and kicking off her shoes. She slid off her trousers and eased off the prosthetic leg, pulling a blanket around her for warmth. The house was chilly with the heating having turned off several hours before. *Half an hour of crap with whatever she could find on the TV then bed*, she decided.

CHAPTER 32

She looked tired, he thought, *and really must get an outside light for these dark nights when she gets home.* He imagined his hands massaging the stress from her shoulders as she sat watching the television.

The news report from earlier had been fairly bland until they had got to the part where the lead officer had mentioned they now believed they had CCTV footage of Piper being abducted. That was of only minor concern. He'd seen the emails with the still attached so knew there was very little they could glean from it. Not that it would trace back to him. He still had so much to do, and the next victim would be in place by the end of the night. He was impressed though with the plans Annie had made to try to get the heights of the abductors and the work she wanted conducted to identify the car. He was confident that even if they did work out the make and model, it was virtually impossible that they would ever stumble across the right vehicle.

The lead investigator appeared a figurehead only from the conversations he had overheard, and the DCI had nothing to go on with the first body. Clarke was interesting and he had enjoyed listening into the dinner Annie had with her colleague's family. He had noted the closeness or otherwise between Annie and all of those she had interacted with today, and they all had some interest to him. When the endgame drew closer, perhaps some would have a starring role. He did like the idea of a personal touch.

He watched Annie sat cradling her glass with her legs drawn up under her. He wondered what her favourite wine was. Maybe he would have a bottle delivered to her. Poor Annie, she had so much to do, and it was about to get a whole lot worse.

SUNDAY 1ST NOVEMBER

CHAPTER 33

S t Nicholas Church was a small wooden building set just back from the beach at Pett Level about six miles to the north-east of Hastings. There was an independent rescue lifeboat station beside to the right and a campsite to the left. It wasn't quite sunrise. The sky was overcast and dark, the wind blowing spray off the white-capped waves as Reverend Francis pulled up in her elderly yellow VW Beetle, the engine sputtering to an eventual stop. She stepped out, pulling her long coat tightly around her and wishing she'd put a hat on as she locked the car and walked from the car park towards the front entrance. She stopped, hesitating; there was something propped up, blocking the doorway. Surely they hadn't had the cross vandalised. It had only been erected and dedicated in the summer of 2018. She drew closer and saw the cross was still to the right of the door. So, what was the other object?

As she took a further step towards the door, she took a torch from her pocket and shone the beam ahead. She could see the horrific blasphemy before her. A large wooden beam was resting at an angle across the door. A figure hung from it, their arms outstretched along the beam. The body was naked except for a small strip of material tied around the groin. She could see the body had been mutilated, the flesh bright pink in patches, and the mouth drawn back in a grimace of agony. A ring of thorns had been forced onto the top of the head and pressed into the skin, with thin lines of blood trailing down over the face.

She backed away, trying to hold down the vomit that threatened to rise from her stomach, and fumbled for her mobile phone, dialling 999 as she bumped into the bonnet of her car, almost falling.

"Please, ambulance and police," she stammered to the operator, trying to pull air into her lungs enough to get the sentence out. "There's a dead body crucified outside my church. Please send someone." She couldn't take her eyes from the grim tableau in front of her, no matter how much she wanted to.

All the while, a soft buzzing came from overhead, the drone capturing the scene as it happened before moving away to the east, where it dropped down, landing gently beside the grey van. The male stepped out from the passenger seat, picked up the drone and placed it carefully in the back before returning to his seat and the van slowly pulled away along the road.

CHAPTER 34

He had been nearly as pleased as the client on this one. The victim, Connor, he had been informed, had played his part well. The industrial steamer burned the flesh away down to the nerves and beyond in a slow process of enduring pain. He had chosen the client and location carefully. Normally this individual's request would have been held back for a more seasonal approach, but it had appealed to him. Undoubtedly, even a basic internet search would turn up the similarity with a crime committed at the turn of the last century, when the killer had been caught at the scene, sitting and staring at the victim nailed to a cross in front of him. They had been quickly convicted and hanged with no attempts to extricate them from their sentence with pleas of diminished responsibility or other defences as you would find now. No, it had been a straightforward crime and punishment, although the police at the time had never bothered to pursue the reasons why the killer had decided to nail their wife to the wooden cross, seemingly just accepting it as another murder. There had been mentions in books, of course, and the method had been copied in a low-budget horror movie, but he had been impressed by his client's diversity from the normal methods of murder. At least this one demonstrated some creativity. The location had been of his choosing. Pett Level wasn't exactly a densely populated area, with less than 800 people living in the small coastal village. There were only two main roads in and out, one to the north from Guestling and the other coming from Fairlight and heading through and on to Rye. He had liked the idea that the murders were slowly working their way east. Connor's death had been captured and recorded for posterity, the client watching the whole ordeal live as per the arrangement. It was only after that it had been uploaded so they could watch repeatedly at their own leisure. He personally had no interest, only watching the live feed to ensure the task had been carried out correctly, as instructed. After Connor's body had been removed to the van, the old farmhouse had been sterilised, with the oven cleared out of any debris and the rooms then bleached clean. Once the van had left, a motorbike with a single rider had arrived and the whole building had been set on fire, using an old cooking stove set in the room where Connor had been held captive. The farmhouse structure was mainly wood, and he had watched from the drone as it had burnt quickly down, almost extinguished, with only the stone walls remaining by the time the fire brigade had been notified and arrived. They had hardly bothered to do any more than damp down the embers. A solitary police officer attended to do no more than the basic paperwork. They had enough to do without worrying about an old building burnt down by what appeared to be somebody sleeping rough in it. There were no bodies and he imagined it would be quickly written off as no crime. There was less paperwork that way. The van and bike had only ever parked on the old concrete drive, the ruts leading from the road now destroyed by the fire engine. No other damage had been caused to any of the ramshackle barns and outbuildings and there were no nearby, nosy neighbours. An ideal location for the purposes.

The only concern had been the drive down from the north-east to Pett Level, with several hundred miles negotiated and countless CCTV, including the ANPR cameras on the Queen Elizabeth Bridge at Dartford. Several different fake, magnetic company signs and false index plates, changed at intervals, ensured that there would be no continuity for the journey. The instruction to torch the vehicle once out of Sussex in some wooded area in Kent meant that there would be no forensics to be recovered from it either. The two males used for the assignment travelled back to their respective areas to hopefully never meet again. They had no names for each other, and no reason to seek each other out again.

It was going to be another very busy day ahead, and Sunday was meant to be the Sabbath, a day of rest as well.

CHAPTER 35

Somebody is seriously fucking with us, Annie thought, as she sped past Bexhill-on-Sea on the A259. The only bright spot was if whoever was responsible for the murders carried on east then they'd be in Kent soon and it would be another area's problem. Kent and Essex MIT teams worked together and had far more resources to call on, although Cornish had mentioned before she'd left the office that they were getting mutual aid from Hampshire, Surrey and a contingent from the Met. Over a hundred detectives would be heading to Sussex from Monday morning to bolster those that had already been working on the first two operations.

The latest was being run as Operation Holt. The weekend on-call SIO had been contacted by the Detective Inspector covering the day shift at Hastings within minutes of the report being placed on the system by the control room. They hadn't even got the first officers on scene, with a response car being sent on blues and twos from the early turn shift, but the DI was switched on enough to quickly realise this was going to be linked to the previous murders that week and had put the balloon up as soon as he'd been informed of the 999 call. He had organised for the duty uniform inspector to follow down to the scene and place a large cordon on, effectively blocking the roads, preventing access in or out of Pett Level. Three vans of officers and PCSOs were deployed to check everybody, and only when authorised and their details verified would the residents be allowed to pass the checkpoints.

Cordons and scene guards were in place and an area DS and team of DCs from the weekend staff were already conducting house-to-house in the immediate vicinity. This would be followed up and completed again in a more coordinated approach in the following days, but there was an urgent need to see what, if anything, could be gleaned along the road passing the church. Annie had set off as soon as Cornish had given her a five-minute briefing and told her to get to the area and make sure it was all being dealt with properly, like he'd know. Livingston was already ensconced with the Chief and several others in a Gold Group meeting to discuss strategy and the media shitstorm that was only going to increase with this latest murder. She'd had updates fed into her on the mobile as she'd driven along. It was going to take at least an hour and a half of travelling time, dependent on the Sunday traffic and the normal groups of middle-aged male cyclists in Lycra heading for the nearest coffee shop, so she'd called up Ged Lake and asked him to meet her at Pett Level. He had been up in Clarke's office when she'd rung him, and they had arranged for the reverend to be taken to the nearest victim care centre so that she could be ABE interviewed as a significant witness to get her account recorded. The process, set out under Achieving Best Evidence guidelines, called for trained officers to take a witness account recorded on camera as opposed to the normal written statement. Lake had said he would get one of his DSs to conduct the interview, assuring Annie they were highly competent, having been on the rape team for many years. Once the video interview had been completed, they would make sure the reverend was comfortable and well looked after so that Annie could see her in person before she left. The sergeant would type up a draft note of the interview and email it to both Annie and Lake as soon as they'd finished, so any urgent enquiries could be taken from it.

What the fuck was going on? This wasn't the work of some maniac out of control on a blitz killing spree. The murders were too specific, all different MOs, with the first two at least being similar to murders conducted decades apart. She remembered the series of murders that happened in Ipswich in Suffolk in 2006; they had been close together but all consistent in method and deposition. Nothing here fitted. The first and latest were on or near to a beach but the way the victims had been dispatched were poles apart. There had to be a link;

there was no way on earth that three different killers had decided to strike in one week. She wondered if it was some initiation rite, but dismissed the idea. They were too well orchestrated to be the work of a random gang. But it had to be someone local; the knowledge of the area couldn't just be from looking at maps on the internet, could it?

A double flash in the rear-view mirror made Annie hit the brake and look at her speedo. Shit, she didn't need any more points on her licence. She thought she was doing about 48mph when she'd hit the brakes, and hoped she was in a 40 zone and not a 30. Maybe the ACC could write this one off if the speed camera had pinged her. There were no blue lights on her MIT Focus and the expectation to follow the speed limits was great until you were told to hotfoot it halfway across the county to a new murder.

Her mobile rang, coming through on the in-car system, and she quickly answered, "Bryce."

"Annie, it's Tony. I didn't get into the office until nine as I had to drop the kids off to their nan before heading in, so I've just heard there's another one. Want me to come over?"

"No, stay put Tony. Can you keep an eye on the staff for Senna and Magenta and make sure they move on anything new. I've got staff from the weekend teams that are going to help on this one today. We can't let the others slide; they've got to all be connected."

"Leave it with me and you concentrate on Mr Crucifixion. Maybe the killer's a fan of Monty Python."

When there was only silence in reply, he continued, "You know, *Life of Brian*, crucifixion or freedom? No? Humour is completely lost on you, DS Bryce."

"Thank you for your valuable input, DS Ali. Call you later."

She hung up, trying to keep to the speed limits and wishing she had Tony with her, but knowing she also needed him to make sure the other two operations continued to be progressed. They couldn't afford to lose track on either of them. There had to be some connection they were missing.

CHAPTER 36

Annie drove through the outer cordon roadblock at the junction of Chick Hill, flashing her warrant card as she turned left onto Pett Level Road. The uniform officers looked frozen already in the damp air blowing in from the sea and they stood hunched against the wind in heavy fluorescent coats, woolly hats and gloves. *Rather you than me*, thought Annie. It was less than a quarter of a mile to St Nicholas Church from the junction. She stopped her car short at the back of a line of marked police cars and a large CSI van. The inner cordon had been set up to restrict access to the entrance to the church, but unfortunately also stopped access to the holiday park beside the church and the promenade that ran along the top of the beach.

She took a heavy black waterproof coat, previously the property of a firearms officer she'd known, and put it on as she got out of the car, zipping it up to the collar and pulling down the flap on the left breast pocket so that the 'Police' label stitched onto it could be seen. Locking her car, only from habit with the amount of police present, Annie walked to the officer with a clipboard standing by the police cordon tape. She showed her warrant card again, "DS Bryce, MIT. Who's here as the CSM?"

A blank look came from the officer, who looked just out of his teenage years.

"Crime Scene Manager. Lead CSI," said Annie, trying to keep the impatience from her voice.

A look of comprehension dawned on the officer's face, "Sorry sarge, hang on."

He looked down at his clipboard, turning back a couple of pages, "Erm, says here it's a Mr Martin. Think they're all over by the front of the church."

He pointed behind him, and Annie could see a white crime scene tent had been constructed to keep off the worst of the weather and salt air. "I'll just sign you in. Can I get your name again, please?"

"DS Bryce, Major Investigation Team," she said, lifting the tape and ducking underneath. "Tom, Tom," she shouted as she approached, and a head appeared out of the tent, covered in a crime scene suit with the hood pulled up and a face mask on.

The mask was pulled down and the beaming smile of Tom Martin greeted her. "My favourite DS is back. You can't keep away from me, can you?"

"Actually, I wasn't expecting to see you; I thought the on-call would be here."

She could still only see Tom from his shoulders up as he leant out of the doorway to the tent. "He gave me a call. He's over at a supposed kidnap and assault in Littlehampton from the middle of the night. Victims turned up within a couple of hours and their story is all over the place. They think the victim was just trying to get some money from his parents, but when this came in, he knew I was nearby and would want to come out, so here I am. This is even better than the last one. Hang on there and I'll get someone to get you kitted out before you come in."

A CSI Annie didn't recognise stepped out and went to the CSI van, returning with a Tyvek suit, overshoes, mask and two pairs or orange latex gloves, asking Annie to double-glove.

She had to remove her warm coat and put it in the van to get the scene suit on and was thankful of the extra layers she put on before she left home as she stepped into the tent. The lights inside created a warmth against the outside cold and Annie saw Tom had Beth with him assisting. The body was a mess.

"What's caused all the injuries, Tom? Any ideas?"
"Looks to me like hot air pressure or steam. See all the bubbling around the wounds? Also, the pink tone all over the body. Reckon he was doused with boiling water. Can't say if he was alive or dead at the time. May get that from the PM, depends what they say about the livor mortis. If the blood pooled all on the back, then

they were lying flat after death. Can't see that they would have been vertical as there's no marks on the upper arms to show they were tied to the beam. If it was just by the hands, then they'd have ripped away from those nails that have been hammered in."

Annie could see a large metal spike had been driven through the palm of each hand, holding it onto the beam.

"There's no pull or tear marks on the hands," Tom continued, "so I reckon they were hammered in while matey boy here was on his back. Might just be for effect. Or he may have still been alive when they did it. There are a few things that will help with his ID though, and I'll put money on his DNA being in the system. There's plenty of needle marks in his arms, and I don't know many addicts who haven't been nicked at one time or another. Also, and here's a clue," he pointed to the victim's neck, "he's got the name Connor tattooed on the side, amongst other ones. So, either he's gay and that's his boyfriend or that's his own name. I'm going for the latter. Before you ask, yes, I've already told DI Lake and he's checking PNC."

With a bit of luck, they could get a fast identification from the Police National Computer on the victim and send some officers to wherever he originated from. There were other tattoos among the burn injuries, and they had a rough age range to search with. Annie just hoped that, if he had been in custody, whoever had booked him in had also taken the time to note them all down. "Is that a real crown of thorns on his head?"

"It would appear so. I'm going to leave it on for the post-mortem. Just have to be careful in the body bag; don't want it poking through and giving some poor soul a prick, do we." He sniggered to himself.

"You somehow manage to find a filthy connotation in anything, Tom. What's it made from, a rose bush?"

Annie was trying to look closer at it without getting in the way of the CSI.

Beth was taking some close images of the crown on the victim's head, "I don't think it is, sarge. I'm not botanist but I do like a bit of gardening. These thorns are way too long to come from a rose bush. I'm getting some images so that we can email them to a chap the National Crime Agency recommended from their database on another job recently. Tom called him just before you got here, and he says he can give us an answer pretty quickly. I haven't seen spikes like that before."

"Tom, can't you just take a couple of pictures on your job phone and do it from here? He might be able to tell us, and we can follow them up with Beth's photos for clarification."

"That is such a good idea, Annie. I don't know why I didn't think of it."

Because you're a technophobe? Annie wondered.

Tom took his phone out, eventually figuring out how to work the camera and then snapping a couple of images before attaching them to an email. "I'll just step out and give the good doctor a quick call and let him know they're on the way," he said, disappearing out the tent flap.

Annie stood back from the body. *There's got to be someone who saw this being put here, surely? A semi-naked man nailed to a six-feet beam of wood; it's not like somebody was dropping off a bag of shopping for harvest festival. There were houses either side, the lifeboat station, the camping park. Whoever chose this location must have known they stood a chance of being seen and there was a CCTV camera at the entrance to the caravan site. This time, there has to be a lead to those responsible.*

CHAPTER 37

This had become far more personal than he had meant it to. Normally, a contract would be agreed, the subject selected and the task carried out, whether in the UK or Europe, spread far enough to seem single, isolated incidents. So why had he agreed to undertake three killings in one week, all in the same small county? Because he had become bored, was the answer. There was more money in his various accounts than he could ever hope to spend, and what had begun as a business proposition over a chance web meeting had started to feel repetitive. Take an assignment, task it out, capture the murder and move on to the next one.

It had been two years and not a single killing had been connected or anyone ever identified as a suspect, let alone arrested. There were murders around the world all the time. He could have taken contracts in North and South America, but there he felt people couldn't be trusted. They were more interested in the killing aspect rather than the money, and that worried him.

They would be careless, and carelessness had risks, and risks could ultimately lead back to those committing the acts. They may not be able to identify him, but they could give the law enforcement agencies places to start looking. This created an unacceptable hazard that he might one day end up talking to the wrong person in a chat room. It happened, he knew. Plenty of stupid paedophiles had been caught because they'd thought they were arranging to meet a 12-year-old girl and, when they'd turned up, had found some burly cop waiting for them. He didn't put himself in their category; they were stupid to get caught with such a simple tactic, but he liked to minimise any risks where he could. As for Africa, well, he had decided they had their own problems, and getting encrypted phones out there made matters far too complex. No, he had more than enough work than he could ever accept just from the European areas.

There was something about this Annie Bryce that intrigued him, though. He could make her life difficult for a while, increase the pressure and see what she did. He had already decided that Livingston was not interested in the outcome unless it benefitted his career and Cornish didn't want to rock the boat if he could help it. They were both content to let Annie do the brunt of the work and certainly run the investigation. If they ever did identify a suspect, he little doubted the pair would be the first to garner the plaudits in front of the cameras.

No, Annie was the real leader. Her interactions with Clarke had been interesting and he wondered if there was some scope there to make matters more personal for her. One more thing to think about.

Without being able to see, he still knew what the police activity at the church would be. Officers out knocking on doors, speaking to the locals who would in turn be on television later telling reporters how shocked they were and how they'd never thought this sort of thing would happen in their village.

He flicked one of the screens in front of him onto Sky News, and the ever-familiar face of their crime correspondent, Martin Crown, doing a piece to camera. He turned the volume up.

"Kirsty, as you're aware, this is the third death in this part of East Sussex in six days. I'm standing down the road from St Nicholas Church in Pett Level, only a short drive from Hastings, where, just a few hours ago, the shocking discovery was made by the church's Reverend Francis when she arrived to open up for the morning's services."

Kirsty Wright, presenting the morning news from the studio, was leaning on the desk, her hands clasped together in front of her, looking earnestly into the camera, "Martin, what can you tell us about this latest incident?"

"Well, the details from the police are currently minimal. However, a source has told me that the victim was found nailed to a wooden beam in a position they are likening to a crucifixion. The body of the deceased has been mutilated, and some kind of thorn crown placed on their heads. Whether this is some symbolic murder or not, there are obvious religious connections."

Clearly Mr Crown has done his homework on the information he's been given prior to transmission, he thought as the reporter continued.

"What is apparent is the placement of the body outside the doors to the church and on a Sunday when, traditionally, the church would be full of local worshippers."

"Martin, are the police connecting this latest murder with the two other deaths this week?"

"Officially Kirsty the police have not made a statement yet other than to say all three are now active investigations being dealt with by their Major Investigation Team, who will be supported by colleagues being drafted in from other forces due to the scale of the investigations. We have been told that the Chief Constable of Sussex Police, Mr Ashley Johnson, will be making a formal statement sometime around lunch today, so we're hoping to get more information then."

"And unofficially?"

"I can tell you that, from the information I am in possession of, the police are currently no further forwards than they were after the second victim, Jack Piper, was identified. They have no suspects and still no identification of the first victim found at Glyne Gap on Tuesday." The reporter paused, suddenly looking over his shoulder and then indicating for his camera operator to follow him as a car began to drive away from the scene. It slowed to negotiate the reporters and cameras in the road and Crown approached the driver's window, pushing his microphone inside as he tried for a quote.

"Officer, can you tell me anything about the latest murder?"

He moved closer to the screen as he saw Annie's face appear, looking annoyed at the intrusion and putting her hand up to move the microphone out of her car.

"No comment at the moment," she said, trying to get her window closed and keeping her face pointed directly ahead.

The reporter continued, "As you can see, the police official line at the moment is not to give out any further details. That was one of the officers involved in all three investigations, Detective Sergeant Anne Bryce, a career detective who has been involved in a number of murder investigations in recent years and is renowned for her thorough approach. She has been a regular visitor to Hastings since Tuesday and I'll try to get a comment from her later in the day."

There will be no chance of that, he thought. Annie would give nothing to the press and leave all briefings to some talking head while she got on with the police work. He continued watching the news report for a while as it flicked back to the studio, rolling out some ex-Met DCI, overweight and sweating under the studio lights, to give their opinion. Pointless, he knew: they would have no more information than the viewers watching. Their comments were pure speculation, the same drivel that he had heard spouted after every murder by some retired officer looking to top up their pension. It always seemed to be the officers of rank, and he imagined that was the only reason the news agencies used them. It gave them a level of gravitas, even though most of their comments were generic rubbish they seemed to repeat no matter what the crime.

He switched to the BBC news channel, then ITV, both giving coverage of the murder from other locations. This would be the main news item for the day, he envisaged, unless a member of parliament was caught with their pants down to bump it back down.

The next killing, though, would hold the front pages, and he intended to have the entire country following it from the outset.

CHAPTER 38

Annie sat in her car down the hill from the police station, putting off the walk past the reporters as long as she could. God, they were parasites; they couldn't care less about the victims, only about which of them could create the most drama and bump up the viewing figures. Not that they needed to there; the killings were creating enough interest by their number and manner alone without having to dramatise it even more. She put her head back onto the rest and closed her eyes. *Why is this happening? There must be a reason.*

A bang on the far window startled her, and she looked across. Ged Lake was bending over, looking in, pointing to the door handle. Annie opened the central locking and he got into the passenger seat next to her.

"Thought you were sleeping on the job. Sorry, couldn't resist seeing if I could make you jump."

"Very funny, Ged. Lucky I'm not armed or I might have shot you. I thought you were still at the scene?" Annie was ruffled, she didn't like to have people creep up on her, no matter if they thought it was funny or not.

Lake was rubbing his hands together in front of him, trying to get them warm. "I was, but Clarke called and told me to get back here. I've left the team with instructions. They're a good bunch; I trust 'em."

Annie was calming back down, "So did you find anything?"

Lake turned to face her. The scar on his cheek looked whiter with the cold and stood out more lividly than usual. "As a matter of fact, we did. There's a camera on the entry to the camping site but that only covers the gate, nothing for the approach to the church. There's no cameras in the car park but there are two at the lifeboat station. One covers the beach side but the other looks directly down past the church towards the road. I haven't seen any footage, but they had managed to contact one of the keyholders via the control room and they were on their way down to allow access. Apparently, it's just straight onto a hard drive, so I've asked TSU to meet them there and provide a replacement and just recover the whole drive. That way, we can look back as far as it goes and see what else might have been recorded."

"There has to be footage of them arriving and dropping off the body. It can't have been the quickest thing to get a person attached to a large piece of wood propped up to the door. Are they bringing it here?"

This could be a decent break, Annie thought.

"No, taking it straight back to their office, but they said they'll do a fast-time review and put some clips and stills onto the system so that we can access them here. They'll call me as soon as they have anything."

"What about the PNC check on the victim's tattoos you were having run?"

Lake checked his phone, "Nothing yet." He scowled at the screen, "I was hoping we'd get a quick hit. I'll chase it up as we walk in, that way I look busy for the cameras, plus I have an excuse not to talk to them."

Annie turned in her seat, reaching for her coat off the rear seats. "Shall we run the gauntlet then?"

"Why not. You lead; nobody wants to see this ugly mug when they're eating their lunch later."

The pair got out of the car and headed up the road to the rear of the police station and the cluster of reporters congregated outside. As they entered through the throng, Annie pointed to a coned-off space in the otherwise full car park. "I take it that's for the Chief? Heaven forbid he'd have to walk through that bunch like we just had to."

"Nah, he'll just get his driver to mow 'em down so he doesn't have to stop," Lake said, swiping his tag on the door and opening it to allow Annie to walk in first.

CHAPTER 39

The Superintendent was in her office, with a large silver pot of coffee on the table in front of her when Annie and Lake knocked on the door and entered.

"Ma'am," they said, virtually in unison.

"I think we can dispense with that; there's only the three of us here."

Between them, Lake and Annie updated Clarke with what they knew. "We should have some footage from TSU in the next couple of hours at the latest," Lake said, "and I'm still waiting on a call from intel on the PNC check they're running."

Clarke looked like she'd barely slept in the preceding days, her face looking more drawn than ever as she picked at a digestive biscuit from the plate beside her. "Help yourselves to coffee and biscuits. Sorry, best I can do. I'll send somebody out later to get some hot food for us. Don't think we'll be sitting down to a Sunday roast today."

Annie looked at Clarke. *You don't look like you've ever eaten a roast dinner,* she thought. Clarke's uniform seemed to be hanging off her. "Jess, are you okay?"

"Fine, I'm just not used to three dead people on my patch in a week and the world's media camped outside my office. Don't get me wrong, murders I can deal with, but this level of scrutiny ... I got home last night and there was some reporter waiting outside my house. My own bloody house. What did they think I was going to do? Invite them in for coffee and let them have a look through my laptop?"

Lake was pouring out two coffees, "So what did you do? Give them dinner and a nice bottle of Pinot?"

A flicker of a smile at least crossed Clarke's face. "Not exactly. I told him if he didn't get off my drive, I was going to beat him with his own tape recorder, cheeky fucker. He was just standing there by the door in the dark waiting for me to turn up. I very nearly twatted the prick with my baton. He must have been stood still as the security light only came on as I pulled up."

"Where was he from?" Annie asked. "And how did he get your address?"

"No idea. Not hard to track down though; I've lived there a while and I suppose a quick run through my Facebook account would probably give you enough clues if you wanted to find me. Never really bothered worrying about it before. Might change my mind now though."

"And that bright red Range Rover of yours with the personalised plate isn't that hard to follow if you want to," remarked Lake.

"Don't tell me: 999JC?" asked Annie.

"Worse," Clarke even looked embarrassed. "JES3Y. Thought it was funny when I saw it on the internet and cost a bloody fortune. Not exactly my cleverest purchase, but when you've had a couple of drinks to drown your divorcee sorrows a lot of things seem a good idea at the time."

So, a large, bright red car with a personal plate, parked in the rear yard of the police station and seen every time she comes and goes. No, not that hard to find out where she lives, Annie thought. Strange that it was a hard copy journalist and not one of the big TV crews with a camera to get her reaction? Perhaps they were a bit too professional to confront the Area Commander on her own doorstep?

Lake's phone began vibrating on the table and he snatched it up. "DI Lake." There was a pause then, "Hi Andy, what've you got?"

He began making notes in his daybook and, after a couple of minutes, ended the call. "That was Andy Smy, DS on the intel team. They've got a hit on our victim. His name's Connor Reece and he was reported missing on Thursday from the hostel he was staying at. Standard paperwork completed but no effort to trace him as he's a regular wanderer. He's a druggie from Middlesbrough. I'll go and give the area DI a call and get a couple of their DCs to go to the hostel and see if they can't get a voluntary search conducted of his room, see what they can turn up. Andy's drawing up a profile but says the age and tattoos all match up with our victim. We can do DNA for confirmation, but I reckon we have our man."

Annie stood up from the table, "I better give the ACC a call. He'll need to put the Chief's press conference off for an hour or so until we get some bobbies around to Connor's next of kin. At least then the Chief can go out to the media with his statement and include who the victim is in one hit instead of holding another conference later. We'll need to make sure that we leave a uniform outside the family's when we find them, to stop any unwanted press giving them a knock on the door. Bad enough they have to find out he's dead without having to contend with the media as well. Give me a minute."

She picked up her coffee and left the room to find an empty office to call Livingston.

After the door had closed Lake reached across the table, putting his hand over Clarke's, "Why didn't you tell me about this reporter when you rang me last night?"

"Why, what difference would it have made? It was just one of them trying to get the jump on the rest and see if I'd drop them a bit of info. Soon as I got out the car and told him to fuck off, he left. No issues. Anyway, what would you have done? Ridden over the hill on a white charger to rescue me. Like I need that."

She pulled her hand away from Lake's.

"Jesus Jess, why do you never want to accept any help? I offered to come back with you last night and you brushed me off."

"And good job I did. How would that have looked? Area Commander rocking up home with one of her DIs in the passenger seat in the pitch-black. Would have made a great bit of press, wouldn't it, and I really don't need that right now Ged, especially not with Livingston over here."

Lake stood up and moved round the table to sit in the chair next to her. "Neither of us are married. I don't see what the problem is."

"You wouldn't because you're a man. Do you understand how hard I've had to work to get here and then I fucked it up having an affair with Livingston." She sighed. "Look Ged, I like you a lot and the last few weeks have been great, but if it gets out we're seeing each other then one of us is going to get moved to another division and it's likely to be me as the senior officer. I don't need another black mark on the books that can be used by the likes of Livingston and his cronies against me. Let's just leave things as they are for the moment, can we?"

"The bloke's a cunt and I'm more than happy to tell him to his face if he tries to stitch you up. Seems everyone but his missus knows he's always over the side."

He stopped, seeing a look of hurt on Clarke's face to his last comment. "Can we just have a drink at yours when we finish tonight? Bit of company outside this place would do us both good. I'll park in a different street, and you can ring me when you're indoors so you don't get seen with me. Even if I get seen coming back out, we can pass it off that I was dropping something urgent off to you on my way home, completely innocent. Come on. Promise to go straight home to my crappy flat after."

He put his hands together in a pleading gesture.

Clarke relented, "Okay, but just one glass and then you drag your arse back to your own pit, agreed? Let's see how late we finish first though. You need your beauty sleep way more than most."

CHAPTER 40

Livingston was, unsurprisingly to Annie, in the Chief's car when she rang him and was put on speaker so that the Chief could listen in. She updated the pair on the identity of the victim and told how she had arranged for the local officers from Cleveland Police to find and speak to the next of kin, plus start some checks around the person who reported Reece missing. She'd draw up a list of actions with Lake and run them by the DCI before they were passed out to be actioned.

"Have we got a new HOLMES team yet?" she asked.

"No, we need to get that staffed from tomorrow," Livingston replied. "I've spoken to Jenny who's in on overtime trying to catch up on Magenta. Once we get some additional staff land, she's going to set up a third MIR to accommodate this latest murder. She thinks she can oversee all three, but I want a manager in each office. She can sit above all of them. Mr Johnson and myself should be with you in about half an hour. Zoe's following on behind us. She's already contacted the relevant people to get the press conference put back until 1 p.m."

That's convenient, thought Annie. *The Chief will leave after the conference and then the lovely Zoe is on hand to drive you back to HQ later. Almost like you planned it that way.*

"See you when you get here then, Sir."

By the time it got to 1 p.m., Annie had established the number for Connor's phone so that they could obtain the call data and cell site history. His parents had been traced and the agony message passed, and she'd had an update from the significant witness interview of Reverend Francis. Lake had been right about his DS: he'd been thorough in both the interview and his typed summary, which he'd sent through. There was no need for Annie to see the Reverend Francis at the VCC, so she'd arranged for her to be taken back home and would go to visit her there later. The reverend had wanted to contact some of her parishioners in any event, not to tell them what she's seen, but to offer her support and that of the church.

Annie had called Tony and he was liaising with Cleveland MIT to get a team to start tracing the Connor's last steps on CCTV, starting with the town cameras. If they were lucky, they might pick him up and be able to follow him and see if he'd been abducted close by. It would take a while, but they now knew a rough time he was last seen from one of the occupants at the hostel who'd spoken to the police when they attended earlier.

Annie was standing at the back of the room next to Lake, the assembled media all in front of her with cameras at the front facing the table and chairs laid out for the Chief Constable. A large board behind where he would be sitting had the Sussex Police crest and the telephone number to call for the incident room, along with the number for Crimestoppers.

Right on cue, the Chief walked in, followed by Livingston, Clarke and Zoe Tims. The group sat down with Livingston and Clarke either side of him. Johnson was in full uniform, his tunic emblazoned with his medal ribbons over his left top pocket. He had an iPad in front of him to read from.

"Good afternoon all and thank you for attending. I'm going to read a brief statement then will take a few questions. To my right is ACC Mark Livingston, the Senior Investigating Officer for the recent incidents in and around Hastings, and to my left, Superintendent Jessica Clarke, the Area Commander for Rother Division. Finally, at the end of the table I'm sure most of you will already know Zoe Tims, one of the headquarters press office team."

He paused for effect, "Shortly before 7 a.m. this morning, the body of a male was found outside St Nicholas Church at Pett Level, a small coastal village on the outskirts of Hastings. At this time, we believe we have identified the victim but will not be releasing their name until specially trained family liaison officers are in place with the next of kin to support them at this very difficult time. I will also not be discussing the details of the victim's death but can say that this is being treated as a murder investigation. As you will be aware, this is the third suspicious death on Rother Division in the last six days. There is no evidence currently to link either the crimes or the victims, but we are exploring all possibilities and a working hypothesis has been developed. Individual teams are working on each investigation and ACC Livingston has oversight of them all. While we do not feel that there is a greater risk to the public at large, we ask them to take care when they are out and report anything suspicious to the incident room on the numbers on the board behind me. If urgent, then please ensure that you call 999 for an emergency response.

"Be assured that we are actively pursuing all lines of enquiry to identify those responsible and I have been provided support to the investigations by my colleagues in other areas of the country. The residents of Hastings and the surrounding areas should expect to see a heightened, visible police presence over the coming days, and I would ask for their patience and assistance if they are delayed in their daily business. I would also like to take this opportunity to offer my sincere condolences to the families of all three individuals and give my personal assurance that every effort will be made to bring those responsible to justice. Thank you."

The Chief sat back as a flurry of hands were raised and voices called out questions. Zoe Tims, trying to bring a semblance of order, worked around the room, going first to the main news channel leads before moving on to the print journalists.

Annie watched as Livingston fielded questions regarding the investigations and their progress without actually saying anything of relevance, before Clarke conducted a series of interviews for the local news groups, reiterating the Chief's comments and attempting to reassure the public.

When the briefing had concluded, Johnson stood up, spoke briefly to Livingston, and exited the room without passing a glance in Annie's direction. Obviously, he'd fulfilled what he felt were his duties and was now going to do a smart about-face back to headquarters. The ACC waved a hand towards Annie and Lake, beckoning them over to the table.

"So, we at least know who this latest chap is, that's a start. What he's doing down by the beach nailed to a lump of wood is another matter. What've you got from Cleveland yet Annie?"

"Speaking to the officers up there, Reece is a well-known Class A drug user, regular misper in and out of custody. All for the usual low-level stuff, some shoplifting, bit of possession. He's been known to them since he was a juvenile and ended up getting kicked out by his parents, who were fed up with us kicking in their front door at four in the morning looking for him. When he went missing from the hostel they just called in the details as part of their normal procedures, no need for an officer to even attend as he'd only come back from his last jaunt a couple of days prior. They just updated PNC expecting him to return as normal. His regular dealer's been traced and says he hasn't seen him since last weekend. They're not convinced they believe him but are checking out his alibis for the days since Reece was last seen."

"Anything else?" Livingston was nothing if not blunt. Annie wondered if he ever bothered to read any of the reports he was copied into.

"Yes Sir. They had an officer do a quick review of the council CCTV. There's a camera on the corner by the hostel, and they've picked Reece up leaving the location and have tracked him through the town to an old car park behind a parade of shops. There aren't any cameras covering the car park but he's not seen to come back out again and there's no sightings of him from that point onwards. They're trying to get some work done on all the vehicles leaving the immediate vicinity in the next hour in the hope they can get some index numbers."

She went on to explain that one of the priorities was to identify the vehicle which had brought Reece down to Pett Level from Middlesbrough. There were countless CCTV cameras along the way, and ANPR, depending which route had been taken. One thing that couldn't be avoided was the Queen Elizabeth Bridge on the M25. She doubted they would have risked coming through central London and they needed to clear the obvious routes down before they considered alternatives. It was unlikely they had deviated from the most direct route, as the less time you drove around with a dead man nailed to a lump of wood the better.

"There's so many cameras on the bridge that they must have picked up whatever the vehicle was. Just the small matter of finding it. I'm hoping they brought him down overnight on Saturday. With it being weekend traffic it should be lighter than on a commuter day and there should be less lorries as well."

Clarke had rejoined them, and they discussed staff deployments and plans for the rest of Sunday. Tom called to say he had arranged for the post-mortem, but it couldn't be done until 10 a.m. on the Monday morning and Ludstein wasn't going to be available. It would be a Dr Kerry Drake, who was fairly new to the Home Office team, but Tom had worked with her on a number of occasions.

Lake offered to attend, "Annie dealt with the last two, I'm happy to go on this one with Tom. Just have to provide an exhibits officer to go with me."

"I'll sort that with someone from my office Ged, thanks." Annie was relieved to not have to spend another half a day in the mortuary and she could see the ACC wasn't about to rush to go in her place.

The day continued with little further progress. TSU had downloaded the footage from the lifeboat station. It showed a white Transit van arrive just after 6 a.m., the footage grainy and dark. The van had parked by the front of the church, obscuring the view of the camera. Less than five minutes and it pulled away again. Anyone who had exited the van must have done so on the driver's side. The index plates couldn't be seen and there was no writing on the van to differentiate it from any other grubby white van. They could put out an image from the footage for as much use as it was. Annie had managed to take a drive out in the afternoon and speak to Reverend Francis, who had insisted she stay for a coffee, telling Annie to call her Steph and drop the formal title. Steph Francis had been at St Nicholas for the past five years and, before that, had worked in different parts of the country along with spending time abroad in South America. Annie heard how Steph had seen sights there she never imagined she'd see again in quiet Pett Level – victims of drug gangs, tortured and left for dead. Annie was surprised at how tiny the reverend was, maybe a fraction over five feet tall and nearly the same width, and it was apparent Steph was shaken by the mornings activities, despite her previous experiences.

It was mid-evening when Annie was called to Clarke's office to join her and Lake. Livingston had left several hours earlier, citing that he needed to get back to his office but would be contactable on his phone. Annie felt it far more likely he was going to make use of his executive bathroom with the lovely Ms Tims, as she saw the pair driving out of the car park in Zoe's car, with Tims skirt just about covering her dignity as she got into the driver's seat. That day he had a perfect excuse to his wife for being late home and for her to not wait up.

When she walked into the room, Clarke and Lake were eating chicken kebabs from orange polystyrene cartons on the table, with a third, unopened, sat waiting for Annie. Cans of soft drinks sat in the middle and Annie picked up a Diet Coke before sitting down, "Take it there's no forks then?"

"Forks to eat a kebab? What are you, some kind of heathen?" said Lake as he shovelled in another handful of chicken and salad. "Sorry if I stink; had to go with the garlic sauce and the chilli."

Clarke was picking at bits of chicken, the pitta bread itself untouched. "Ged got them. Yours is a basic doner kebab, no sauce. I did tell him to hang on so you had the option of that or the chicken, but he seemed too starved to wait. You can share mine if you don't want meat of doubtful origin."

Annie would have happily eaten grilled rat, she was so hungry, and opened the carton, taking a bite of the still warm kebab and washing it down with the coke. They ate in partial silence, Lake devouring his food as if it was going to be his last supper and Annie not far behind him. Lake looked at Clarke's only partly touched food, "You gonna eat that? Wouldn't want it to go to waste."

Clarke pushed the mostly uneaten carton of food across to him, and he briefly indicated if Annie wanted any, to which she declined. She knew exactly where her kebab was going to sit like a meat baby in her stomach for the next few hours and was already regretting having 'dirty food', as they often called takeaways at work. The eating habits of a police officer on long hours was not one that would be recommended by most dieticians or doctors, unless they wanted to induce heart attacks in their patients.

Lake cleared the cartons away when they'd finished, Clarke asking him to put them in the bin in the corridor as she didn't want to come into the smell of them in the morning.

There was little else that could be done by that time; all the enquiries were being conducted and results would drip through in the next twenty-four hours or so. There was so much to go through, and Annie doubted she would get any sleep even when she did get home, with all the information running around in her head needing to be unscrambled. She'd text Kevin to ask him to keep Bella at his for the next few days. Much as she wanted her dog home, she was only there to sleep. He'd been fine with it, having seen the news bulletins, and said Bella was currently fast asleep on his sofa. *Good to know she's not picking up any bad habits there!*

She called Tony and arranged to meet him at the office first thing, so they could go across to Hastings together. At least that way they could discuss things in the car as opposed to over a phone and, the truth was, she needed him to bounce ideas off. They had always worked well together and, while he had a far more laid-back approach, they complemented each other. Yin and yang.

She told Lake she would be over no later than nine in the morning and then headed out to walk to her car. There were still a few reporters outside the gates, with bright camera lights on them as they gave yet another version of the day's events to the viewers. They'd yet to come up with a catchy name for the killer, but give them time. They didn't have one thing to fix on yet, but they would. She opened her car and threw her coat and bag onto the back seat, started the engine, and decided to go straight home in the job car. No point in adding an hour to the journey to go to the office and swap over to her own.

CHAPTER 41

He had the most recent three files open on the computer screens in front of him. The police should be getting snippets of incorrect information from across the country now. They'll soon be chasing up on potential CCTV opportunities at garages and motorway services in the hope of finding the van, if in fact they'd even established it was a van yet, which it didn't sound like. He'd gone through the emails on Annie's phone, and until they identified a vehicle, they wouldn't be able to try and track it on a route. Sadly for them, when they picked up the van that Reece had been unceremoniously bundled into, and he hoped they would eventually, it would vanish within a few miles. The false plates, signage, and removal of the wraparound giving it the appearance of a rusty, decrepit van would mean police would spend days looking in the wrong places.

He knew there were cameras at the deposition site. It was one of the things he'd made sure of when he selected it. There was no fun if he didn't have the investigators running around like headless chickens.

The news conference had been played earlier and he'd taken an instant dislike to Chief Constable Johnson; a pompous individual in his opinion, assuring the public they were safe and how there'd be extra officers out. As if that would make a difference. You were hardly going to grab a person off the street if there was a marked car parked next to them. Even if they flooded the area around Hastings, they couldn't do the whole county. It was a PR exercise, plain and simple. He had a feeling the Chief may be looking for more suitable employment in the coming days.

The comments he'd heard from Annie's phone had been more interesting. The ACC was one for the ladies, it seemed. Well, carefully created reputations could be destroyed in a heartbeat if it came out in the media that while he was meant to be leading three murder investigations, the ACC was getting it on with his press officer. There was some scope there for a piece of work. No more than a distraction, but he'd taken a dislike to Mark Livingston. If Sussex police headquarters was similar to most others with their security, then it would be no hardship to get a camera in the ACC's office. Old habits and courtesies to hold a door open for someone created opportunities to walk inside many buildings if you had the correct looking ID. From his experience, if the paperwork looked right, it got only a cursory glance. The key was to look and act as if you were meant to be there.

There were going to be dozens, if not hundreds, of new people going in to help on the investigations at headquarters, the MIT office and Hastings. People would be far too busy to check each individual properly, and it would be nice to mingle and meet a few of those he'd recently come to know only on screen. Yes, now would be an opportune time to take a personal involvement.

He began to draw up the necessary arrangements, sending messages via darknet chat rooms to obtain what he required. There was a lot of work to be done, some of which had already been arranged for that night, which would throw the whole of Hastings police, the ACC and most certainly the Chief into a state of utter panic. After all, if you can't look after your own, how can you be expected to look after the general public?

CHAPTER 42

It was a quarter to eleven when Lake put his head into Clarke's office as she was putting a plain, padded jacket on over her uniform shirt. "Still on for a quick drink? I know I could do with one."

She looked at her watch, "I'm not sure Ged. It's late, I need to get some sleep."

He stepped into the office, shutting the door behind him, and moved across to stand in front of her, pulling her jacket closed then placing his hands on her arms. "Jess, I think it's safe to say you aren't gonna be sleeping whether I come round or not, even if you do look shattered. Come on, a bit of decent company will do us both good and I promise, one drink, then I'm gone." He made a crossing gesture over his heart with his right hand.

She looked at his face; a bit of human comfort would be good. "Park a couple of roads away though, just in case that reporter's hanging around again. When I get inside I'll give you a call and you can walk round."

Lake grinned, "Give you time to slip into something more comfortable?"

Clarke rolled her eyes. "Don't push your luck, handsome." She kissed him briefly before continuing past to the door, "No, it'll give me time to turn on the lights and pour us a drink. I'm more than comfortable in what I'm currently wearing tonight, thank you."

Lake gave her a few minutes' head start then walked down to his first-floor office to collect his jacket and keys. He was just switching the light off when the landline on his desk rang. He swore to himself, considering leaving it for the answer machine to pick up, but thought better of it and walked back to his desk, throwing the jacket over the back of his chair as he sat down. "DI Lake," he answered.

"Evening boss, wasn't expecting you to still be in the office, was about to leave you a message. It's Andy Smy."

"Hi Andy, what can I do for you? Been a long day for all of us." He looked at the time displayed on the phone: 10.55 p.m.

"We've been doing some work on vehicles coming out of that car park in Middlesbrough and think we've got a van around the right time. It turns up about ten minutes before Connor arrives and then leaves soon after he's last seen on CCTV."

"That's great, Andy. Got an index for it?"

"Yeah, and that's about as far as it goes. It's a standard white Ford Transit, looks like it's seen far better days, but the index is bollocks. Comes back to another Transit in the town. I've checked with the locals and they sent a unit round to the registered keeper to do a bit of covert. Turns out it's just some builder, his van was parked outside his house, not even similar and he's not had his plates nicked. Looks like they just cloned 'em. Must have a contact in the motor trade or got the kit to do it themselves. Either way, means they could use the same vehicle and just keep changing the plates every couple of hours. Run the risk of being stopped by a mobile ANPR but if they got lucky and stick to cloned Transit plates, they could just keep swapping them around. All they'd need to do is go on Autotrader and look up white Transit vans then copy the index plates and nobody would give 'em a second glance. White van man syndrome."

"Fuck. How many white Transits are there driving around the country d'ya reckon, Andy?"

"You see Ford's TV adverts, boss? If you want to know, I googled it before I rang you: there's over half a million. Great, eh?"

Lake sat running his hands through his short hair thinking, *this takes us fucking nowhere.* "Have you got a decent image of the van, Andy, going in and coming out?"

"Yeah, reckon so boss. It's the council system, so it's digital."

Lake was thinking ahead. They could check the images of the van entering the car park and compare them with the images of it coming back out. There were some very clever people who could look at those images and tell if the weight had changed. It was more than likely Andy had the right van, the false plates being the main reason, but if they could say with certainty, then they at least knew it was the right vehicle.

"Get some stills to me as soon as you can. And get the locals to run the CCTV again. I want all white Transits in the area checked no matter if they look the same as our target or not. Check every one. If they've used ghost plates on one, then they'll have done it again. Cross-reference against the registered keeper to see if they check out against the van's movements. Run them through ANPR as well." *This could be it; just need to do the leg work.*

"Will do boss, but nothing's happening until tomorrow. There's only sad sacks like us still working tonight."

Lake checked the time again, "I know, you're right. Thanks Andy, at least it's something. Get off soon and we can pick this up again in the morning."

"Will do, cheers boss."

Progress, Lake thought, considering momentarily if he should call Annie. Deciding against it on the basis it would make little difference tonight, he wrote a short email updating her of the conversation so at least she'd have it first thing in the morning. Then, picking his jacket back up, he headed downstairs to his car. That glass of wine with Jess was looking very appealing right now, not as much as her company but still, the day was ending better than it started.

CHAPTER 43

Clarke pulled up onto her drive, only noticing as she turned the engine off that the security light by the front door hadn't come on. *Shit, and I don't have a spare bulb,* she thought.

She stepped out of the car then leant into the back seat to pick up her laptop and bag. As she took hold of the bag, the opposite door opened, a figure appearing in front of her, and a hand clasped over her wrist. Shocked, she tried to pull back away and out of the car but was pushed from behind as she stood up, striking her forehead on the top of the doorsill and a sharp stab of pain stunned her as she was forced into the car and dragged across the back seat.

Clarke tried to roll over, kicking back with her legs, but the figure who had her wrists used it to stretch her arm out straight and a needle was plunged into her forearm where her coat had ridden up.

The air had been knocked out of her and it was difficult to breathe lying on her front. She grabbed through the front seats with her left hand, attempting to pull herself away from whoever these people were, and lifted her head to shout for help. But then the figure behind her was pressing her face into the leather of the seat covers. She thrashed against them, but the more she struggled, the less she could breathe, the lack of oxygen starving her brain and slowing her down.

They, whoever they were, had injected her with some substance, and she knew she had to quickly get out of the car and get help. She could feel her legs getting heavy. *What the fuck had they injected her with and where was Ged? He should be right behind her. She needed to warn him. She needed to, needed to what?* Her thinking was becoming foggy as, inevitably, she lost consciousness.

Clarke's limp, unresisting body was folded first onto the back seat, as a set of plastic cable ties were placed around her wrists and ankles and a strip of tape put over her mouth, before she was rolled into the footwell, and a blanket thrown over her. One of the figures immediately got into the driver's seat and started the engine, backing the car slowly out of the driveway, before turning up the hill away from her house and heading to The Ridge. They had a few hours until she came round to get to the location where Clarke was to be delivered and secure her in place, as instructed.

The second figure had calmly walked away from the house, removing the balaclava from his head so as not to draw unnecessary attention to himself. It was late and he didn't expect to bump into anyone, but if he did it was no consequence. He had a dark Puffa jacket and jeans on, head down, minding his own business. He set off back to the motorbike parked less than half a mile away, the crash helmet stashed in the hedge nearby. Ten minutes later he was already on his way out of Hastings.

Lake parked his car two roads away from Clarke's house. It was a far nicer location than where he had his flat, and he supposed she could afford it, even after her divorce. The road was all high hedges and long driveways for privacy. Expensive it may be, but the streetlights were still out at that time of night, the same as in the cheaper parts of the town, and he used a small LED torch as he walked the short distance to her home. He was later than he'd meant to have been, slowed down by the call and then emailing Annie, but Jess was meant to have rung him when she'd got home to let him know if that reporter was still hanging about. She'd probably gone indoors and completely forgotten. He imagined her sitting down already, with a wine or gin and tonic, only to be surprised when he knocked on the door.

He turned into her drive and stopped. Where was her car? She'd left well before him and he'd expected to see lights on in the house. Jess can't have stopped off for anything; she wasn't the type to buy wine from a garage and, anyway, she always had a well-stocked drinks cabinet. No security light had come on either, which was puzzling. He knew she had one fitted by the front door.

He took out his mobile and dialled her number, listening as it rang three times before the answering service cut in. He texted her, "Jess, where are you? Car trouble?"

He doubted the last; her car was only a couple of years old and regularly serviced. In any event, if it had stopped for any reason, he'd followed the same route she would have done so he'd have seen her. Where the fuck was she? He banged on the door, knowing it was futile, but couldn't think of what else to do at that moment. The dark house was silent. He dialled her number again with the same outcome. Now he was beginning to be concerned. He dialled the control room supervisor.

"Hi, it's DI Lake from Hastings CID. I need a marked car to my location now on silent blues. I've just come to Superintendent Clarke's address and the house is in darkness with no sign of her. There's no car and she spoke to me before leaving the nick saying she was going home. With all that's been going on, this doesn't feel right."

"Sir, it's Sergeant Wright. I'll get a car dispatched to the address, I've got it in front of me, and I'll transfer you to Oscar 1 now."

The line went silent before a female voice spoke, "DI Lake, I'm Inspector Bryant. What's the issue?"

"As I just told your sergeant, Superintendent Clarke left Hastings police station about half an hour ago telling me she was going directly home." Lake paused, framing his next words carefully, "I was just dropping by to give her an urgent update on the most recent murder and she's not arrived home. I tried calling her mobile but it goes straight to voicemail."

Lake could imagine the Inspector sitting there wondering why he'd felt the need to go to the Superintendent's address in person rather than just phoning to update her. Added to that, why did he know where she lived?

"There's a car on route to you. I've just got the Super's mobile number up on my screen and we'll try calling it from here. Is there anything where you are to suggest that something's happened to her?"

Lake shone the torch around the drive. Nothing. Then he heard a crunch of glass under his right foot and looked down, shining the torch at the ground. Fragments of glass littered the porch by the door and he swung the beam up to the security light. The LED unit in the housing was shattered. He felt his stomach lurch.

"Her security light's been damaged. I think she's been grabbed."

Bryant's voice was calm in comparison to Lake's, "Okay, this constitutes an immediate threat to life. I'm more than content under the circumstances to authorise a trace on her mobile number to see if it's still active and moving. I'll let the Authorising Officer know so they can give a verbal authority on it. Units should be with you in a minute."

Lake swore. *Fuck, not Jess. Not one of our own.* He didn't even cast a thought that it would be anything other than connected to the recent murders. None of the local villains would be stupid enough to go for a copper. He saw the blue strobes of the approaching unit in the darkness and walked to the side of the drive to make his way to the road to meet them.

Clarke's phone was in the pocket of the motorcyclist heading up the A21 towards London. Somewhere on the M25, he planned to drop the phone on the road, where it would be repeatedly driven over and smashed to pieces. The trace would follow a false trail away from the town and no amount of convoy checking on ANPR would link it back to the bike. Despite that, there were already arrangements in place to dispose of the motorbike in one of the less salubrious hamlets in London, where it would either be stripped for parts or ridden ragged and set on fire. It mattered not to him.

CHAPTER 44

Annie put the phone back down. Never for a minute would she have thought Jess may have been a target. There was no reason to. She could hear the anguish in Lake's voice when he made the short call to her, saying that they'd had a location for Clarke's phone, but it had cut out on the M25 near Bromley, so may have been switched off. Clarke's car hadn't pinged any of the ANPR cameras on the A21, so whoever had grabbed her most likely had dumped it for being too easy to spot and transferred her to another one. There were plenty of officers at the scene along with a forensic team, but nothing obvious and no calls from a kidnapper. This made it even more of a possibility that it was linked to the murders and there would be no ransom demands. The Chief had been informed, along with Livingston and several others of the command team, and a Silver Cell, staffed for kidnap situations, had been set up in the event that there was contact from the abductors, but that was more hopeful than expectation.

Annie had offered to head straight back across, but Lake had told her to stay put. If she was awake all night, then she wouldn't be around for Monday. He said he'd hold the fort for that night and take the lead until stood down by a more senior officer but would call her if there was any progress.

She put the phone down on the kitchen counter. *This can't be happening; police officers don't get snatched from outside their home address.* It wouldn't be for money, so there was only one other alternative, that she didn't want to be true because if it was, it meant Jess was going to be the next body found.

***

He sat watching the monitor, wondering how each of those involved would react to the latest developments. The only reason Lake had discovered Clarke missing so quickly could only be because he had gone to her address, and at that time of night after a long day together he doubted very much if it was to give her a report that could have been passed over the telephone. No, rather he felt it was a romantic liaison that the pair wanted to keep quiet from others. This created an interesting new dynamic: how would Lake react now that it was personal and someone close to him? He could tell by the way that Lake spoke to Annie that he was trying to hold himself together, and she obviously wasn't aware that there was a relationship going on. Lake must have decided to keep that information to himself for now, even from Annie, which was interesting. How was Livingston going to take the latest turn of events as well? Would he come running to rescue the situation? Unlikely. Rather, this may be a convenient get-out if Clarke was to die. He better hope though that there was nothing on her phone that showed the pair were more than just business acquaintances. Once the call data and text messages were recovered from the phone service provider, he imagined there was a strong possibility it would contain more than enough to put the ACC in a very uncomfortable position with a lot of explaining to do, not least to his wife. Well, he intended to add to the man's problems. His wife was either naïve or turned a blind eye to his dalliances because Livingston kept them quiet. She'd have a change of heart soon enough.

Everything was in place for him to go to headquarters in the coming hours and create a diversion for the media. Pretty Zoe would be collateral damage, but she only had herself to blame.

He would watch for a while longer; he wasn't tired and wanted to see Annie safely off to bed. He turned in his chair and looked over at the figure lying on the metal-framed bed behind him. Clarke was still sleeping off the effects of the anaesthetic, which would take several more hours. It was difficult to predict how different individuals would react and the dosage was more to render them quickly unconscious than to have them wake at a set time. He had considered giving a Narcan injection, but there was no rush; he had plans and things he still needed to do before he spoke to her. It wasn't like she could go anywhere. He decided to give her a top up before he left. It wouldn't do for her to come round and find herself in a strange location with nobody to talk to, after all. He swivelled back to the monitor.

***

Annie walked upstairs and sat on her bed. *This is all rapidly going to ratshit and out of control.* She had begun to feel like she was in the eye of a whirlwind with everything spinning around her. She downed half the glass of wine she'd poured herself. It was probably a bad idea to mix it with the two paracetamol she swallowed at the same time, but it wasn't like she hadn't done it on many occasions before. She was exhausted, her leg hurt and now Jess was missing. She doubted she would get more than an hour's sleep at best the way her brain was buzzing, trying to make sense of it all, but she had to rest. The prospect of falling asleep driving and crashing her own car was not going to help her or anyone else.

She continued her routine with her prosthetic, taking more care that night after seeing the redness around the stump. Wearing the false limb for long periods was never comfortable towards the end of the day and she felt she'd only taken it off for a few hours' sleep each night for the last week. Eventually she downed the rest of her wine and lay back, not bothering to remove her underwear. What had made them go for Jess now? There had to be a purpose, a reason? There was no way it wasn't part of some larger plan.

MONDAY 2ND NOVEMBER

CHAPTER 45

He arrived at 5 a.m., the same time as the other cleaners would have been starting their work at headquarters, and waited for an opportune moment to gain access to the main building which housed Livingston's office near the top floor. As a female cleaner came walking out the doors, he quickly approached, making as if to swipe his access card just as she pushed the door open from the inside. As expected, the woman barely gave him a glance, happy to keep her head down and get on with her work as she pushed the trolley loaded with black sacks of rubbish away to the large bin shed. He was all too aware there were CCTV cameras around the complex and located at points within the building but was confident that, unless they had reason to, they were not routinely checked. They were there more as a deterrent and not monitored in live time. In any event, he knew where the system was sited, in a small room behind the reception, and it was there that he made his first stop. It would be too obvious if he were to damage the system in any way.

Far better to just make some adjustments to the date and time. If somebody did have a cause to view it later, it would take a while before they realised they were checking the wrong days. Simple but effective, if only in the short term. He made his way up to Livingston's office, expecting it to be accessed by a swipe pass and to have to dismantle the lock. He was surprised to find the office door propped wide open with a bin. Either they had no security concerns at this level, or it had simply been left this way by the cleaner. It mattered not; it took minutes to place the covert camera in a suitable position out of sight. He hadn't bothered with a microphone for this one. Pictures, after all, paint a thousand words, and he was expecting to have some results within the next forty-eight hours. He was very good at reading people and there was a certainty in what he had seen with Livingston and Zoe, even if there was a major incident now occurring in the county and one of their own senior officers had gone missing, possibly taken. He'd decided Livingston was the kind of individual who wouldn't let the small matter of murder and kidnap get in the way of satisfying his own carnal pleasures. Livingston should make the most of his next flirtation. It was all about to change for him in a big way.

He left the door open as he'd found it and walked back down to the ground floor. The beanie hat pulled low on his forehead and the thick black-rimmed glasses were enough to alter his appearance along with the padding around his waist and shoulders. Not that they would be looking for him, but it always paid to anticipate the opposition's next move. If a person were to look at the CCTV footage and check his clothing closely, they would see that it was lacking the cleaning company logo on the front. Other than that, it was a standard blue sweatshirt and black combat trousers, nothing to make him stand out from the rest of those working that morning. He walked back to his car, changing in the front seat into a black, long-sleeve police shirt and putting a Sussex Police lanyard around his neck. The warrant card in the holder was a copy of that of an officer who was based to the far west of the county, so the chances of the security guard knowing them and wondering why the photo didn't match the face was minimal. Look the part, then a security guard on minimum wage at the end of a night shift was not apt to bother you very much when you were leaving. As usual he was correct, the guard at the gate waving him distractedly through, the car barely slowing down before heading back to speak to the waiting Superintendent Clarke.

CHAPTER 46

Annie had slept fitfully through the few hours' rest, frequently drifting in and out of sleep, concerned over Clarke's disappearance. By half past five, she had completely given up and rolled over in bed, picking up her mobile from the unit. She dialled Lake first, figuring he'd still be working. He answered on the first ring, "Annie, hi."

"Any news on Jess?" She held the phone in the crook of her neck as she pulled on the dressing gown.

"Nothing." He sounded tired and drained, not surprising as he must have been up for over twenty-four hours, and Clarke going missing had obviously hit him hard. "There's been no calls into the Silver Cell, no demands and the trace on her mobile was a dead end. It's either switched off or been dumped. She had a Ring doorbell fitted recently and TSU came and took it to see if they can get a link to the footage from it. Soon as they got it off the wall they noticed the camera lens had been covered over. Nothing that would be instantly apparent, just a small grey adhesive disc the same size as the camera lens placed over the top of it. It may have been done days ago, depends when she last checked the camera viewing history. Whatever, it won't have caught what happened last night."

"What about the neighbours?"

"We woke them all up in the night. Not too happy at first but, as you can imagine, they were quick to apologise when we told them what it was about. Both neighbours either side of Jess have cameras, but they only cover their frontage. Big hedges obscure any views outside. The three houses opposite, only the middle one has a doorbell camera, but they have it switched off from ten at night until six in the morning as they don't like the phone going off with notifications. I mean, what the fuck is the point of having CCTV if you turn it off at night?"

Annie couldn't quite believe what she was hearing: nice houses in a decent area and nothing on CCTV. They might pick up some a bit further afield, but there was no quick win for Clarke's drive, meaning that the abduction wasn't captured. How was it possible, with all the cameras there were now, that they had three murders and a police officer grabbed from outside their home and not a single piece of useful footage to help them?

"Didn't any of them even hear anything?"

"Nothing. They were all in bed except the husband of next door who was downstairs until the early hours bingeing *Game of Thrones* on catch-up. He's no use either, though: puts on his Bose noise-reducing headphones so as not to annoy his wife and heard nothing. Didn't even hear us knocking on the door; it was his wife who answered and went through and shouted at him to turn it off."

Nothing was going their way. It was ridiculous.

"You had any help overnight? You sound knackered."

"I'm running on adrenaline, anger and coffee right now. Yeah, I've had DCI Cornish calling me on and off. Said he's updating the ACC who's gonna be in touch today after briefing. Tom turned out, bless him. Came over with a couple of his CSIs but they found nothing. No scuffle, no blood, nothing. Her car hit one of the ANPR on the A21 at Flimwell, but nothing after that. They had to move her to another car if she still had her phone on her as her Range Rover would have pinged another camera further up around Tunbridge Wells, but it didn't."

"That's if she was with her phone and they haven't taken it in one direction and Jess in another." Annie was thinking of all possibilities. They had three murders in and around Hastings; if they were sticking to that area, why would they take Clarke towards Bromley? It felt to her that, with the precision and care that had been taken to date, they wouldn't have slipped up like that. It had to be a decoy.

"Ged, I think Jess is still in East Sussex. I reckon they've just taken the phone towards London, knowing we'd put a quick trace on it and hoped we'd then spend days with the Met trying to locate her. She's still on your patch, I'm sure of it."

"There's nothing else to say that, Annie. The evidence puts Jess in her own car with her phone heading to London. We lose the car but the phone continues to Bromley area. There's no evidence to say that she's still in Sussex. The bosses will want to concentrate their efforts where the evidence is and it's not down here."

There was an element of panic in his voice as well as tiredness now. "Annie, you've got to know something. Me and Jess ..." he stopped, unwilling to say further.

Annie would like to have said she was surprised, but she had seen this kind of relationship develop so many times. With two recently divorced individuals working closely together, she'd have been amazed if there hadn't been something really. It was the police, after all. It wasn't like it affected anybody else, was it? Clarke had to have been divorced some time if both her and her ex were settled in their own properties. Lake, from what he'd said, was recovering from what he no doubt took as the embarrassment of being dumped for a younger model. The problem was that now she knew and wondered who else he'd told. You can't be investigating the disappearance of your own partner, police or not. The bosses would haul him straight off the investigation if they found out.

"Ged, who else knows? How long's this been going on?"

The line stayed silent before he replied, quieter, "Only a couple of months. We've been friends for years, both had a rough time of it recently with divorce and just ended up having a drink back at hers to start with after work. Nothing else to begin with, but the last few weeks it's gone further."

"You know if they get the footage from the doorbell camera and look back over the preceding days then they're going to see you turning up late at night and, I guess, not leaving until the morning. Gonna be a bit difficult to say they're all just urgent investigation updates, isn't it?"

"I know," the realisation hitting Lake. "Best get in first and tell Cornish, hadn't I."

"Better he hear it first from you rather than see a set of clips from TSU and you have to stand in front of him and explain them."

Annie felt for Lake. For no reason other than wanting to have a relationship, he was left with having to go public to the boss.

"Maybe leave telling Cornish until a better time. Get yourself home and try to have some sleep. I'll sort out the PM for later; I'll speak to Tony and get him to cover it. Call you if anything develops."

"Thanks Annie. I'm gonna hand over to the day's DI at six. I'll be in later, drop you a text and let you know what time."

She hung up, then dialled Tony. It took a few rings until he answered, "Hello?"

"Tony, it's Annie. Take it you heard about the Superintendent?"

He sounded muffled as he spoke, "Sorry, just took a bite of toast. Yeah, any news?"

Annie gave him a quick update from her conversation with Lake, missing out the part about Clarke and Lake's recent relationship.

"Fuckin' hell. This is mental." As ever, Tony was concise in his conclusions. "I take it from the early-morning call you need me to do something for you?"

Annie was grateful to her friend that he always offered before she had to ask. "Can you cover the PM at the Conquest mortuary at ten this morning? It's a Dr Kerry Drake conducting it, I've not met her before."

"Sure, no issues." Annie could hear him eating as he spoke. "I've read the current situation report, which I take it she's been sent. Is Tom Martin going as the CSM?"

"As far as I'm aware. I know he was out in the night with the Super's abduction, but he went home after so should have grabbed a few hours. He's taking one of his CSIs and I've got one our civvy enquiry officers to meet you there to scribe and do the exhibits. They can take them straight back to the MIT property store with them. There's a briefing at eight thirty; you can dial in from your car when you're heading this way."

She knew there would be dozens more officers arriving that day who would need to be brought up to speed and then tasked onto the different operations. There had been emails flying around, that she was now reading, to say they were going to put a new DS onto each job to dish out the actions and work from the MIT offices, leaving Annie free to have oversight on them all, as well as Clarke's abduction. It was far more important for her to be out and active instead of tasking out actions and handling phone calls. She'd seen the names suggested and they were all sergeants who'd worked with the MIT before, so knew the ropes. It would take several days to get all the new staff settled in and deployed, but that was the way it had to be. There were now four investigations to deal with and the Chief was going to declare a critical incident to get even more backing.

Annie swung her legs out of bed, letting her head fall to either side on her shoulders and stretching her arms high above her head. Quick shower and then she could make the rest of the calls from her car. Like Tony, she would dial in for the briefing. No point in sitting there and losing half a day; time was critical. Somewhere, Clarke was alive, she hoped, and she meant for it to stay that way.

CHAPTER 47

At the same time Annie was getting into her car, another vehicle was just arriving at an isolated cottage on Hurst Lane, to the east of Sedlescombe. The property had been on the market a while. From his research, the elderly owner having been found dead. She was only noticed when the taxi driver, who would pick her up to take her to the village once a week to do her shopping, arrived to find no reply to his knocking and had seen her slumped in an armchair through a window. She'd lived in the cottage for over fifty years with no heating and only a hand pump in the garden to get her water. The interior was full of old books and magazines and bags of clothes dating back years. It had been cleared and marketed as a potential project for a buyer, a listed building needing gutting and complete refurbishment. Something that, in the current climate, nobody seemed too interested in. It had been a simple matter to have Clarke deposited there and had the added benefit of a garage where he could store the car without any passers-by noticing. The chances of an agent turning up was as remote as the location. No neighbours for hundreds of metres in either direction. It would be more than sufficient for his needs for the short duration he intended to be there.

He entered by the back door, first going up the thin wooden stairs to check the two Bluetooth cameras he'd installed at the front to look up and down the lane. There was a third that looked out onto the open fields at the back, all three having excellent fields of vision, both night and day. The electricity had been by-passed so there was power, although he hadn't bothered to try the lights; there was no need to run the risk of a passer-by seeing lights coming from what was meant to be empty premises. A call to the police to come and check for squatters was an inconvenience he was happy to do without. Clarke had been placed in the back room of the cottage, next to the kitchen, and he had told them to make sure the windows had been covered over before Clarke was dropped off. With the heavy sheets that had also been hung across the doors, there would be no light to escape towards the front. Happy that everything was in place and working correctly, he walked back down the stairs, through the kitchen and opened the door to the room containing Clarke, pushing aside the sheets as he entered and letting them fall back into place behind him.

Jess Clarke was still unconscious on the narrow bed. The cable ties around her wrists and ankles were now fixed to the top and bottom of the bed, a strip of tape across her mouth. He checked first to see if she was feigning sleep, pinching her ear lobe between his forefinger and thumb. When he got no reaction, he cut the ties at the foot of the bed and swung her still-bound legs around, so they were at a right angle to her body. Kneeling in front of her, but still frequently checking her face, he fixed a metal cuff to her left ankle, attaching one end of a lead to the inside of it, the other end of the lead finishing beside a large, heavy-duty car battery. He pulled her legs back up onto the bad and then went around behind her. He inserted a cannula into the small of her back, packing the area around it to prevent Clarke rolling back and damaging it. Into the cannula he then injected a large dose of lidocaine, a drug commonly used as epidural pain relief. Used for the correct purpose and it would help reduce pain in a lengthy childbirth. Used for his purposes, it would numb Clarke from the waist down, reducing the risk of her trying to escape and having an added side effect of making her groggy and drowsy. She would be awake enough to converse but incapable of causing him any problems.

He then went across to the single table in the room: an old, pitted, heavy wooden piece of furniture atop which sat his laptop and monitors, a chair in front of it. He switched on the equipment; one screen split into three, showing the views from the three cameras upstairs. A second monitor showed the interior of

Annie's home and the third gave a view from the corner of Livingston's office. He bent over, picking up a bottle of water from a tray beside the chair and twisting the top open. By his calculations, and if they had given the correct dosage, Clarke would be coming around in the next hour or so. Maybe he would have a little bite to eat before. He wanted to give her his full attention, after all.

CHAPTER 48

Annie listened into the briefing from the ACC to the assembled teams. She had arrived early at Hastings and linked in online, although turning off the camera on her laptop so she couldn't be seen working while the ACC was talking. To his credit, Livingston kept a sombre tone from the start, welcoming all the new officers and staff before outlining the events of the previous night and Clarke's abduction. She noticed the press officer – make-up perfectly applied for the cameras, tight-fitting cream dress – sitting to the right of Livingston. Who does that for a briefing? Annie rarely had on any make-up other than a dab of blusher and a bit of eye shadow, working on the basis it only came off in the day anyway. Zoe Tims, on the other hand, always appeared ready for her next Instagram shoot. Style over substance, as far as Annie was concerned.

After giving a summary of the four investigations, the floor was opened for any updates. Jenny, the HOLMES manager, was taking notes and was first to raise her hand.

"Sir, we've had a number of calls into the incident room and via the Major Incident Public Portal to say that the murder of Connor Reece is very similar to one committed in 1902 by a Thomas Smyth in London. I've had a look on the internet myself first thing and it seems that Smyth was a bit of a religious nut. He found out his wife was having an affair and decided to punish her by nailing her to a cross, pouring boiling water all over her body to cleanse her sins, according to him. He then left her body outside their local parish church. He was found sitting beside it and confessed to the murder. Sentenced and hung within six months. There's no other murders linked to him, but there's an obvious similarity to Reece.

Annie made a note to look for herself when she got the chance, see what else came from the post-mortem later. The rest of the briefing gave her nothing new and, at the conclusion, Annie and several others were asked to stay online for a management briefing which was even less inciteful.

CHAPTER 49

He was sat beside Clarke as she came to, opening her eyes and slowly focusing on him. He placed a hand on her shoulder as she became aware of her surroundings, disorientated from the after-effects of the drugs and her brain trying to put together the events which had brought her there.

"Don't try and roll back, Jessica; there's a needle in your spine and it would be most uncomfortable to press on it." Clarke stiffened under his touch. "Now, I'm sure the first question out of your mouth will be to ask what you're doing here, so let me clear that one up for you. I have brought you here to prove a point, that being: nobody is safe. If I can take you, the Area Commander for where all the murders are taking place, then all these comments around reassurance to the public from your Chief Constable are shown to be false, aren't they? I can take who I want when I want. Nobody knows where you are. In fact, I have made efforts to have your colleagues looking well away from here. I have no doubts that the brighter ones will expect a decoy, but the problem is, with three murders already, resources are strapped, aren't they? Plus, the leadership leaves a lot to be desired, doesn't it? How do you feel about Mr Livingston now? Regretting that fling you had with him? I imagine so. Don't worry though, Jessica, I have plans in place for him and you are in the perfect position to watch them unfold."

Clarke's mouth felt like it was full of cotton wool, her arms ached from being pulled above her head and her legs felt strange, almost detached. "Who are you?" she struggled, not expecting an answer, but it was all she could think of to say. She needed to get her head clear.

"And that, Jessica, is what I was fully expecting you to ask next. You don't mind if I call you Jessica, do you? I find Jess sounds too childlike. Let's call me Janus for the time being. Do you know Roman mythology, Jessica? Janus was the god of beginnings and endings, transitions and time, and is normally shown with two faces. I like to think we all have two faces: the one we are happy to show in general and the other which we like to keep private. You have your public face as the Superintendent for your Division, sadly divorced, dedicating yourself to your work, all very legitimate and above board. Then there is the private face, which is far more interesting, the illicit relationship with a married senior officer who, let's be honest, just used you as another bit on the side then discarded you. And then there's Detective Inspector Lake. He is desperate with you missing. Such a shame, if he hadn't been delayed, he would most likely have turned up just at the point you were getting out of your car. He may even have rescued you from your assailants. Imagine how he must be feeling."

She looked at the man calling himself Janus. He was dressed casually, a blue sweatshirt with a gilet over the top of it and blue jeans. She couldn't distinguish his age; he may be 30 or 40, his features smooth and wrinkle-free. What made his appearance strange was the complete lack of any hair on his head or face, the missing eyebrows only enhancing the bright blue eyes looking down at her.

Clarke's mind was beginning to focus. She knew she had little chance, if any, of getting out of this alive. This male Janus was content to let her see his face, hear his voice. It seemed unlikely, therefore, that he would be letting her go free at any point to divulge that information to anyone else. Her only hope was to try to prolong her life by engaging in whatever he seemed to want which, to start with, appeared to be a conversation.

"Are you responsible for the other three murders?"

"Responsible depends on your perspective, Jessica. I have neither seen, engaged with, or touched any of the victims that have been found in the last week. I did not seek them out, decide who they should be or why they should be the ones to die. Rather, I provide a very bespoke service. I let very wealthy people with very specific tastes live out their sadistic fantasies with no comeback for them. They get to watch their subject die in a manner they have chosen, and they get to watch it happen in real time. I select the personnel to undertake the tasks and large sums of money changes hands. I obviously take an amount for myself to cover my time and planning. It is a business arrangement, no more, no less, as far as I'm concerned. I have no interest in personal vendettas; this is about fulfilling people's needs and desires. I'm certain that I'm not the only one in this line of business but I like to think that I have a very professional approach." Janus paused and moved his chair slightly so that Clarke could see him better. "You will have to excuse me; this all feels a bit like a Bond villain doing the exposition to explain the big plan before failing to then kill 007 and thus allowing him to thwart it. Rest assured, there is no possibility that you will be alive at the end to perform that role."

Clarke felt the tiniest fragment of hope that had been there shatter as the full realisation that she was going to die sank in. It was no longer a matter of if, just when.

"So why bother telling me this if you just intend to murder me like the others?" She spat the words out despite her best attempt to remain calm.

Janus was sitting back, his hands clasped in front of him, and Clarke couldn't help but notice the nails looked manicured. "Jessica, I told you, I haven't murdered anyone. Yet. I decided that I needed to change my usual methods. You can only sit back and watch for so long after all before you want to experience what something feels like. The thrill of being involved. And I wanted to meet you, let you see your Mr Livingston brought down to earth as it were. At least you get the satisfaction of that."

"But why here? Why now? If you run a business, why dump it all on my area where it's only going to generate national interest and have the whole country looking at it?" she asked.

"Because it was different, and I like to watch you all running around without a clue what's happening as body after body piles up with no connection. Part of the remit I set out is how people will die. There's so much choice with the internet to search through. Killers have been documented over and over. They might be a one-off murder such as young Connor, or serial killers who've had books and documentaries covering their exploits such as James Whittaker for poor Mr Piper. There are so many to choose from and that's just in the UK. Go abroad and there's countless to select from; some of the Eastern European countries have really pushed the envelope when it comes to originality. Do you see? Clients get to live out their particular fetish vicariously and can then watch it over and over again."

Clarke could see the computer set-up and monitors behind Janus and seemed to recognise the room on one of the screens. "So why do it? Is it the money or do you like to sit and jack off to the killings like your clients?"

If she was hoping to get some emotional reaction from Janus then she was disappointed. "Come on now Jessica, let's not be crude. I've told you; this is business. I saw an opportunity and a vacuum and decided I could fill it. There was a certain amount of time I had to put in to find the right websites and chat rooms, but the web is such a useful tool. You don't really need to get out of your own room if you know what you're doing. I'm more than comfortable financially, none of my clients or associates have ever met me so, with the exception of you of course, I can move around freely from country to country, conducting my business from any location I choose. Don't get me wrong, I do have my preferences as to an office, if you want to call it that, but I so love the freedom." Janus was enjoying the conversation; it made a pleasant change to talk to another person openly about his work. "Please, don't think I grew up in a deprived home or was beaten and bullied as a child. I have never tortured small animals and am no psychopath. This is the modern world and how it works. I know of places where you can go and hunt people as if they were big game. Where you can inflict every sexual depravity that could ever be dreamed of, and it all comes back to how much the person is willing to pay. There are large numbers of very wealthy individuals in the world today who are bored with their life, wanting to have the next thrill that you can't buy in the normal marketplace.

Not every millionaire wants a ninety-second weightless experience at the edge of space in a rocket. It's simple supply and demand, and I am happy to supply because, if I don't, then somebody else will."

"Is that how you justify this to yourself so you can sleep? That somebody else would do it if you didn't?" Clarke wanted to gouge out those blue eyes staring down at her.

"I have no problem sleeping, I can assure you." He glanced over his shoulder, checking the monitors on the table, and Clarke noticed he had a small earpiece in his left ear. "It seems that the latest briefing has concluded. Let us have a look and see shall we. Don't you recognise the office on the left?"

It was very familiar to Clarke and then it came to her: it was Livingston's office at headquarters. She recognised the photos and certificates on the wall behind the desk. What the fuck? How was there a camera feed coming from there. The monitor to the right showed three views looking out onto a road and fields and the final one showed what looked like the interior of a person's house. As she looked, she saw the corner of the door as it opened in Livingston's office as he walked in, followed by Zoe Tims. The latter stopped and turned back to the door as Livingston walked to sit behind his desk.

Janus picked up the chair he had been sitting on and moved it across to the table, placing it so Clarke could still see the screens. He began typing on the laptop's keyboard and Clarke watched as Zoe walked around the desk before sitting on it in front of the ACC, perched provocatively, her short skirt hitching up on her thighs as she crossed her legs. Clarke saw another image appear on the laptop but gave it only a cursory glance, the image of Livingston and Zoe of far greater interest.

She saw Livingston lean towards Zoe and slide his right hand along the top her leg, slowly disappearing out of sight as it went under the skirt and Zoe's head move towards Livingston's. The camera angle obscured the view slightly but there was no doubting what the pair were doing with their heads together, Zoe uncrossing her legs and moving closer to the edge of the desk, Livingston's hand still out of sight.

Clarke could only see the back of Janus's head as he spoke to her, "Ever heard the phrase 'revenge is a dish best served cold' Jessica? Take note, I've done this for you. There's a lot of unfairness in the world and this is me doing my small part to put one right. Keep your eyes on the monitor now; wouldn't want you to miss the highlight when it happens."

As much as Clarke didn't want to watch Livingston and Zoe with their tongues down each other's throats and the ACC's hand up Zoe's knickers, she was stuck with facing that way and unable to turn over. If this was to right an injustice against her, then why was she being forced to watch Livingston as he made another mockery of his marriage. Zoe slid off the desk and stood to the side, in front of Livingston, lifting up her skirt and hooking her thumbs in the top of her knickers and pushing them down, before stepping out of them and sitting on his lap. Clarke heard Janus begin laughing to himself and wondered what was so bloody funny about making her watch as her ex-lover was about to fuck his press officer over his desk.

Suddenly, she saw both Zoe and Livingston flinch and jump apart as if an electric shock had passed between them, Zoe backing away from the ACC and reaching down to snatch up her discarded underwear. Both Livingston and Zoe were looking panic-stricken in the direction of the door, then back at each other. Clarke wished there was sound, as she saw Livingston fumble with his trousers and walk towards the door, Zoe stuffing her underwear into her small handbag, then sitting down opposite the desk and trying to compose herself as Livingston reached for the door and stood back. A figure walked into the room at speed, pointing first at Zoe and then looking around at the walls. Clarke recognised the late entry as being the Deputy Chief Constable, whom she recalled as having the office on the same floor as Livingston. He was waving his arms around and she could see he was shouting. The DCC pulled out his phone and was looking at the screen, then at the wall beside the door. Clarke watched as he waved his left arm and moved towards the direction the camera was filming, before his hand obscured the image on the screen and it went black.

Janus turned back towards Clarke, "It would appear that while he should be leading several high-profile investigations, all subject to intense media scrutiny, the Senior Investigating Officer is spending his time instead using his office to fuck his pretty little media assistant. You see, the benefit of understanding human nature, particularly that of a misogynistic serial philanderer such as Mr Livingston, is that they are very easy to predict. I've watched the pair in their briefings to the press, coming and going together, never seemingly apart, and it was just a matter of time until this was caught on camera. Although I must admit, I didn't expect it to be quite so quick and graphic, especially with you being abducted less than twelve hours ago. It's almost like he couldn't care less. I'm sorry Jessica, this must be hard for you to watch."

Clarke had the feeling that the compassion in his voice lacked the sincerity he was aiming for.

"You will, however, be pleased to know that this wasn't just for your benefit. It was live-streamed as they entered the office and is now circulating across the media. I did take the opportunity to make sure it was also sent directly to all the larger news teams along with your Chief's team. I would imagine that it was a bit of a surprise when they clicked on the link." He could barely keep the smile from his face as he looked at her.

CHAPTER 50

The message had come into the Deputy Chief from the media head almost at the same time as they had started getting phone calls about the footage. He'd left his own office, going immediately along the corridor to Livingston's and knocked hard on the door before trying to open it, finding it locked. That only added to his frustration and, as the door was pulled open from inside, he saw Zoe Tims sitting sheepishly to one side of the desk. Livingston was sputtering some comments about having a meeting to discuss the next media release even as the DCC was looking around the office, now seeing himself on the screen of his phone, indicating the footage was live. He was beside himself; this was being seen by the press and anyone logged into the internet who had chanced across it. It was a media disaster for the force. On top of everything else happening, they would now have to contend with their chosen lead officer being seen as a national disgrace. It would knock the murders, even the abduction of the Hastings Superintendent, off the front pages of the news and all the bulletins. There would be referrals to the Independent Office for Police Conduct. Hell, they would probably get an HMIC inspection on top of that. All the Command team's jobs were at risk by this; their selection of Livingston as the lead officer would be pulled apart and their own roles scrutinised. If this was happening under their noses, then what kind of leadership example were they setting? It was catastrophic.

***

Annie was still in Lake's office when Tom Martin burst excitedly in the door.

"Annie, have you heard? The ACC is all over the internet. Somebody stuck a camera in his office and he's just been caught over the side with that press officer he's had with him and his hand up her skirt."

Tom could barely contain himself, grinning from ear to ear

"What?" Annie was confused. What the hell was Tom talking about?

He had already made his way around to her side of the desk and was thrusting his phone at her, "Look, you can view it again and again if you want." Tom seemed to find what he was watching hilarious and Annie looked at the screen of his phone. She couldn't believe what she was seeing.

"This has gone out on the internet?"

"Too right. Watch it to the end and you get to see the DCC come in and find the camera. His reaction is quality. Think it's safe to say Livingston's going to be looking for a new job and somewhere to live by the time his wife sees this. I don't know her but, God, I feel sorry for the woman. What a way to find out your old man's over the side."

Shit, as if things couldn't get any worse than they already are, Annie thought. She couldn't care less about the ACC, but this would deflect from the investigations and what they were trying to achieve. The news would be all about the scandal of the ACC when they needed it to concentrate on Clarke and keep her at the front of the public's mind.

She looked back at Tom, "Shouldn't you be down at the post-mortem?" she realised.

"I've got another of the CSMs to cover it for me. I had so much to catch up on with the submissions on the other operations and Dr Drake has kindly said she'll come to the station and speak to us both when they've finished. That way we get a full summary from her in person."

Annie looked at the footage playing on repeat. Well, at least it would get rid of Livingston. The question was, who would they put in his place?

CHAPTER 51

Janus held a water bottle out to Clarke, a straw in the top so she could drink. He seemed satisfied with what he had seen on the screen earlier.

"I'm afraid that I can't let you use the toilet on your own. Your legs won't fully support you with the drugs you've been given, however, I will provide you with a sheet for decency's sake. I'm sorry it has to be that way, but I'm sure you understand."

It was early Monday afternoon and Clarke was still none the wiser as to what her role was to be in Janus's plans. The image of Livingston's office had now been replaced by a further view looking at the back door to the cottage, Janus having gone out after the ACC debacle to site a further camera on one of the small outbuildings to the rear. He'd explained that the coverage to the rear was predominantly to see if there was any approach across the fields. The additional camera was to show if a person had somehow come from the sides, evading the other cameras. What he hadn't mentioned were the motion sensors placed either side of the house. Those would set off a silent alarm on his phone, allowing him to be prepared for any unwanted visitor.

"Are you hungry? There's only sandwiches and fruit but I imagine you could do with something by now."

"I don't want you feeding me, thanks." Clarke wanted to be off her side. If nothing else, the opportunity to be sitting up would allow her to get a better look at her surroundings.

Janus stood up, "I tell you what, I'll release the ties to the top of the bed and help you to sit. First though …" He moved out of sight at the bottom of the bed and Clarke felt a vague tugging on her left leg. Numb as it was, there was still some sensation. Janus came back into view holding a small grey plastic box in his right hand. It looked like a garage door opener.

"Here's the thing, Jessica: you've had a significant amount of lidocaine pumped into your spine which is what's making your legs feel so heavy. That in itself will slow you down should you get free of the ties around your ankles. In addition, I've just connected a lead from your left leg to a battery and this," he held up the clicker, "when pressed, will send a jolt of electricity into you. Now, it's not enough to cause you any permanent injury, but it will knock you off those unsteady feet should you attempt to walk. I'm sure I won't have to explain that more than once." He pocketed the clicker in his jeans and then used a small lock knife to cut the restraints holding Clarke's wrists to the bed, leaving the pair binding them together in place, then helped her to a sitting position. "Tuna or cheese? Not much choice but beggars can't be choosers."

The wave of nausea that hit Clarke as she sat up was enough to make her refuse either and she put her head down towards her knees, expecting to vomit. It passed slowly and she managed to raise her head as Janus placed a pre-packed cheese sandwich on her lap. She looked down at her ankle, seeing the cuff and lead trailing away from it to the battery in the corner of the room. Apart from her bed, the table and chair, there were few other items in the room. A couple of lamps provided the illumination, with the cloth over the door and the covered window preventing any light from seeping out and being noticed. Power leads ran from the monitors and a large blue cool box sat by the door. The walls were yellowing, flaking plaster, the floorboards grimy, and a smell of mould lingered in the air.

"Can I ask where I am? Based on what you've said already, it's hardly going to make any difference if I know, is it?"

Janus had moved his chair back to the table, an opened pack of tuna sandwiches beside the laptop. He finished his mouthful, washing it down with a swig of water from a bottle.

"You're still within your own division, just not in an area likely to be searched." He took another bite of the sandwich, chewed and swallowed before speaking again. "Now, apologies, but I must get on. He placed a small round mirror to the right of the laptop as he turned away towards the monitors. Clarke could see herself reflected in it. She considered the possibility of throwing herself at Janus, coming to the conclusion that, with her hands still restrained and no real feeling in her legs, the likely outcome would be that she would end up flat on her face on the floor with him still well out of reach. She decided to bide her time for a better opportunity. If she was at least allowed to remain seated then there was a better chance of … she had no idea what.

CHAPTER 52

I t was just before four that afternoon when Tony arrived back at the station with the pathologist. He'd called Annie to tell her they were on the way, and she'd said to meet in Lake's office. He had come in just before midday and looked terrible. Tony introduced the pathologist as they took two of the chairs between the desks.

"Annie, this is Dr Kerry Drake. Kerry, this is DS Bryce. She's the one who's actually running things until we find out who's going to replace Mr Livingston."

Word had got round very quickly about the video footage and the ACC's immediate removal and suspension.

"Hi, thanks for coming here," Annie said, standing to shake the pathologist's hand. "Behind you is DI Ged Lake who's working on the investigations with me." The door swung open and Tom Martin bustled in, all smiles and bluster.

"Kerry, Tony, how are you both? Seen that video of the boss yet?"

264

Annie wondered if Tom was ever aware of a time to be appropriate.

"Tom, if we can stick to the PM and leave the dirty videos until after?" Annie asked. Kerry Drake was petite, with short, cropped brown hair, and Annie noticed a tattoo on her left forearm of a barcode. The pathologist saw her looking.

"It's my partner's date of birth. Better than a name in case you ever split up, I told her. She didn't find that as funny as I did."

Drake had an accent Annie couldn't quite place, somewhere between Australian and South African. Drake went on to give the details from the post-mortem conducted that morning.

"The victim, identified as Connor Reece had multiple burn injuries all over his torso, legs and arms. None of which would have caused his death although, if they had been left untreated, the blistering would have become septic with a possible result of sepsis. He had a heavy metal spike inserted through the palms of each hand into the beam he was found nailed to. My view is that these were caused pre-mortem due to the blood patterning indicating his heart was still beating at the time. All his internal organs appeared to be healthy, insofar as they would in any habitual drug user. I've asked Tom to get the toxicology sent but if he was a heroin user then it will be nigh on impossible to differentiate between that in his system and any other opiate that he might have been injected with. The dosage may be an indicator though. The crown of thorns pushed onto his head caused superficial puncture wounds only. Again, my view is he was still alive at that point. What may well be the ultimate cause of death is the boiling water that his body was doused in from head to foot. This may, and that awaits further examination, have created enough shock in his system to have killed him. Currently though, C.O.D is pending further work."

Tom chipped in at this point, "That crown of thorns thing; the botanist came back to me. She says it looks like a plant called, hang on," he flicked through his papers, checking some notes he'd written, "Euphorbia Milii. I've probably pronounced it completely wrong. She said it's a species native to Madagascar and it may have been introduced to the Middle East in ancient times. It's believed this was the plant for the crown of thorns worn by Jesus Christ. If you go in for all that kind of thing."

Tony turned to Annie, "It gives us something to work on, if nothing else. We can get somebody looking at who imports it and how common it is to get hold of. With any luck, it'll be rare as hen's teeth in this country and might point us in the right direction."

He had a large family bag of Haribo he was working his way through as he sat with the others.

"I'm getting the feeling that it won't be that easy, Tony. With the care that's been taken so far, I can't see them slipping up on something so simple. Don't get me wrong, we'll check it, but I'm expecting another dead end."

Annie felt the weight of expectation on her shoulders: three murders and a missing police officer and she, a Detective Sergeant, was the senior officer dealing with it. Where the hell was Cornish?

After they'd finished, Tom took the pathologist back to his office and Tony told Annie he was going to check on the progress of the other investigations, leaving Annie alone with Lake.

"How're you holding up?"

It was difficult to tell where his grey hair stopped and his skin started, with its pallor. "Pretty fucking badly, if you want to know. I'm just waiting for them to pull me in and drag me off all the investigations."

Annie could hear the pain in his voice, "Look Ged, I've told them nothing about you and Clarke. Whatever is between you, that's up to you to sort out. But it's not healthy being this close working on her abduction. Help me by all means, but take a step back."

Lake looked Annie straight on, his eyes red-rimmed, "When was the last time you had someone you cared about snatched by a fucking nutter going round killing people, Annie? Last I heard, it was just you and your dog, so don't lecture me about not being involved."

She knew the anger wasn't directed at her; he was venting the frustration and concern for Clarke, but his comments touched a nerve and she answered more angrily than she meant to. "I want to find her just as much as you, Ged. She's one of our own. Just because I'm not the one shagging her doesn't mean it affects me any less."

She stopped suddenly, seeing the way her words hit him, as he stood up and walked to the door.

"Ged, I didn't mean it to come out like that. I'm sorry."

He slammed the door behind him, leaving Annie to sit alone in the office.

CHAPTER 53

Janus had listened to the conversation with the pathologist, pleased to note that the crown of thorns had been correctly identified. He prided himself on his attention to detail, wishing them good luck in finding where he had sourced the item. Surely, they weren't so moronic to think that he had walked into a florist and ordered it? What interested him far more, was the exchange between Annie and Lake. He knew from other conversations he had listened into from Annie's cloned phone that Lake and Clarke were in a relationship, but it was good to hear the effect Clarke's abduction was having on the formerly stoic DI. Janus had plans for him as well.

Clarke was lying on her side again, staring across at him. She had her legs pulled up in a foetal position, her arms in front of her chest as if praying.

"It would appear that your DI Lake is a bit upset about you going missing," he said without turning round. "He should be careful; it might affect his judgement."

Clarke had no way of knowing how Janus had come by this information, at first thinking that he had an officer on his payroll. No, she couldn't see Ged talking openly about them to people at work. He was too private and knew she would want it kept between them. So where was Janus getting his information? "He's a good officer, and professional."

"I'm sure he is, but this is different, isn't it? Not every day your lover goes missing. He must be beside himself." Janus appeared to find this amusing, and Clarke could see a half-smile on his face in the mirror.

"I don't know what you think you know, but he's one of my officers."

"Yes, of course he is, Jessica." Janus swivelled in his chair to face her, "And that's why he parked his car two roads away and walked to your house near midnight instead of pulling up on your drive. Bit odd if he was there on official matters, isn't it? Almost like he didn't want to be seen there." The laughter came from him then.

"You sick cunt. You say this is business yet you're sitting there getting a kick out of other people's pain and suffering."

Janus gave a feigned look of hurt, "Oh Jessica, it is business. That doesn't mean I can't get a bit of enjoyment out of it on the side. You are all so righteous, upholding the law, yet you have your dirty secret little flings, all on the taxpayer's time and money. It's good for the public to see what you're all really like. As for DI Lake, well, isn't it nice for you to see how much he cares?" He turned away back to the monitors, the conversation apparently over.

Clarke lay trying to get her thoughts in order. She knew there would be a major operation to look for her on top of everything else that was going on. If she could get to the laptop when he was out of the room, try to send a message somewhere. There had to be a way to communicate her location to the outside world; she just needed Janus out the way. She jerked suddenly as a shock of electricity surged up and around her body, sending it rigid and making her clench her teeth. The pain was mercifully short as the electricity was cut back off.

"Just a test so you know how it feels, Jessica. I have plenty of experience and you are no doubt trying to think of ways to get out of your situation. Rest assured, whatever you think of, I have put measures in place to prevent it. Now, lie still and let us see what we can do in the meantime." Janus didn't even bother to glance at her as he said this. To him, she was just a means to an end. Another pawn to be moved around a board and sacrificed as and when he wanted.

CHAPTER 54

Matt Cornish sat contemplating the poison chalice he'd been handed. After the ACC had been summoned to the Chief's office and suspended with immediate effect, Cornish had fully expected the Deputy Chief or one of the other ACCs to be put in charge of the investigations on Rother Division. It came as a shock, therefore, when he'd been called up in front of the Gold Group and informed he was now going to be heading up all four of the enquiries on the east. He made a half-hearted protest. Surely the high-profile nature and national interest meant that someone more senior should be leading? But no, they wanted him at the front, reporting directly back to them with twice-daily briefings morning and afternoon. The Chief would sit above it all, but Cornish would be the face of Sussex Police.

Cornish knew they didn't want their careers on the line. He was walking a fine line and was under no illusion that he was completely expendable as far as they were concerned. They had promised promotion if he was successful, but with the knowledge he already had, he felt that was highly doubtful. There was still no identity for the male found at Glyne Gap and no suspect or motive, so Op Senna was at a stalemate. It was similar with Op Magenta. Oh, they knew who the victim was, but that was all. Then there was Op Holt, the murder that had really got the media excited. Nothing like a body pegged out like Christ on a Sunday to really get the press clamouring.

Now, to top it all off, he had the Area Commander, a police officer, snatched from her home. The press were creating a panic with their half-hourly bulletins going on about how no one could feel safe if police officers were being murdered as well. A bit presumptuous, he felt. No body had been found yet and they were all clinging on to the hope Clarke was still alive. God, he prayed that she was. If Clarke turned up somewhere dead, displayed for the world to see in some grotesque manner, it wouldn't only be the public after his head: his own colleagues would be demanding it as well. They had to find her. Fuck it, he was on a very high wire with no safety net underneath him when it broke.

Cornish had been given a male press officer; they obviously didn't want to run the risk of any further scandal. The media team were doing their best to keep the press focused on the investigations, but all they seemed interested in was running bits of the footage of Livingston and Tims. It was all over the internet as well, with people posting and sharing the footage on social media, YouTube, anywhere there was a platform. As for the comments, he was confident the ACC wouldn't ever work in the police again. Cornish wondered if he would see Livingston on the television standing outside his house on Monday, his wife and children by his side as he made a statement that he was sorry, how he'd let his family down but they were standing by him and he just wanted to get back to work serving the public. He'd seen enough MPs doing it, although the wife on the receiving end standing with a fixed smile always looked like they wanted to drag the guilty party inside and scream at them.

He had no sympathy. It was one thing to be over the side, but to do it in your own office at HQ in the middle of all that was going on ... Livingston deserved all the shit coming down on top of him, especially as it now meant the responsibility sat firmly on Cornish's shoulders.

He picked up his mobile, and dialled a number. It was answered on the first ring, "Annie, it's Cornish. Where are you?"

"In the DI's office at Hastings, guv." She had called and given him the PM update after hearing about the ACC. He was, after all, her direct line manager, so she had come to him in lieu of anyone else.

"You need to know I've been put in as SIO for all four investigations. I want you in as my deputy." When there was no immediate reply from Annie, he continued, "Look, I know that you don't have a lot of time for me, and do us both the courtesy of not trying to tell me otherwise, but this has been dumped on me and I've no alternative. It wasn't exactly a request. I need your experience; we have to find Clarke alive."

On the other end of the call Annie felt like taking off her prosthetic and smashing herself over the head with it. So, her Senior Investigating Officer had gone from one who was completely useless to one who was vastly inexperienced. It was as apparent to her as to Cornish that the senior officers were arse-covering for when it all went tits up if Clarke was found dead. There was no way one of them was going to take the fall when they could delegate someone else to do it for them.

"Sir, surely you want an officer of a higher rank as your dep? It's not gonna look great if it's a sergeant, is it?"

"I don't care how it looks. You know you're the best chance Clarke has of being found alive before this fucker decides to make another public display. We can't let it happen." Cornish almost sounded like he was pleading with her. "I'll be over in an hour. I want you to meet me at Clarke's house so we can have a look around."

A team had made a cursory search inside, finishing late afternoon, and found nothing to help with what had happened.

Annie agreed, looking at the clock on the wall and seeing it was already nearly seven. There were hundreds of additional officers swamping Hastings and the surrounding towns and villages, detectives making house-to-house enquiries, uniforms on hi-vis patrols. How could it be that there was no information coming in? Tony had stuck his head in the door earlier to say he was heading back to the MIT office, he wanted to check in on the various incident rooms and get a briefing ready for officers on Tuesday. Not that they had much new to tell them.

Lake, meanwhile, had been conspicuous by his absence. She hadn't seen him since he'd left the office after their conversation. She'd called his mobile, but he was blanking her. She knew he was chasing his own team hard to find something, anything, to help locate Clarke, and at some point, she was going to have to have a conversation with Cornish. But not yet. She knew how much it meant to Lake to be involved, and she knew there was nobody better to be doing it from what she'd seen in the last few days. She'd give it until nearly eight, then head over to Clarke's to meet Cornish, although she couldn't see what he was looking for or why they were going.

CHAPTER 55

Janus knew there would be nothing for the DCI to find at Clarke's address. He'd never sent anyone inside, so what was the point? They were purely a snatch and grab team to pick her up and deposit her here so he could deal with her in private. He had left her for a while earlier; he had work to do outside, and had returned to find she had barely moved. He injected more lidocaine at regular intervals, enough to keep the dosage topped up. He would give her a further sedative later to help her sleep as well. He didn't want her to see Annie getting home later and there was no point in her lying awake all night. He had no plans for her until later tomorrow and he would need to get some sleep himself. Only a few hours, just enough to keep fresh and alert. He imagined they would be going over the CCTV at police headquarters by now, looking to see who had been in and placed the camera in the ACC's office. They would no doubt also be conducting searches to see if there was anything else hidden that could add to the force being the current national object of ridicule. This would drag in more officers, using up valuable resources they couldn't spare. Create chaos and panic and have them waste their time looking for something that wasn't even there when they should be concentrating on their missing officer. It showed him where the Chief Constable's priorities lay.

In a way, he wished he had taken the time to get a download of Clarke's phone before it had been destroyed. It would have been interesting to see the communication between her and DI Lake. He'd needed it disposed of faraway though; better to not run the risk of a trace picking it up anywhere near him. He'd asked Clarke about the relationship, but she seemed reluctant to share. So be it, he would find out soon enough how she felt about Lake. There was plenty of time. He could have got the information out of her if he really needed to; there were subtle methods which were exquisitely painful to the recipient, but he had no need to go down that route just yet.

"So, do you need to have me unable to move before you kill me? Does that make it easy for you?" Clarke was trying to provoke a response, but she got nothing in return.

"Dear Jessica, just enjoy that you are comfortable for the time being. Nobody is harming you and I have certain matters to put in place first. Your time will come when I decide it, and not before." He didn't even look at her directly as he spoke, merely glancing into the mirror as if she wasn't worth the extra effort to turn around.

TUESDAY 3RD NOVEMBER

CHAPTER 56

I t was nearly 1 a.m. by the time Annie pulled up on her drive. A faint glow from the moon was all the light there was. She realised she must have switched off the timer for the lamp Kevin had set for her.

The meeting with Cornish had been, as expected, fruitless. All he'd wanted was to have her tell him what he needed to do. He'd needed the privacy for the conversation, worried that someone else may overhear a phone call. All about ego then, even after what he'd said about wanting her help. He did, but only in private so he didn't come across as floundering. Some leader. As she entered the house, she half expected Bella to come bounding up, forgetting for a moment she was still with the sitter. She missed her and the house had an empty feel to it.

She looked at her watch then decided, fuck it, a glass of wine would help her sleep. She felt so wired from the conversation with Cornish, but she needed to get a few hours' shut-eye. Lake had finally called her on the drive back, and she'd told him the latest. He said that there had been no progress in the hunt for Clarke. The phone signal around Bromley had been a dead end and there was no joy in locating her car either. He had finished for the night and was back in his flat, unable to get any sleep himself. He still hadn't told Cornish or anyone other than Annie about the relationship with Clarke, and Annie couldn't help but feel that it would only complicate matters. The bottom line was she needed Lake on the investigation, if for no other reason than he would leave no stone unturned in his search to get Clarke back alive. She finished the call by promising to call him if she heard anything, saying she'd be back over first thing in the morning.

Annie took her wine upstairs. At least she'd eaten that day, Thalia having sent what Tony had referred to as one of his wife's special Red Cross packages across with him. "She said I've got to make sure you're eating something decent. Never says that about me."

Hardly surprising, as Annie couldn't recall Tony going more than half an hour without putting some kind of food in his mouth. He should be the size of a house and she could never figure out how he wasn't.

She sat on her bed, unbuttoning her trousers and sliding them off before starting the process of removing her prosthetic. She went into the bathroom, gave the limb and herself a clean, before returning to sit on the edge of the bed. She tried to run through everything that had happened in the last week and see if she had missed something obvious. With all the CCTV cameras available, how could they have not captured an image of the suspects that would help? There had to be a group doing it? It wasn't possible for a single individual to be in so many places at once or to have left the bodies in the manner they were found. So how come nobody was talking? There was always a grass out there who had some information to share for a bit of cash or letter to a judge for a bit of leniency on a sentence. Everybody talks. She had never worked on an investigation where one of the suspects hadn't blabbed at least part of what they'd done to a girlfriend or a mate, yet now she had three murders and an abduction and all of them conducted by this group working in total silence. It didn't add up.

***

Janus sat watching Annie. It was strange, he was completely comfortable with observing all manner of atrocities being conducted on his fellow man and yet, looking at Annie sitting in her underwear made him feel wrong. *I wonder what she's thinking about?* So much responsibility was being piled up onto those slim shoulders, perhaps he should lend a helping hand? He had decided on the time he would conclude this latest enterprise and had already sold the viewing rights to a selection of clients. He had set a fee and taken his pick from those willing to part with their money. Arrangements had been put in place for his departure and he would perhaps leave it a while to start a new venture. He was bored, after all; this was too easy. If it had been a case of having to personally locate the right people to get the work conducted then he would still be making arrangements for the first murder, but the inception of the internet, in particular the dark web, had allowed for like-minded people to be in contact where previously they would have been too frightened to discuss their particular tastes with anyone for fear of the disgust it would engender. Depravity and perversion were seen by Janus merely as things to be exploited for financial gain, and he had gained so very much.

Janus knew that this time, however, he had deviated from his set routine by becoming involved. But what was all the money in the world if you didn't do something for yourself occasionally? He was confident that he could disappear once all this was over. He looked back over at Clarke, sleeping on her side facing him. It was a shame really, what her outcome was to be. He had no personal vendetta towards her, or the police in general, taking it that they had their job to do, and it was all part of the thrill for his clients to watch the law running around on the television, never once getting anywhere close to identifying those responsible. Janus sat back in his chair, switching the monitors that covered Annie's house off. No need for Clarke to waken and see those just yet. There would be a time for that as and when it fitted his needs.

CHAPTER 57

I t was almost ten that morning before Cornish had finished briefing the various different teams and sat in Clarke's office with Annie, Tony, Lake and Tom Martin, going over the plans for the next few days. All of them were aware that, the longer Clarke was missing, the less chance they had of getting her back alive.

"Tom, I can't believe we've got nothing in the way of forensics on any of the murders or Clarke."

Cornish sounded as desperate for a bit of good news as the rest of them felt.

"I know, but what can I say? The toxicology is going to be several weeks yet before we get a return, the same with the histology samples and the brains from the unidentified male at Glyne Gap and Piper. It's not like *Prime Suspect* or *Silent Witness* on telly where they get all their results back the same day. This happens to be real life and things take time, even on a high-priority submission."

Tom wished it was different and was a drama show, officers never seeming to understand the processes the labs undertook on the samples he asked to be submitted. It didn't matter how much money you threw at an investigation, some things just took time.

"And there was nothing from Clarke's address?" Cornish asked, running his right hand over his bald crown.

Tom had gone over this more than once, but repeated himself, "No, nothing. The drive is gravel, so no footprints. No sign the house was entered at any point. The tape over the camera lens on the Ring doorbell had no DNA and was far too small for any print ridge detail to be lifted. We checked all the windows but no prints that come back to a suspect. There are some unidents, but until you find a suspect, we've nothing to compare them against."

Tony, out of courtesy, put down the croissant he had been eating, brushing the flakes from the table onto the floor, "We still have no idea who the male is from Glyne Gap. No matches on the national missing persons database, charities, or other organisations. He may as well have just dropped out of the sky onto that beach."

Cornish had his four separate operational notebooks in front of him, "We have male one dumped on a beach a week ago and we still don't know who he is, a second local male murdered with no apparent motive, a third taken from hundreds of miles away and left in some symbolic religious gesture, a police officer abducted, and nothing to link any of them together. Am I missing anything?"

Annie spoke up, "Well, there is a link of sorts." All eyes turned to her, "The first three either have a similarity or are identical in method to a previous murder. The first was found in the same location and in a similar M.O. used by Charlie Knights in 2000, the second is a copy of a murder by a James Whittaker in Devon in 1955 and the third bears a striking resemblance to one committed by this guy Smyth in 1902, with the exception that it was a male and not a female. So, apart from the Superintendent, we have someone committing murders copying the M.O. of old crimes."

She paused, letting them all take the information in fully. "There is no pattern because there's no link between the crimes. They're decades apart, two of the offenders are dead and the other one's well past his pension in prison."

"So, what's with Jess being taken?" Lake asked.

Annie was hoping Cornish hadn't noticed Lake hadn't referred to the Superintendent more professionally. Maybe he'd just put it down to them working together. "I think that's for us. All three murders in less than a week, then the Area Commander is snatched. They've got us running around chasing shadows and we just keep letting it out on the news we have no idea who's responsible. There's hundreds of cops working on this now, and as far as the public's concerned, we're no further forwards than day one. Then add on the shit that's come from that video of the ACC. Somebody went into our headquarters without being seen and put up a bloody camera in his office. How did they know he was going to try and shag his press officer?"

Cornish told them there had been searches conducted by teams at headquarters and Hastings police station and no other cameras or devices had been located. They'd stripped his office and Clarke's, where most of the briefings had been conducted from, even to the point of air vents and changing all the computers. It didn't matter how many officers they had to throw at the investigations if there were no leads for them to chase down.

The meeting ended, and Annie went with Lake to his office, the pair going over all they knew and ending up back at the same place: a dead end.

It was early afternoon when there was a break. Clarke's Range Rover had been found burnt out on National Trust land near Burwash. One of the trust workers had been out clearing footpaths and found the remains of the car on a patch of scrubland. There were tracks through the woodland off a road which ran from the A265. The first unit to attend had found the number plates burnt away, so had checked the vehicle identification number on the plate fixed to the chassis against PNC and it had come back with an immediate alert.

Annie's first question was to ask if there was a body inside the car, swiftly followed by had the officers checked it thoroughly? She was put through to the officers at the scene on their radio and went over what they could see. One of them had the foresight to use his phone to send a 360-degree view of the exterior of the car plus images from the interior directly to Annie, being careful to steer clear of any footprints they could see on the ground around the car. She shared these with Lake to give him some small comfort and hope that Clarke was still alive.

Tom called to say he was going down to check the ground around the car for any footprints and get it recovered for a full examination under cover. Cornish was arranging for a PolSA team to do a fingertip search once the car had been moved and set out the track to be taped off back to the road. TSU were dispatched to recover any available CCTV. Annie looked at Google Maps to work out potential routes the vehicle may have taken to end up where it was found. If it had come off the A21 at Hurst Green then it had to have gone through Etchingham and Burwash, two decent-sized villages which would provide numerous CCTV opportunities. The other, most direct route was via Battle, an area she knew was well covered due to its tourist footfall. This was the best chance they'd had so far. The car was easily identified and stood out well.

A quick phone call and Cornish had agreed to divert more resources to the CCTV scoping and collection. It was going to be their best option and the more bodies on the ground collecting footage and viewing it, the quicker they may get a result.

CHAPTER 58

Janus listened as Annie made several calls, setting out how and what she wanted done and making the necessary arrangements with Cornish. It had taken a little longer than he'd wanted for the car to have been discovered; he'd anticipated that some group of elderly ramblers or the like would have stumbled across it on Monday, alerted by the smell of smoke, but today was better than tomorrow. It would give the police another area to concentrate on. He could imagine all the efforts they would take to get an image of the driver of the car. Shame, really, that all they would see was a pair of bearded figures in matching green wax jackets and flat caps. Hardly a description that would stand out in the middle-class areas where the car had been taken to. He'd tasked the pair to simply walk away across fields after they had torched the Range Rover. It was less than a kilometre to where they had left the other vehicle in Batemans Lane. A simple matter of two gentlemen out walking in the countryside in the early morning sunrise. Even if they were seen, there was little that would assist from their descriptions, and the false plates on the old Land Rover they had used as a second car would lead nowhere either. Time was of the essence for the police; he had more than enough to accomplish what he needed to.

Clarke was awake behind him, unaware of the developments, the earpiece Janus wore hiding the information from her. She had been fed and watered and helped to go to the toilet before being secured back to the bedframe. There would be a further sedative later. He needed to go out that evening and make a social visit. Clarke would be conscious enough to see the monitors but unable to move. Janus wanted her to be actively involved in the next part of the process; there was no point her being there if it was to only be a passive observer.

He turned to face her, "Jessica, how do you feel now that Mr Livingston has been punished?"

She glared back at him, "What, you expect me to be grateful?"

"Well it wouldn't go amiss. He has, after all, managed to lose his career, family and, I'd imagine, his home, all for the sake of a quick fumble in his office. Very low-class, really. I'd have thought you'd be pleased after the way he's treated you. A little exotic bit on the side to screw with as and when it suited him before he trotted off back to the happy family home for a cosy dinner with the wife and kids." Janus could barely keep the smile from his face.

Clarke would have happily used her nails to scratch that smirk away, "So you did that for my benefit, is that what you're telling me?"

This time he did smile broadly, "No my dear, I did it because I wanted to and I could, and it's destroyed him both professionally and personally. At the same time, it's detracted from the investigation into your disappearance and the murders by the media lapping it up. There's nothing they like better than chopping the mighty down and exposing a dirty little secret. Shame, isn't it, when a bit of video of a person in power shagging a pretty young female takes precedence over death and kidnap? Says a lot about society, doesn't it?"

"And this is how you enjoy yourself, is it? Sick fuck." Clarke spat the words with as much venom as she could.

Janus just sat calmly in his chair, arms folded across his chest, "No Jessica, I get no enjoyment out of it. I am purely showing people for what they are as opposed to what they wish to portray. The great and the good are so very rarely that, so why shouldn't people see them for what they really are? I could bring so many of this country's men of power down, all their supposed secrets, drugs, illicit affairs, odd sexual habits, the list really is endless. Information is power and power is what can make my life and my business possible."

Clarke had no idea what Janus was talking about. Did he have men in positions of power that covered for him, that knew what he was doing but were prepared to ignore it so that he kept their secrets from getting out?

"Tonight, Jessica, I shall be leaving you for a brief time. Don't fret, I will be back, and you shan't be going anywhere. I'll even leave you some entertainment." He turned away, leaving Clarke to ponder on his words.

CHAPTER 59

I t was almost 9 p.m., and Tony was still at his
borrowed desk, one hand holding his phone, the
other a mug of tea, when Annie walked in. He
gestured for her to sit down as he finished the call.

"Coffee?" he asked, putting the phone on the desk.

Annie shook her head, "Heard anything?"

Tony picked up a half-eaten prawn sandwich and
started to demolish the remnants, "Only that they've had
to stand down the search teams for the night as it's too
dark out Burwash to continue. They'll be back first light
in the morning to go again. In the meantime, there's half
a dozen officers on points to keep the area secure. Tom
got a load of footprints, but the trouble is, the worker
who found the car stomped over most of the ones already
there. The car's undercover and Tom and his team will
go and examine it in the morning. Doubtful they'll find
much due to the fire but, who knows, might get lucky."

He didn't sound as if he believed his last comment
any more than Annie did. "How's Ged holding up? Must
be hard with Clarke being his boss and all."

Annie trusted Tony above anyone else but she still held back about Lake and Clarke's relationship. She didn't want to put Tony in a difficult position and, as far as she was concerned, it still wasn't relevant to finding out where Clarke was. "He's coping is about the best I can say. Don't think he's hardly slept since Sunday but we're all running on empty at the moment."

Well, except you, she thought as she watched her friend shove the last piece of sandwich into his mouth and wash it down with a large swig of tea. It was both an endearing and annoying quality that her colleague had the ability to continually eat no matter what may be happening around him. Food fuels the brain was his oft-quoted response to her when she mentioned it.

"More importantly, Annie, how are you? You look tired."

He cared for her a great deal; she knew that. They had been colleagues and friends for a long time. She'd seen his children grow up, sat round his house for dinner enough times to feel she was almost a part of his family, and he was as close to her as any brother to a sister. She didn't have any siblings, but if she had, she couldn't have asked for any better than Tony.

"Like everybody else, just worn out getting nowhere fast. We've got to find Clarke and find her alive. We can't have her being the next in this bastard's line-up of copycat killings." Annie dreaded the call to say Clarke had been found dead, set up in another murder tableau for the media to plaster all over the news. She didn't just want Clarke found alive though: she wanted the person setting all this up. If he happened to get killed in the process then that would save a lot of court time, just so some smarmy barrister could try to argue a shitty, diminished responsibility plea for their client. That was the problem with only specialist officers being armed – most offenders managed to get a comfy prison cell when caught and convicted, as opposed to the punishment she felt some of them deserved. Oh, there were the cases where they were genuinely insane, but the majority were just happy to kill, safe in the knowledge the worst that could happen was a lengthy sentence inside before eventually they managed to convince a parole board they were a changed individual. Meanwhile, families of victims spent the rest of their lives grieving for loved ones taken long before their time. The years had made her bitter at the same system she worked in.

"Go home, Annie. I'm gonna be here a while and I'll call you if anything changes. Promise." He held up three fingers beside his head in his best attempt at a Scout's honour."

"Thanks Tony. Give me a ring when you finish, okay? I'll be up. Get home and see Thalia before she forgets what you look like."

Tony winked at her, "Not possible, mate. Who could forget something this sexy."

He was still laughing at his own joke as Annie left the room.

WEDNESDAY 4TH NOVEMBER

CHAPTER 60

It was just over an hour's drive from Sedlescombe to the address, and Janus had calculated the dosage for Clarke to keep her incapacitated enough to not be a concern, but at the same time awake. He wanted Clarke to see what was happening on the monitors. He'd left the cottage just after eleven, letting the car roll quietly out of the garage, then shutting the door. He drove cross-country instead of taking the main roads, figuring the chances of being stopped by a random police car were more remote. Nevertheless, he had changed plates on the car twice before he arrived, parking well away from his destination and any nearby houses. He made sure to leave a note on the windscreen telling any concerned passer-by that the car had run out of fuel and the occupant had gone to the nearest garage. That way, the car had a valid reason for being in an otherwise obscure location. He would go the rest of the short distance on foot.

He stood in the darkness of the garden, waiting as the lights downstairs went out one after another and only a single glow was left coming from an upstairs room. Pulling on latex gloves, Janus let himself in through the patio doors, leaving the small bag outside. He pulled a pair of slip-on covers over his shoes and then slid the doors silently closed behind him. He sat in the kitchen listening to the sounds of the house. There was some music playing softly from upstairs, he couldn't place the melody at first, then recognised the tune as 'Clair de Lune'. Excellent taste, and one of his favourites. He moved soundlessly into the front room; the night vision goggles he wore giving a monochrome green tinge to his vision while at the same time producing a clear image. He took a seat under the window so that he would be facing the door and took in the surroundings. Minimal items on shelves, a large flat-screen television fixed to the chimney breast, some photos on the unit next to him. He picked one up for a closer inspection. It showed a smiling Asian family of mum, dad and three children, a posed formal picture taken in a studio and no doubt a larger version, made to look like a canvas, was fixed in the parents' family home. It must be dull to be living that life, he mused: get up, go to work, come home, put the kids to bed, maybe a glass of wine. Then, if they were lucky, the parents had a fumble under the bedsheets, hoping none of the kids would wake up and disturb them before they fall asleep to start the whole process again. How very predictable their life must be.

Janus placed the photo back on the unit as he noticed the light extinguished upstairs. He waited a full half hour then rose, walking through to a small office set up in a room off the hallway, the carpeted floor cushioning any small sound his footsteps may have made. A pile of framed certificates sat on the floor to the side of the desk in the room, hidden from view to casual visitors to the house as if they were of little consequence to the occupant. Under the window was a large dog bed, chewed around the edges, with an old frayed blanket on top. Janus was acutely aware that he would need to change and destroy his clothes after this visit to prevent any evidential link to the address. Even a dog hair, if you knew where it originated, could be compared to one found on clothing. He was far too careful to allow that to happen. There was a collar hanging on a hook on the door which he took down and slipped into one of the side pockets of the black combats he'd put on specifically for this visit.

He moved to the bottom of the stairs, listening intently for any sound of movement, before slowly heading up. He walked to the very edge of each step, placing his feet carefully and anticipating any creak that could disturb the householder. At the top of the landing he paused again. He knew which room they were sleeping in, and the door was wide open. He moved towards it and stopped, looking at the figure lying in the double bed. They were, as expected, on their own, and he could see the top half of the person where the duvet had been pushed down to their waist. They were facing away from him, towards the bedroom window. Janus stood listening to the soft breathing coming from the room. He had no intention of waking them, wanting only to see them in person. Nonetheless, he held a hypodermic syringe in his right hand in the event that they awoke. He hoped not to have to use it, the sequence of events for the next forty-eight hours having been meticulously planned for his audience. A light shone from a mobile phone on the bedside table. It vibrated a single time as it received a message. Janus stepped swiftly back out of the doorway, continuing to watch and see if there was any movement from the bed.

Minutes passed with no sign of disturbance and Janus capped the syringe, returning it to a pocket on his left sleeve. He took out a small video camera. The GoPro had night vision capability which, while not as efficient as his goggles, still produced decent enough images for the purposes he required. His clients would have a sneak preview of what he was offering. He entered the room and crossed the foot of the bed, recording as he moved silently. Janus felt his senses acutely, his heart rate raised as the adrenalin coursed through him. This was what he missed with others doing the work for him: the closeness to the targets, being so near as to touch them while they slept, totally unaware of his presence. He knelt down in front of the sleeping figure, their heads barely apart. If they should stir now, then he would have to take extreme measures. He stared intently, seeing their eyelids flutter as they went from deep to REM sleep and back again.

He stood slowly, backing out of the room and retracing his steps down to the ground floor and into the kitchen. He found the coat sitting on the worktop and placed the small piece of paper into the top left pocket. It was possible that she would find it in the morning before leaving the house, but he doubted it. In his experience, the majority of people placed items in the pockets at waist height, rarely using the top ones. He hoped this was the case. It would be confusing for them to find it earlier than suited his purpose.

Janus let himself out the patio doors, relocking them after him. He placed the goggles in his pack now slung over his back and made the short walk back to his car. Again, he waited before he approached it, checking the note was still in place on the screen under the wiper blades. Taking the note off and crumpling it up, he put it in his pocket. Another item to be destroyed. He started the engine and began the drive back to the cottage. It would be around 3 a.m. if there were no issues, and he would still be able to catch a few hours' sleep before the day began to take shape.

***

Clarke had lain watching the monitors in front of her after Janus had left, having no alternative from her fixed position. She could see several views of the interior of a house and another covering the driveway. She watched as car headlights had turned in and been switched off, a female getting out of the car. As they approached the door, she instantly recognised her: Annie Bryce.

Janus had cameras in Annie's home. She could do nothing but watch as Annie moved around the downstairs and then up to the first floor and into a bedroom. There was no sound. Janus had switched that off prior to leaving, so Clarke never heard the patio doors open, only seeing a shape in dark clothing with what looked like a set of binoculars over their eyes. She recognised the goggles for what they were as she watched the person, whom she could only assume was Janus, moving around. She saw Annie turn off the bedroom light and then Janus sit motionless until eventually leaving the living room where she lost track of him on the screen. He appeared in the bedroom, standing at the foot of the bed as Annie slept. Clarke felt powerless as she watched Janus move round and kneel in front of the sleeping Annie. Please, please don't let her be next was all she could think, not when she was so helpless. But then Janus stood, and she saw him make his way back through the house, pausing by a coat before leaving. What was all of it for? Just so he could show Clarke that he could get to any of them? Her current situation meant he didn't need to prove that to her of all people. There had to be a purpose, and it was unlikely to be just for her benefit.

CHAPTER 61

Annie woke with a start and looked at her watch. *Shit, six-thirty.* She must have forgotten to set her alarm. Then she remembered she'd told Tony to ring her when he finished and got home. She rolled over, picked up her phone from beside the bed and touched the screen. No calls but there was a WhatsApp from Tony, "Hey slacker, just letting you know the real workers have finished. Home and eating a warmed up roast dinner before giving Thalia a surprise".

There was a leering emoji at the end of the message, which Annie thought was too much information by half. She checked the time of the message: 12.50 a.m. She'd left her phone on silent and hadn't heard it vibrate when the message came through. She sent a reply, "Sorry, I know you're the one who's holding it together really. Such a knob. XX."

She showered quickly and was surprised to see Tony had sent an answer when she returned to the bedroom, rubbing her hair dry with a towel. "A knob that's clearly up earlier than you! See you at Hastings loser x".

Annie dressed and headed to the kitchen downstairs, making a coffee for the drive across. She planned to call the office on the way, hoping Jenny or one of the other managers would be in the MIR to let her know how they were coping. She grabbed her coat and headed to the car, nearly leaving the coffee on the roof as she went to pull out the driveway. She put in a call to Lake before ringing Cornish; she didn't want to find out the wrong way if Lake had decided to tell the DCI about his relationship with Clarke and be left fumbling as to if she knew or not.

Lake answered after a couple of rings, "Morning." He sounded like he'd used gravel for mouthwash.

"You sound like shit. You sure you're good for work?"

Lake almost growled his reply, "Of course I am and what d'you expect? Sunshine and fucking roses?"

Annie was in no mood for his attitude, no matter what Lake and Clarke had been up to on the side, "Don't give me any pissy crap, Ged. I'm on your side, unless you've forgotten. If you aren't going to be any use to me then stand down and I'll find somebody else that will."

Lake at least had the decency to be contrite, "I'm sorry. Shouldn't have spoken to you like that, just feels like we've got nowhere and Jess is out there with this cunt doing God knows what."

Annie took a breath before replying, "I understand Ged, but if you can't focus then you're not helping. I need you and so does Jess."

"Again, I'm sorry. I'm on my way into the nick. What time'll you be here?"

Annie looked at the clock on the dashboard, "Be there by eightish. Cornish wants a meet once he's done the daily brief, much use as it is."

Lake said he'd meet her in Clarke's office so they could listen into the briefing, and ended the call.

When Annie arrived, she was surprised to see Cornish walking through the back doors to the police station just ahead of her. "Boss, hold the door," she shouted.

He turned and waited for her as she entered, "Thought it best I be here to run the briefing. Also, this way, I avoid the Chief and the rest of the Command. I've got better things to do than sit telling them the same information so they can do nothing with it."

Well, well, well, maybe there's hope for you yet, thought Annie, as she followed Cornish up the stairs to the second floor.

She sat through the eight-thirty briefing to the teams, listening as any hope of some new information quickly evaporated. No sooner had it finished, than Cornish dismissed everyone apart from Annie, and then he was on the phone arranging batches of uniform officers to be deployed in the villages, moving out in concentric circles from Burwash. He wanted them checking any empty properties, farms, disused buildings. If they saw anything suspicious then they were to pull back and inform either Annie, Lake or Tony while keeping obs on the premises. Annie sat listening in. He seemed to be thinking for himself instead of waiting to be told.

Cornish put the phone down from his latest call and looked over the desk, "I know what you're thinking. Since when did I start making decisions before deciding how it would affect my career? Ever since we lost one of our own. Fuck it, Annie, if they don't like the way I'm doing things then they can put somebody else in charge. I know why they picked me, and it's not because I'm the best of the best. I'm expendable to them. So, if that's the case, then let's use every resource there is until we run out or find Clarke."

She stared at him, stunned, "Guv, it's not …"

"Yes. It is. I know what you and all the rest think of me, so do me the courtesy of not denying it. Let's just get the job done, agreed?"

She nodded, "What do you want me to do?"

His reply was brief, "Find her. Alive."

***

Janus was unconcerned by the conversation between the DCI and Annie. It was nearly twelve and a half kilometres as the crow flies between Burwash and Sedlescombe; it would be days until they managed to get as far as his cottage, and by that time all of this would be over.

CHAPTER 62

As Cornish and Annie were talking, the Chief Constable was sat at headquarters waiting to start the media briefing. He had no alternative now but to appear himself before the cameras, after three murders, a missing officer, and the lead investigator all over the internet with his hand up a member of staff's knickers. It was an utter disaster. He was due to meet the Police and Crime Commissioner later that morning, and already there was talk of the Home Secretary considering his position. By rights, he should have put someone in charge of the investigation with more experience and a higher rank than DCI Cornish. He'd made a mistake and couldn't see a way out of it. He knew now he should have had an SIO for each operation. The media were hanging him out to dry, saying he was more concerned with his own reputation than finding one of his officers alive.

He looked out at the faces and cameras in front of him, feeling beads of perspiration run down the middle of his back under his tunic.

"Ladies and gentlemen, if we're all ready then I would like to make a brief statement. As you are aware, three days ago, one of my own officers, Superintendent Jessica Clarke, the Area Commander of Rother Division, was abducted from outside her home. At this time, the suspects remain unidentified, and no demands have been sent. Every effort is being taken to locate Superintendent Clarke, safe and well, and would I urge anybody with information to please come forward. We are supported in our efforts by colleagues from several other police forces, for which I am grateful ..."

He stopped, noticing the assembled journalists suddenly looking down at phones and tablets. He felt a sharp tug on his arm as a laptop was pushed in front of him. The screen was showing a video clip of Clarke bound to a metal-framed bed, her surroundings blurred. There was a blindfold over her eyes and tape across her mouth. She was still in her uniform, with the crown on her epaulettes visible on her shoulders. A banner running underneath the image repeated the same phrase, over and over, 'Remember, remember, the fifth of November.' The Chief looked at his press officer, who just stared straight back as a clamour of voices came from the massed crowd in front.

"Where's this come from?"

"You said there hadn't been any demands?"

"What are you going to do to get her back alive?"

Johnson had no idea what to say. He sat staring, open-mouthed, as the image repeated itself in front of him.

***

Annie's phone rang at the same time as the landline on Cornish's desk and a loud knock at the door. It burst open without waiting for an answer and a constable Annie didn't recognise blurted out, "Turn on Sky News, now."

Cornish grabbed for the remote, switching on the large flat-screen on the wall and turning the channel over to the news. The clip of Clarke was playing on repeat as the reporter spoke over it, saying how this had been uploaded to several social media sites from an unknown location. They were already speculating as to the significance of the message attached to it, questioning if it were a countdown.

Cornish picked up the phone, talking rapidly, trying to establish if there was an IP address the footage had come from. Annie knew that was clutching at straws, with all that had gone before in the last nine days. She doubted very much if the footage would go back to an address and even if it did, it would be a false trail. It would have been bounced around from different locations, making it untraceable. But it did show one thing: Clarke was alive. There was a time and date stamp in the top corner of the video showing it was recorded not much more than an hour or so before. Time stamps could be faked, that wasn't overly difficult, but why bother? It seemed from the message they had until the following day to find Clarke. Whether that time ran until the Thursday morning or last thing at night, she had no idea, but she was convinced more than ever that Clarke was still local, somewhere close by.

She left Cornish on the phone, running down the stairs to Lake's office. The door was open, and he was at his desk, looking at the same footage she had seen moments earlier.

"Ged, she's still alive, the video proves it."

He stared back at her, his face taught, the scar white, "For how long?"

CHAPTER 63

There was nothing on the video clip to give any indication as to where it had been taken. The metadata was removed at source, leaving just the images. The bed was a simple metal frame, cheap and available anywhere, and the white plaster wall that could be seen behind Clarke gave nothing to help. The lighting was artificial, with no visible windows and no sound in the background at all. Whoever had uploaded the footage had covered their tracks sufficiently to give no more than they intended: proof that Clarke had been abducted and was being held, alive for now.

Annie stared at the yellowing white walls of the office feeling utterly useless. They had all the technology, cameras, science, and yet they were being toyed with, made to look helpless while the killers selected individuals seemingly at random with no fear of capture and then taunted the police with one of their own. All they were doing was treading water; they had no leads, nothing to help to find Clarke. It didn't matter how many officers they could throw at it now; it was only a matter of time until she was killed. Yet another statement murder.

Lake had gone AWOL again, chasing up leads of his own at the same time as assuring Annie he wouldn't do anything stupid, whatever that meant. Outside, the sky was grey and heavy, the rain pouring down the window. At least, she hoped, this weather might keep some of the usual idiots and their bonfire parties from going ahead tomorrow, if it continued.

There had to be some significance and connection to Guy Fawkes night. The words on the video clip had been quickly identified as coming from the first line of an old children's nursery rhyme. She looked and read again the printout on the desk:

Remember, remember the fifth of November,
Gunpowder treason and plot.
We see no reason
Why gunpowder treason
Should ever be forgot!
Guy Fawkes, guy, t'was his intent
To blow up king and parliament.
Three score barrels were laid below
To prove old England's overthrow.
By God's mercy he was catch'd
With a darkened lantern and burning match.
So, holler boys, holler boys, Let the bells ring.
Holler boys, holler boys, God save the king.

And what shall we do with him?
Burn him!

There was no way that all this related to some plot to bring down the government, so why quote that line? Bonfire night in Sussex had a history going back nearly 250 years. Guy Fawkes for most of the country meant going to large public firework displays, families with small bonfires in the back garden setting off coloured rockets and Catherine wheels. Sussex was different: it would have vast parades through town centres, predominantly in the south-east. Lewes, where the police headquarters was based, was traditionally transformed every 5th of November, with bonfire societies converging to march through the town and roll lighted barrels down the cobbled streets, their members in elaborate costumes with painted faces. An effigy, normally mocking the government or a celebrity in some way, was carried through the streets before being set ablaze, and it wasn't unheard of for the town's small population of just over 17,000 to be swelled by a huge influx of thousands more spectators for the night. Celebrations, similar to those in Lewes, were duplicated across the east of the county with large numbers of police on duty to cover public order. It was always a busy night for the force, with officers' rest days cancelled to provide sufficient numbers.

Annie knew already they would be losing part of the teams investigating the murders to cover events the following day. Battle, only a few miles to the north of Hastings, was another of the towns where the public descended in their masses to celebrate Guy Fawkes Night. Generally this meant an excuse to get drunk and cause chaos outside the pubs along the High Street. Roads into the town would be closed and traffic diverted for part of the evening to accommodate the parade, with a huge bonfire in front of Battle Abbey and firework display from the abbey grounds being the culmination of the night's events. The abbey itself backed onto hundreds of acres of woodland, fields and nature reserves; you could have put the whole police force for Sussex in the area and still been unable to cover it all.

At the back of her mind was a feeling that this was just a decoy. Nothing so far had shown any links to the 5th and none of the murders had any connection to that date. Her phone vibrated next to her and she saw it was only a message from Kevin telling her that Bella was fine. She thanked him, wondering when she would get to see her dog again. It was the least of her problems but she still felt guilty over keep palming her off.

Cornish had put the wheels in motion to have the bonfires in all the larger towns checked and then checked again the following day. The last thing they wanted was to find a body in the embers of one of them once it had burnt down. This pulled even more resources away from the investigations, with dozens of sites to check. Once it came to tomorrow, they would be stuck with thousands of additional people milling around towns, making it impossible to track anyone in the crowds.

Annie's phone went off again, and she picked it up ready to swipe away a reply from Kevin. She didn't have time to discuss how much fun he was having being paid to look after her dog. Her finger paused over the screen. There was no name or number for the message, which puzzled her and she frowned, pressing the icon to open it, thinking it was only a scam to buy insurance. Instead of a worded message, there was a single photo of a brown leather dog collar hanging from a hook on a plain white wall. She checked the image, but there was no data behind it to say where or when it had been taken. She was just about to delete it, figuring it had been sent to her in error, when she stopped, using two fingers to enlarge the picture. That couldn't be possible, surely? But it looked just like Bella's spare, the one she kept in her office at home. Annie tried to make the image larger, losing some of the definition as she attempted to zoom in on the metal tag attached to a ring on the collar. It had to be a coincidence, the same bone-shaped blue metal name tag, too out of focus to make out what was written on it.

Leaving the office, she went down the corridor to Tony, whom she found talking to a couple of detectives she didn't recognise. Seeing Annie walk in, Tony waved her over as he finished his conversation, "Get one of the locals downstairs to point you in the direction of Netherfield. If the Superintendent's car went cross-country instead of coming off the A21 then it will have had to go through there before going north either by Wood's Corner or Cackle Street. Have a scoot round and see if you can tip up any CCTV; the TSU boys have their hands full and need extra bodies for the scoping. If you find anything then let them know on this number and they'll sort the download." He handed one of the officers a slip of paper and they left for the ground floor.

"We've got DCs and DSs coming out our ears and all I can do is throw them out into the countryside and hope they stumble across something to help. I give them some of the names of places and they look at me like I'm taking the piss. I mean, Cackle Street, seriously?"

His desk was strewn with the detritus of what could only be several days' worth of sweet wrappers, crisp packets and balled-up clingfilm. He saw Annie looking down, "I told the cleaners to leave it all alone." He pointed to a note pinned to the back of his computer screen with the simple, "DON'T MOVE ANYTHING".

So much for the clear desk policy then, thought Annie. "Tony, is Thalia home today?"

"Yeah, expect so. Kids should all be at school. Why?"

Annie paused before asking, "Can you ask her to take the spare key I gave you and nip round to my house and meet a couple of bobbies there. I just need someone

317

to go and look at the back of my office door where Bella has the bed she's supposed to sleep on instead of mine. I just want them to check the hook on the door and send me a photo."

Tony looked puzzled, "Sure she can. What's this for? You lost something?"

Annie went around the desk and put her phone down, opening the message she'd just received and showing him the photo. "It looks like Bella's spare. I leave it hanging on the hook on the door, so how is it on a photo I'm being sent from an unknown source?"

Tony picked up the phone, attempting to zoom in on the image much in the same way that Annie had when she received it. "Could be any brown leather collar, can't see a name on it. Must just be chance, surely?" His voice was calm. He didn't need to spell out the possibilities otherwise.

Annie took the phone back, placing it in her pocket, "With all that's been happening, what do you really think the odds are that I get sent an anonymous message with a picture of a dog collar identical to one I should have hanging up at home?"

Tony was already on his mobile, dialling his wife's number. "Thals, it's me. Need you to take the key for Annie's. Think it's in the drawer by the front door. Can you drive over there and meet some uniforms? I'm going to get a car sent from Burgess Hill. Just give them the key and get back in your car. You're not to go inside."

Annie could hear a muffled reply before Tony spoke again, "They'll be in a marked car. If you get there first, sit tight and wait. You are not to just go bowling in."

He then said the words Annie had been fervently hoping she was wrong about, "It's possible someone's broken into Annie's. Don't know if it's recent or not, which is why I don't want you going in, okay." A brief reply then, "Thanks honey. Call me when you get there. Love you." A response from Thalia and he ended the call, putting the phone down and looking at his friend, saying what she already knew. "If there's no collar on that hook then they've been in your house. Once we know, I'm going to get the pair to pull back and sit tight. CSI can go over and check and then we can stick a PolSA through. If they can hide a camera in the ACC's office at HQ …" He left the rest of the unsaid, as there was no need to finish the sentence.

Annie was acutely aware of what he was going to say: had someone been watching her as well?

CHAPTER 64

Clarke sat looking at Janus. He'd changed the glasses she's seen him wearing previously from wire-framed to frameless. She'd been certain he was wearing contacts, the eyes surely too blue to be his own, but unless the glasses were purely for effect, the colour hadn't changed. It wasn't the only thing about him that made him stand out, of course; bald and lacking eyebrows would certainly draw attention to you in the street. She doubted that he went out looking that way, it was a simple matter of a bit of wigs and make-up and he could look completely different. He appeared to change his clothing regularly, now attired in a black roll-neck jumper, grey trousers and, bizarrely to her, a pair of cheap flip-flops.

Janus saw her staring at his feet, "It's not just a comfort thing you know, Jessica; shoes, trainers, they all leave a pattern which can be matched. Not quite the same with these, is it?" He waved a foot towards her, "Easily disposed of in a bin near to a beach and nobody gives you a second glance in the summer. Oh, obviously it would be different if I wandered along Winchelsea beach in these at the moment, but the other benefit is they're only made of plastic and rubber. Easily destroyed in a fire. Shame it has to add to the carbon footprint, and not exactly ecologically sound, but that's not really my main concern." He smiled pleasantly at her.

She imagined, in other circumstances, and with the addition of some hair, he would be pleasantly attractive. Not too handsome that he would stop a room when he walked in but good-looking enough that he probably wouldn't have an issue with attracting the ladies, or men if it came to that. There was no accent to his voice. He'd not raised it towards her at all so far. If she'd been asked to place it she would struggle; he had to have spent time learning to cover any trace of where he originated. He spoke eloquently and politely, and nothing about Janus or his actions led Clarke to believe he didn't plan down to finite details.

"What time is it?" she asked.

Janus looked back at one of the screens behind him, "Ten past two in the afternoon, and it's Wednesday the 4th. I understand that time here can be a little confusing, what with the sedatives combined with the lack of natural light."

Clarke didn't really want to ask the next question, fearing the answer, but did so anyway, trying to keep her voice steady, "How much longer?"

"Less than a day for you, Jessica, then this will all be over with." His voice was measured and calm, showing neither pleasure in his comments nor indifference. What he was saying was merely factual for her personal information. He had no malice towards Clarke; she was simply a means to an end and the knowledge of her relationship with Lake had given him an opportunity he didn't want to deprive himself, or others, of. He was confident that her knight in shining armour would come charging to her rescue on cue, but only when he was ready for it to happen.

She couldn't understand Janus's motives or methods. If he was intending to kill her, then what was the point in keeping on feeding her? He may as well have let her starve for the few days she'd been in the room; it would have made her weaker, minimising the risk to him of her causing problems. He'd been courteous, almost caring at times. When he had arrived back from his visit to Annie's she'd asked him why he'd left her to watch what he was doing. His reply, a simple one: he wanted her to understand this whole situation wasn't just about her. He'd explained there was no vendetta; he had no axe to grind for some perceived slight by Sussex Police. It was the same with the three people he'd arranged to be murdered, confirming to Clarke at least that the male found at Glyne Gap beach had been the first in the series. He'd had no previous contact with any of them. They were selected to fulfil a purpose. The manner of their demise, again, selected at the request of unseen third parties, purely to fit the correct scenario. When Clarke had asked his reasons for setting up the deaths, his answer had been as matter of fact as if discussing a venture to open a new shop or restaurant. He had spotted a gap in the market and filled it. The world was so much smaller now with the internet. He helped his clients pursue their interests, such as they were. It was just supply and demand. He refused to discuss any part of his background, again, something that puzzled Clarke. If he intended to end her life, what did it matter anyway? She was resigned to her own death now, knowing no amount of pleading would make any difference. Better to die with her dignity intact if she could. The problem with that was she knew what the three previous victims had gone through.

CHAPTER 65

Tony came to find Annie to update her that Bella's collar was no longer on the hook where it should have been. Thalia had given her mobile to one of the officers who had arrived and he had entered using the spare key. The constable had gone as directed, straight to the office, taken a photo of the back of the door and returned without even knowing what he was looking for. Tony held out his phone so Annie could see the image on it: just a bare brass hook where the collar should be hanging. She shivered involuntarily as the realisation there had been someone in her own home sank in.

"I've got the two bobbies to start a scene log and make sure the front and back are secure until we can get forensics over to have a look. When did you last see Bella's collar on the hook?" Tony had pocketed his phone and pulled up one of the other office chairs and was now sat next to Annie.

"I couldn't tell you. It's hung there so long I probably wouldn't have known it was gone now until I had that picture sent to me earlier." She was thinking about where else this person had been in her house and, even worse, when.

It was Tony who gave voice to what else had been running around at the back of her head, "What I want to know is how the fuck whoever this is knows where you live? Are they following us?"

Annie had no clue. She had never left Hastings at a set time, travelling in either her own car or the works Focus. There was never a pattern as to if she went back to the office or directly home, and it was always late at night, dark on the roads. If someone had been following her all the way back then they would have stood out. There were a lot of quiet roads she drove back to Ditchling on. "I don't know. I can't really see us all being followed, can you?"

"There'd have to be either a lot of them or they just picked on you and Livingston. Think about it, Annie: the ACC gets targeted at work and humiliated nationally. They had to already know what he was up to, or have a bloody good idea, else why stick a camera in his office?"

She shrugged, "Well last I knew I wasn't touching up any of my colleagues, male or female, so why should I be of any interest?"

Tony looked at her, incredulously, "You're shitting me, right? Who gets shafted every time a difficult job comes in? Who is the one always on the side-lines telling the bosses what they should be doing so they don't end up in front of the press with their dick hanging in the wind because they missed something obvious on a murder? It's you. It wouldn't take the IQ of a hamster to find that out. Just go through all the cases on the internet. Your name's over all of them."

Annie stood up, walking away from the desk before turning back to face him, "Come on, Tony. I'm just the DS, nobody special. I live at home on my own with a bloody dog for company, for fuck's sake. What's the point in targeting me?"

"Because you're the one most likely to find that small piece of evidence that this clever fucker has messed up on, that's why. If they can unsettle you, put you off balance, then there's less chance of you spotting something."

"So why not grab me instead of Clarke then? Kill two birds with the same stone, so to speak. They get me out of the way at the same time as using me as bait or whatever she is."

She was angry. She didn't like the feeling of being toyed with for another person's amusement while people were being killed.

Tony sat forward, his elbows resting on his knees and concern over his face, "I think it's a game to them. They seem to know everything we have, which is obviously the square root of fuck all at the moment. They're messing with you to show that it's not only Clarke they can get to: it's any of us. Hang on." He stopped, taking his mobile out of his pocket to make a call, "Thalia, soon as the kids get home from school, get a bag packed for you all and go stay at your mum's for the night. No, don't argue, just listen. If they've been in Annie's house then I don't want any little shit coming in ours while I'm stuck over here. Please, just for tonight, then we can talk about it tomorrow."

Annie could hear Thalia on the other end of the conversation, clearly unhappy with the situation. She'd been married to Tony long enough to know his job came with the occasional risk, working on cases involving organised crime groups where you were targeted by association for upsetting their business. She'd go to her mum's; she'd do anything rather than put their kids at risk. It was the other side of Hove and they could work out a longer-term arrangement if need be.

Tony put the phone down on the desk. "Where's Ged? If they've been to the trouble of going halfway across the county to your house then I imagine his flat in town would be a damn sight easier."

Annie stopped to think. When had she last seen Lake? Sometime this morning? "Give him a ring, Tony, see what he's up to. I think he's got the hump with me for some reason."

Lake answered Tony's call almost at once, telling him that he'd been visiting some of his local informants, but come up blank. Tony told him about the photo Annie had been sent and that there was no doubt that a stranger had been into her house. Lake said he would go back to check his flat and arranged with Tony to meet a patrol car there just in case.

"See he listens to you then. You two been doing some male bonding?" Annie couldn't help feeling put out.

Tony stood and walked to the door, "Not that I know of. Maybe it's just my incredible personality. I'm sending out for food. Want anything?"

The last thing Annie wanted right now was food, with her stomach turning at the thought of people wandering around in her home uninvited. "Not for me. I don't think I can stomach anything right now. You go ahead."

"Gotta feed this giant investigative brain. Thalia's pack-up can only get me so far. Seriously Annie, eat something. I can't see us getting back across to Brighton any time in the next twenty-four hours, can you? We're here for the long run now until we find Clarke tomorrow, one way or another."

She relented, "Okay, just a sandwich of some kind. I might have it later."

"Sorted," Tony said as he shut the door behind him. Annie sat down at her desk, staring at the screen. None of them were going home that night.

CHAPTER 66

It was past ten in the evening and Annie was sitting in the Superintendent's office with Cornish and Lake. Left-over food cartons and wrappings spread across the table in front of them along with a number of Costa coffee cups, none of which improved the aroma of the room. A first sweep by CSI at her home had turned up nothing other than some minor scratches around the lock mechanism on the patio doors. No footprints inside, no other signs of disturbance. The PolSA team had already found several cameras set up around the house, the most disturbing being the one in her bedroom. She'd been watched, and it could have been for days. She thought back to her movements around the house, getting undressed, taking off her prosthetic. *Was this bastard getting off on it?*

"The cameras and battery packs have all been photographed in situ by CSI and they're swabbing them for any possible DNA before they get bagged." Cornish was looking at his notes taken form the call to the PolSA team leader a while ago, "The skipper over there sent me a picture of the first one they found when CSI had finished with it, same kind that was found in the ACC's office the other day. The make and model have all been taken off by some means, so there's nothing to easily track it back to. I'll get the lab to take them apart when they arrive. There must be serial numbers or something on the inside that can identify where they came from. This is high-end kit, not the kind of crap you get off some shitty spy wannabe site on the net. There'll have to be a way to find out where they come from and track it back to a buyer."

Lake spoke up before Annie could even open her mouth, "Boss, with respect," that phrase again, "I hardly think they've been purchased by the normal channels using a credit card. There's a ton of shit you can find on the dark web if you know where to look, untraceable back to the person. It's worth a punt, but don't hold your breath."

Cornish sighed, took off his heavy, framed glasses and rubbed the bridge of his nose. He looked as tired as Annie was starting to feel, the long hours and stress now beginning to take their toll on all of them. He had his jacket over the back of the chair and shirt sleeves rolled up to his elbows. "Well we don't have an awful lot else to go on, do we DI Lake? So, let's just do what we can with what we have, shall we?"

As SIO, Cornish had got the Chief to put all the shifts across the county on twelve-hour duties for the next two days. Unpopular as it would normally be, everyone realised the situation they were in, whether frontline uniform or plain clothes detectives and backroom staff. He'd also asked the Chief to try to get the local town councils to cancel, or at least postpone, the bonfire festivities planned for the following day. There was a flat refusal on that one; it was too late in the day and they had nothing factual to say that there was even any link with the night's events other than a single line from an old poem. Hundreds of thousands would be attending displays across the county and they needed to police them, end of story.

So far, nothing had been found in the search of Lake's flat, and unmarked firearms teams had now been deployed to patrol Rother Division so they would be close by if needed. There was also a full PSU on rotation at Hastings, each van having at least a pair of method of entry-trained officers on board and carrying enough kit to stop a riot. A firearms Tactical Advisor, or Tac-Ad, would be on-call to be deployed at a moment's notice, along with additional direct-entry firearms officers. The Silver Cell continued to run in the event a hostage call for Clarke did come in. The only thing that was missing was the information necessary to do anything with all those resources.

Annie and Lake headed back down to his office when their meeting with Cornish broke up, Annie stopping off first to check in with Tony, who told her

Thalia had rung to say she was at her mum's with the kids and it was already driving her up the wall. Tony had smiled, "Least I'm staying here and not having to hear how it's all my fault from the father-in-law." He'd then gone back to what she could see was his second portion of cold chips.

Lake was looking out of the window into the dark when she walked into the office. The rain had petered out to a fine, misty drizzle, almost a fog as it rolled over the town. The streetlights glowed among the mist with the spotlights of the press teams shining as they supplied their latest bulletins to the viewing public.

"You know this could all be finished in the next couple of hours or he could go until midnight tomorrow to really string us out." Lake's voice was flat, and he didn't bother to even turn away from the window to look at Annie as he spoke.

"What do you want me to say, Ged? Everyone's doing all they can. I want to find Jess alive as much as you do."

"We're not going to though, are we? Be realistic, 'cos I am. They've killed three people so far and taken another and we've got no idea even who's doing this or why after nearly ten days. What makes you think that's suddenly gonna change?" His voice was now raised and he turned, his eyes red-rimmed, "They're going to kill her and do you know why?" Lake didn't wait for a reply, "Because they fucking can and we can't do a thing to stop them."

Annie stepped towards him but he put his hand out to ward her off, "I need to get out of here for a couple of hours. Call me if anything happens; I won't be far away."

He brushed past her, leaving the door open as he left. There was no point in trying to stop him. What were they going to do? Sit and talk about all the things they didn't know? She slumped down in a chair. They were just being played with, like a cat with a mouse, until the cat decided it was time for the final, killing stroke.

CHAPTER 67

Janus, if he could be bothered to feel pity, would have felt it for Annie at that moment. Through no fault of her own, other than being in the wrong county when he chose to conduct his business there, she had become embroiled in a deviation from his norm. It could have happened to any detective, but there was something about Annie that had drawn her to him. Bend the stick enough and eventually it must break. He had decided he would break them all in different ways by the time he had finished with this venture.

He had been busy at the cottage from the moment dusk began to fall. There had been enough ambient light to work in outside, without the need for head torches drawing unwanted attention. It had taken time and care but, in less than two hours, he had completed the task and was back inside with Clarke. He had no concerns over the police finding the cameras in Annie's house. The manner and process of the purchase of the items meant that they could never be traced directly back to Janus or any of his connections. By the time the police managed to follow the paper trail from seller to buyer, they only would find dead ends and false locations. Surely, by now, they would have realised he would be unlikely to order next-day delivery from Amazon? He supposed they had to cling to hope in these circumstance. With nothing else to go on, they had no alternative. In less than twenty-four hours this latest venture would be concluded and he would disappear into the ether, leaving them wondering what motive he had when he chose this small county on the coast to create panic.

Losing the visual feed to Annie's was even less of a concern. She would not be returning home that night, so there was no point in maintaining a view of the premises. Give them another puzzle to figure and spend more resources searching and providing security for families. Every minute extra they were having to concentrate on that was another minute they lost in looking for him.

Janus had now removed the cannula in Clarke's back along with cutting off the sedatives he had been giving her. She would become fully alert in the coming hours and the feeling would begin returning to her legs. She was still restrained to the bed of course, with the cable ties around her wrists again firmly secured to the top of the frame, but she was free to move her legs when she could. He wanted her to understand what was happening now, to be clear as events occurred so she missed nothing. He had given Clarke very specific instructions around any desires she may have to scream or call out for help, leaving her under no illusion as to the consequences should she try. The cuff was still attached to her ankle and he had given a further demonstration of the pain that she would endure at the press of a button. That, in itself, may not stop her from calling out, but the glinting scalpel he had held before her eyes as she lay on the bed certainly drove home the message. He had promised that any sound made, unless in response to a direct question from him, would now result in her finding out exactly how excruciating it was to have your lips sliced from your face. Her eyes had told him that she didn't doubt his threats would be acted upon if he felt it necessary.

Of course, when he wasn't in the room, Clarke may think differently. If he was gone for an extended period she may seek the opportunity to scream from the top of her lungs, hoping a passer-by would hear her cries and come to her aid. This, again, was no issue for him. He had chosen the cottage due to its remote location, and there were hardly going to be any dog walkers after dark. The nearest properties were too far away to hear and, if it came to it, she could scream as much as she wanted. In fact, it was to be a requirement at the right time.

As soon as she was able to sit unaided, Janus had made her turn to the top of the bed and he had spent an endless time brushing her hair before plaiting it at the back, all the while talking to her as if they were sharing an intimate moment together. He told her Lake was beside himself trying to find her, that her colleagues were searching towns and villages in the hope they could locate her before time ran out. He had even turned one of the monitors on so she could see the news bulletins, telling her it was her fifteen minutes of fame. Clarke took this to be her captor's idea of psychological torture, building up to the coup de grâce of her death. Whatever was to happen, she would try to find a moment to fight back, do something to shatter his confidence and throw him off balance long enough to make an error. If she was to die at his hands, she wanted there to be a chance at least that he would pay for it.

THURSDAY 5TH NOVEMBER – BONFIRE NIGHT

CHAPTER 68

A nnie felt herself being gently shaken on the shoulder. She must have dropped off curled up on the one soft chair in the corner of Lake's office. She opened her eyes to see Tony kneeling beside her.

"Shit, what time is it?" She rubbed her eyes, seeing the dim light coming through the window. It was pitch-black outside when she'd turned off the main lights thinking she'd needed to catch a few minutes' rest.

"Half-six. Sun should be up in a bit."

Was it around three in the morning when she'd closed her eyes? "Bollocks, sorry Tony. I only meant to get half an hour." She looked at her phone, sure that she had set an alarm. She had, but then not turned it on.

It was always difficult with Tony to know if he'd slept or not, as he generally had the appearance of having just rolled straight out of bed in the clothes he was standing up in. He held up a mug of coffee, "There's a McDonald's breakfast on the desk, about the only hot food I could find at this time of the morning." He indicated behind him and Annie saw a paper bag with the familiar logo on the front.

"Thank you." Her stomach rumbled, more at the prospect of having something to eat than the actual contents of the bag.

"I did come in to see you earlier but you were out for the count, thought I'd let you catch a bit of shut-eye. You need it for the day ahead." He raised a hand to ward off any argument from Annie before she could start with him, "Nothing's happened in the last few hours that you being awake would have made any difference to anyway. Cornish kept on top of it all and I had a couple of hours as well. He got his head down about five so I said I'd make sure we had some breakfast to go on with. Although a full, greasy fry-up would have gone down better."

Annie winced as she took a mouthful of coffee, burning her throat in the process and wondering how they could make a drink that stayed that hot in a polystyrene cup without it melting. "Where's Ged?"

Tony handed her the bag from the desk, "He's down the corridor with some of his DCs going over the areas to cover today. There's no point in a briefing and I don't think Cornish wants people sitting around when they could be out with boots on the ground. Got to admit, he's starting to feel like one of the team at last now he's come down from that pedestal."

Annie had taken a bit of the warm McMuffin which, despite the somewhat disconcerting plastic appearance of the contents, tasted like gourmet food to her hungry stomach. "Don't suppose there's a muesli and yoghurt to go with this, is there?"

Tony laughed, "No, gave you one of my hash browns though; lots of good calories and fats to keep you going."

She balled up the waxed paper as she continued eating the muffin. The hash brown could wait until hell froze over as far as she was concerned. It was a step too far. "You have it, Tony. I'm hungry, but I'm never gonna be that hungry."

There was no hesitation from her colleague as he finished the fried potato slice in two quick bites. "So, today's the day. Any chance they're just going to dump the Super off on the promenade by the pier alive?"

Annie wished it to be the case. They had no basis to even hope that Clarke was going to survive. All the indicators were that she would be found dead, set up in another scenario taken from an earlier killer. Unless they found her, or the person who had her, first.

***

Clarke sat observing Janus as he went about the room wiping down every surface meticulously, the smell of ammonia strong in her nostrils. He'd removed everything else in the room apart from the laptop and one of the monitors, now showing the spilt-screen format of the four cameras covering the front and rear of the cottage. A bottle of water with a plastic straw had been left within her reach on the bed. He'd taken the coverings down from the window, and even though it was grey and miserable outside, it seemed like a beautiful day to Clarke, having not seen daylight for the last four dawns. From her position on the bed she could see no more than the tops of some trees in the distance and the clouds in the sky, dark and brooding, heavy with more rain. It was obvious that Janus was no longer worried about somebody looking in, which told her he was confident that no one was likely to.

CHAPTER 69

It was mid-morning and Annie sat across the desk from Cornish, listening in silence as he spoke on a video call to the Chief. He'd not mentioned she was in the room and it was apparent to her that this was intentional so she could listen to the conversation.

"Sir, if we can concentrate on the two main events for tonight: Lewes and Battle. If there is any association then they have the largest attendance by far if you wanted to make a statement. I understand that you won't ask for them to be cancelled, but we need to flood the area with as many bodies on the ground as possible: uniform, plain clothes, firearms, and use whatever tech support we have. We can get a drone up at each location if we need to."

She could tell by the tone that the Chief wasn't over-enamoured by the idea.

"We don't even know if it's related to the Guy Fawkes parades, let alone those two specifically. What use is a drone going to be with thousands of people milling around?"

Cornish was prepared for this, "They have thermal imaging capabilities. I've had them used on missing persons out in fields and picked them up. There's vast expanses of open ground that we can cover outside of the main areas where the public will be congregating to watch the parades. Thermal imaging will be far more use in unpopulated areas and woods than using officers, and we can send people in to search if it indicates anywhere."

The Chief took the point and it made sense. There were acres of woodland and fields around Battle, but the main site for events was at the rear of the abbey off the High Street. Lewes was more problematic; seven different societies would be attending, each having their own bonfire in a different part of the town. There was also the added factor of up to a 100,000 people that would be in attendance. It was an impossible situation to police effectively if you wanted to look for somebody. There were mutual-aid PSUs coming from five other nearby counties but, even so, they would still be thin on the ground with everything else that was going on.

The conversation continued and Annie heard the Chief go over the two media drafts, ready should they be required, for whatever eventuality. It seemed bizarre on one hand to listen to him talking about what a wonderful officer Clarke had been, a valued member of the force who left behind two children from her former marriage. There was the usual epitaph remembering her achievements, concluding with how they would leave no stone unturned in the endless pursuit of her killer. For fuck's sake, she wasn't even dead yet. The second spoke of how the efforts the investigating officers and all the support teams had finally found Clarke alive, and they now continued their pursuit of her attackers. To Annie, this latter one seemed a lot less hopeful than it sounded. No press conferences were planned for the day. They would wait it out until there was no other alternative.

Annie couldn't sit and listen to any more. She nodded her head towards the door and quietly left the room, heading back down with the intention of speaking to Lake. She wanted to go over to Battle with him, get him to show her around in daylight before the multitudes began to arrive. As far as she was concerned, if there was to be any show made then, it wouldn't be at Lewes. All the murders had happened on this division, so it made no sense to her to suddenly move to another area. Showy as it may be to commit whatever was planned on the doorstep of police headquarters, it didn't fit with the only pattern they had. It all focused on Rother. She'd only ever driven through Battle on her way elsewhere, never having had cause to stop there. Despite its name, the Battle of Hastings in 1066 had not been fought in the town. It was actually in nearby Battle where William the Conqueror defeated King Harold II. Swathes of visitors annually came to the small town, predominantly to see the historic abbey, which had stood on the site since 1071, and wander around the picturesque grounds behind it. There would be a different type of visitor tonight.

Lake wasn't in the office, so she went through to ask Tony if he'd seen him.

"He was sitting talking to a couple of lads when it looked like he got a message. I saw him looking at his phone, then he just shot out the office like a scalded cat. I thought it was probably from you?"

Annie looked at her watch: 11.55 a.m. "How long ago?"

Tony shrugged, "No more than fifteen minutes. Let me ring him."

He dialled Lake's mobile from his own, getting no reply. He then tried from the landline, figuring Lake might answer if it came from a withheld number, knowing it might be the office. He shook his head, "He's not picking up; straight to voicemail."

"Anyone got a radio?" Annie shouted across the office.

A uniform sergeant was behind her in the corridor, "Here, what d'ya need?"

Like most of the MIT, and many of the older detectives, Annie had got out of the habit of taking a radio around with her, relying on her mobile phone instead. Bad habits come back to haunt you and all she could recall was that hers was sat in a locker back at the MIT. She didn't even know what her call sign was and probably couldn't work one of the new Motorola sets if she had to. "Can you call up control and see if they can locate DI Lake. It's urgent."

The sergeant tried to call Lake direct on a point-to-point first, but all he got back was a tone that the other radio was uncontactable. He went via the control room next, asking them to contact Lake, as DS Bryce needed to speak to him urgently. Annie heard a call go out over the airwaves using Lake's callsign. Nothing came back. It was less than a minute and her mobile phone rang, the control room supervisor on the other end. "Is that DS Bryce?"

She was told they had checked the location for Lake's radio, but it was switched off. The last place it had been active was at the police station in the early hours of the morning. She turned and ran back to his office and saw it behind his desk, sitting in its charger on the shelf. She still had the control room supervisor on the line, "Can you trace his work phone? Tell the authorising officer it's a threat to life. I think he's had some information about Superintendent Clarke." The phone was put on hold.

She had no basis for this assumption. *Surely Lake would have said something if he had? But what if he'd been told not to?* It took a further couple of interminable minutes before the supervisor came back on the line. "We've got a hit on the phone. About five minutes ago it pinged a mast near Sedlescombe Golf Club heading north on the A21. Nothing since, but out that way the

347

mast coverage will be a lot further than in a town. That's the best I can give you until he hits the next mast."

Annie waved at Tony to join her as she continued on the call, "Can you see if his job car's hit any of the mobile ANPR traffic units. That might give a better location."

The radio next to her gave out the details of Lake's allocated car, asking all units to be aware and to call up immediately if seen. Annie was thinking frantically. She didn't know the area well. "How far is that last hit from Battle?"

There was brief silence, then the supervisor came back, "About four miles, give or take."

This had to be the connection; no chance it was a coincidence.

"Can you get some units to be in the vicinity of where that mast is. Did you say Sedlescombe?"

The supervisor confirmed the location and Annie asked for a firearms team to meet her at the entrance to the golf club. She'd go with a marked car from Hastings on blues and be there as soon as she could. She heard the call go out for a response as she turned to Tony, "Tell the boss what's happened. Tell him I'm on my way out there and I'll call him as soon as I have anything."

Tony didn't even bother replying, pushing past and heading up to Cornish. The uniform sergeant shouted to another officer to head down and get a car started; they'd meet him in the back yard. "Jump in with me. Reckon we can get there in about ten minutes, tops."

CHAPTER 70

Lake had been in the main office getting an update on how far from Burwash the teams had got when his phone had beeped, the tone indicating a text message. He'd taken the phone from his jacket pocket, looking absently at it as he talked, then stopped. The message came from a withheld number and said only, "truffles.inch.removed". What the fuck was that all about? It beeped again, this time a picture. He opened the image: it was Clarke sat on a bed, her wrists bound and fixed to the frame. There was a figure behind her, only seen from the chest down and dressed in a blue forensic suit, a gloved hand holding Clarke's head up to the camera by the ponytail. In her hand was a small whiteboard, and across it, written in Clarke's own handwriting were four words. 'Come Now. Come Alone.'

He looked at the first message again, recognising it now as a location address. Emergency services nationally had begun using the what3words app a couple of years previously. If you were lost somewhere and had the app on your phone, you could send the location and it would direct searchers to within metres of you. It had to be where Clarke was being held. Lake knew it was a mistake and he was probably putting both of them in danger, but what other options did he have? With the camera in Livingston's office, and Annie's home being entered, he didn't know if they were being followed, if there were contacts in the station or on the enquiry passing on information. He at least should call Annie, but she would only tell Cornish, and half the force would head to the location he'd been sent in the message. He had to take the chance on his own, stupid as it might be.

As soon as he was on his own in his car he checked the wording from the message against the app on his phone, and it came up as halfway along Hurst Lane, near Sedlescombe. He could be there in a quarter of an hour. He'd call Annie when he was near the location. That way, he could have a good ten minutes at least before the cavalry arrived, figuring that would give the outward appearance that he'd followed the instructions and come on his own.

The unmarked car shot out of the rear yard onto Bohemia Road, swerving to narrowly avoid another vehicle, and headed up Bohemia Road, turning right onto the A21 towards Sedlescombe, the accelerator as flat to the floor as he dared. Within a few miles he turned off towards Sedlescombe village, slowing as he approached and turning onto Brede Lane. He stopped just short of the junction with Hurst Lane, parking the car on the entrance to a field. He should call, he knew he should call, but not yet. Check out the address first, then call. He turned his phone to silent, not noticing that there were no call bars showing, got out of the car and began to walk slowly up the lane towards a small cottage in the distance.

Lake kept close to the hedgerow as he neared the building. It sat on its own, a whitewashed front facing the road behind a small front garden and dilapidated wooden fence tilting precariously outwards, the paint flaking away. There was no gate; it had probably long since rotted away, if the rest of the fence was any indication. As he drew closer, he began to fully appreciate the condition of the place: plaster on the walls was cracked and falling off, old single-paned sash windows filthy with dirt. The whole building had the appearance of being ready to fall down if you slammed a door too hard. To his side of the house was a garage in no better condition than the rest of the property. The door was pulled down and there were no windows to allow him to see if there was a vehicle inside.

He moved on to the back garden, and it was a stretch to call it that. It had a similar picket-style fence as the front and there were a couple of sheds that sat in disrepair, bushes and weeds sprouting all over, long since unattended. An old hand water pump sat near the back door.

Any approach from the lane at the front would be easily spotted. Lake figured he could use the cover of the outbuildings to get close enough to at least glimpse in the downstairs windows, work out if this was just another decoy or not. He could then make a decision as to his next move. As much as he wanted to get Clarke back, there was no point him acting rashly and getting both of them killed if he could avoid it. If she was inside, he would hopefully see how many others were with her, without being spotted. The message had said to come now, but he had the benefit of the sender not knowing where he was when he'd received it, or when. As far as they knew, he might still be sitting at Hastings and not yet even noticed it on his phone. He had to use that as his advantage; he had nothing else.

A metal baton and a can of pepper spray weren't going to be much use if they had guns. It was now he fervently wished he worked in America; at least then he'd have had an arsenal of weapons in the boot of his car, if the reality cop shows were anything to go by. It wasn't until he'd arrived that he realised he hadn't even picked up his bloody radio. Now he had to rely on using a phone, when he could have just pressed the orange emergency button on the top of the radio and had officers descending on his location without having to say a word.

He moved across from the hedge to the back of the property, the long grass soaking his trousers and his shoes sticking in the mud. He paused at the back fence. Shit, this was fucking stupid. What was he thinking, running off down here with no backup? It worked in the movies but, in real life, it never ended well. He had no idea if there was one person with Clarke, or ten, or if she was even inside.

A low gate hung loose on its hinges, and he moved through it to stand behind the shed nearest the back door. So far, nobody had appeared in response, the problem was, with the filth and dirt over the windows, he wouldn't have been able to see if there was someone looking out or not. He noticed a couple of the windows on the first floor at each corner of the cottage looked cleaner at the bottom of the panes than the others, seemingly out of place against the rest. Had whoever may be inside given them a wipe over so they could see across the fields? He edged around to the side, eyes sweeping across the whole back of the building. There were three ground-floor windows on this side, one nearest the door and two at each corner.

Lake crouched down, hoping it would give him some cover if anyone was looking, and moved to the window on the far corner, stopping directly underneath it. Slowly, he raised his head to gain a view inside and stopped instantly as he saw through the murk coating the window a figure sitting on a low bed. They were side on to his field of vision, facing a table, and there was light coming from what looked like a computer monitor set on top of it. He couldn't see what was on the screen with it angled away from the window, but the figure was certainly transfixed by what they were looking at. Lake knew this had to be Clarke. He moved slightly, standing up with his back flat to the wall, to try to get a better view into the room. Clarke seemed to be alone. It was possible that an attacker was sat below the edge of the window out of sight, but at least she wasn't surrounded by a group waiting for him. He desperately wanted to tap on the window, draw her attention to let her know he was there.

Kneeling down, Lake half-crawled along to the next window a few feet from the back door before edging up to look inside. Nobody. Just an old kitchen table and a couple of chairs. No plates or mugs or any signs that there had ever been other people present. But there had to be? The image he'd been sent had a person standing behind Clarke, meaning at least one other individual had been at the cottage. His problem was, where were they now?

He pulled his baton out from his belt, extending it as quietly as he could. There was no point in taking the pepper spray out as well, he needed at least one hand free to try the door to see if it was locked and he doubted he'd get the chance to accurately administer the contents against an attacker in a confined space without getting most of it on himself as well. Lake had suffered the effects before from an over-enthusiastic colleague and knew how incapacitating it was; the last thing he needed was to be blind and unable to breathe dealing with an opponent. Better to smack whoever you needed to around the head with a lump of metal as hard as you could if you got the chance. No matter how big they were, he reckoned he could swing a baton with enough force to nearly take the top of someone's head off with it, and that was certainly what he had every intention of trying to do if the opportunity presented itself.

CHAPTER 71

Clarke saw the male walking down the lane towards the cottage on the monitor. They were hugging the hedge line. They walked in an unusual manner and then disappeared from view, having crossed the road towards the fields at the rear. She had no idea where Janus was; he'd left the room some time ago, but she was unable to read the time on the monitor from the bed. It could have been an hour, maybe more. Was he in the next room or outside somewhere? The photo he'd staged after cleaning the room had been sent to someone for the purpose of getting them here, that much was obvious. He'd told her to write the four words down, with whoever it was intended for told to come on their own and immediately. It depended on when he sent the image as to how immediate that was. He could be lying in wait outside, ready for them. If she shouted to alert them then she would alert Janus as well and he'd already told her that would result in two people dying instead of one. She wasn't prepared for someone to die on her behalf.

She watched as the male disappeared behind the hedge, presumably to approach from the back of the cottage. She couldn't yet make out their face, but they were wearing a grey suit. It had to be a copper. Who else would he have sent the image to? It was hardly going to be her ex. The one person she knew who would come on his own in response to the message would be Lake, and as much as she hoped she was wrong, there were no alternatives she could think of. He wouldn't think twice about putting himself in the firing line; he had that bloody self-confidence about him that he was bulletproof. He went into stupid situations always thinking he would be the one to come out unscathed. Surely that scar down his face should be a constant reminder to him that he wasn't invincible? No, if he was the one the image was sent to, she didn't doubt for a second he would go there on his own to try to rescue her, the bloody idiot.

She had stopped trying to pull at the restraints holding her to the bed, her wrists were now raw and bleeding where the plastic cable ties had cut in. She had known there was no way she could break them, but that hadn't stopped her trying. The bed was fixed to the floor with bolts, so she couldn't even drag it across to the table and try to use the laptop to contact someone. Janus was no fool; they had learnt that clearly in the last week or so. Every detail, every step was set out in advance and the response to every action by the police anticipated.

She waited, scanning the four views on the screen to see where Lake had gone, but he hadn't reappeared. He must be at the back somewhere but one of the cameras only showed the fields, the other a tight angle on the back door. It must be set up virtually opposite to the door and she could see the corner of a window to the right of the frame. How she wished she could see all the back of the cottage. If Janus was out there somewhere, Lake would be easily spotted. If it came to a one-on-one physical battle then Clarke was more than confident who the victor would be: not only was Lake physically bigger then Janus, but she had also heard more than once how he was in a fight. No Marquis of Queensbury rules for him, and he wasn't one for police control and restraint tactics, either. His methods were to take his opponent down as quickly as possible, and if that meant elbows, knees or any other method, he was more than happy to apply it. She hoped in a way it would come to that. The issue was that she knew Janus was far too clever to get himself in a position where Lake had his hands on him. He had to have planned for this eventuality and she desperately wanted to shout a warning. She imagined Janus sitting in the field behind the cottage, waiting to hear her scream, ready for it and acting on it. She would stay silent; he couldn't have planned for that. Don't let him have the satisfaction.

Suddenly, the view of the rear door in the bottom corner of the screen showed Lake approaching it. She could see him moving, his back flat against the wall, his right arm reaching across to try the handle. The door swung open, and Lake stepped towards the threshold.

CHAPTER 72

Annie sat in the rear of the car behind PS Murray and PC Curtis, waiting for the armed unit to arrive. They were heading towards them from the opposite direction and had already called Murray on the radio to say they hadn't seen Lake's car as they sped down the A21. Murray turned to her, "ETA is less than five."

He was wearing an earpiece connected to his radio so was relaying the comms back to Annie as he received them. Curtis had the engine running, ready to go as soon as he was given the word. Problem was, Annie had no idea where Lake was, other than somewhere nearby.

Murray looked back at Annie, "The Tac-Ad wants to know if there's any information at all with regards to a property or suspects?"

Annie shook her head and Murray relayed back over his radio. They may as well still be sitting back at the nick with their thumbs up their arses for as much use as they were to Lake right then. *Why didn't he answer his phone? Did he think he could deal with it on his own?* If he did then he was fucking stupid. It wasn't how things worked; there were no lone heroes in real life. The only way they could get Clarke back alive was by a planned response, use the resources they had to control the area and make sure the perpetrators didn't escape. One officer acting alone wouldn't accomplish that.

She saw the blue lights on a large BMW 4x4 approaching where they were sat at the entrance to the golf club, and the other vehicle swung in next to them, the passenger opening his window as they pulled up alongside.

"Sarge, Terry Knight and that's Damian Rush," he indicated his passenger with his thumb without turning. "Where're we going? Tac-Ads said to wait, but we're happy to go whenever you want us to."

Murray told them to sit tight for the moment. They had nothing to go on and there was no point driving aimlessly around in marked cars waiting to be spotted and put Lake in more danger than he had himself. They would stand out to anyone.

Annie looked at her watch. It was past twelve-thirty, so Lake had a good half-an-hour head start. Murray had checked but there had been no further activations on the phone mast, which meant Lake had to be local to them. Trouble was, the intel cell had told her the mast covered almost as far as Battle to the west and Cripps Corner to the north, a radius of almost two and a half miles in each direction with a lot of ground in between. She tried Lake's phone again. Straight to voicemail.

That was when they all heard the explosion.

CHAPTER 73

The image on the screen went white a faction before the thump of the explosion ripped through the cottage, Clarke throwing herself down onto the bed to escape the blast. The last she had seen of Lake was as he had placed his foot at the entrance to the door, baton raised above his right shoulder ready to swing it. Her ears were ringing and dust was billowing into the room from where the door and curtain had been flung in from the concussive force. She sat up, tears streaming down her face as the dust began to settle, the image from the camera slowly clearing. The back door had disappeared completely, along with part of the wall surrounding its frame, and there was a crater in front of it in the garden. There was no sign of Lake but there was dark red blood over the faded white plaster around where the door had once stood. Chunks of what could only be flesh hung in places where they had struck, now fixed in place.

As her ears began to clear, Clarke could hear sounds from outside. It was Lake. He was screaming in agony, but he was alive. He must have been thrown back by the explosion, out of view from the camera that covered the doorway, and there was nothing she could do to help him. She raged against the restraints, blood now flowing freely as she pulled repeatedly on the ties, writhing to free herself. The monitor suddenly went dark, all the images stopping at the same time. Clarke was left with nothing other than her imagination as she heard Lake's cries from somewhere outside.

***

Janus sat in his car. He'd watched as Lake approached the cottage. He knew the detective wouldn't go from the front, preferring to attempt entry by the back where there was more cover from the outbuildings. The charges he had laid with pressure sensors were set so that anyone trying to enter by the back door would have no way of not triggering them unless they had jumped through the doorway into the kitchen. That was not going to happen. He had planned on Lake trying the door from the side first, leaving those areas clear, and had left the door unlocked. He wanted him to see Clarke, to think he had a chance of getting her back in one piece. It was the hope that had killed the detective, and he fully expected Lake to now be dead, or at the very least in a terminal condition. There had been sufficient explosives left to cause considerable harm, if not an immediate fatality. In the very unlikely possibility that Lake had survived, it would be a miracle if he made it to hospital, the injury trauma from the detonation would make sure of that.

There would be calls to the police of the explosion, but with the risk of a secondary device, they would be told to hold back at a rendezvous point until the army explosives experts attended. Paramedics would have to wait as well until they were given the go-ahead to get to the victim, all the while with Clarke sat in the cottage having seen her lover blown into the air and not knowing if it would be her next. The police response was so predictable. They had their protocols in place for explosive devices and he knew they would stick rigidly to them. He tapped a few buttons on his laptop, killing the cameras at the cottage and then wiping the hard drive of the computer he had left behind. They would get nothing from that other than a make and model available at any major store. He would have liked to have kept the camera running and watched as officers sat and waited to be called in while their former colleague lay dead or dying in agony, but he didn't want to run the risk of any interference to the laptop and leaving compromising information on it. Better to destroy it now; his clients had already enjoyed the pleasure of watching a police officer die. Clarke had been unaware that the laptop left open had also been streaming video of her as she had watched events. It mattered not that she was alive still. He had clients who wanted no more than just to watch her suffering. There was no need for her to die as well.

The army would take their time in getting Clarke out, moving at a snail's pace through the cottage, fearful of further tripwires, pressure pads or anything else that could trigger another explosion. He had one last task before he moved on to the final stage. Janus took a clip from the moments of Lake's approach to the door and the explosion, edited it down and then uploaded it to as many false social media accounts and news outlets as he could. They could concentrate on this for a while yet. That way, he could complete what he intended before he left for good.

CHAPTER 74

PC Curtis hit the accelerator hard and headed off with strobes and sirens wailing as soon as he saw the plume of black smoke off in the distance to their right, the firearms team following closely behind, gravel spraying out behind them as they sped off. Sergeant Murray was on the radio to the control room giving the commentary as they headed towards the smoke rising into the sky, feeding in the details as they got closer, calling for others to be sent on an emergency response to their location and asking for a rendezvous point where the rest could convene with ambulance and fire. Annie could only pick up one side of the conversation, but Murray knew what he was doing, an experienced sergeant organising the response with sharp commands over the mike. The two vehicles were driving at the limit of their capabilities, covering the ground between the golf club and Hurst Lane in less than four minutes. Curtis stopped their car a few hundred metres into the lane from the junction.

The cottage lay ahead, pale smoke still visible over the property.

Murray turned in his seat, "Oscar 1 is running this now from the control room, we need to sit tight and keep obs from here. Another unit is going to put a block on at the other end of the lane. Once bomb disposal arrive then they can clear the building and we can go in. They've given a travelling time of forty-five minutes from Kent."

His voice was steady and in control, but Annie could see he wasn't happy with the directions he'd been given as she spoke, "That's what the top table have said and we know that's what we should do. Problem is, we know that Ged Lake was heading to somewhere here and that's possibly where Clarke is. There's no way in the world that this isn't the place he was coming to so I can't wait here if Lake's lying there injured."

She was already trying to get out the rear of the car, forgetting the doors could only be opened from the outside to prevent prisoners escaping. She pulled repeatedly on the door handle nevertheless before the door was pulled out of her hands and swung open, Murray standing beside it. Curtis was also out of the driver's door, and the two firearms officers were heading over to the group.

Murray looked at Annie as she stepped from the car, "If you weren't going, I was. Easy to give orders of the right thing to do from behind a desk. Bit different when you're standing down the road. You coming?"

They were already moving up the Lane. The firearms pair, Knight and Rush, had a quick conversation and then split up, Rush heading to the front of the cottage and stopping fifty metres short, kneeling down and training his G36 rifle at the front of the building. Knight joined Annie's group. He had a large medic kit on his back and had taken his Glock handgun from its holster on his hip, pointing it in front of him as they moved along the field behind the hedge to the back of the cottage. Lake's cries had now become softer moans as they got near, and without any communication between them, they all broke into a run.

Knight held out his left arm to stop Annie and the others at the back of the garage, still keeping his handgun pointed at the cottage. He called his partner on a point-to-point over the radio, "Damo, white face still clear?" He waited for the response, nodding to Murray as confirmation before relaying back to his partner, "Black face clear, one victim down. No movement seen from any of the windows. I'm moving in to see what I can do. Stand by." Most of the windows at the back were now shattered or completely missing.

He turned to the three behind him, "Any of you fired a handgun before? I need someone to provide cover while I see if there's anything I can do for the DI."

Murray was the only one to respond, "I was firearms in London before I transferred down her a few years ago.

Not saying I can hit a cow's arse with a banjo now but I can certainly get off enough rounds to make anyone get their head down."

He stuck out his hand and Knight handed his Glock over to him, along with a spare magazine from his belt. "It's loaded and ready, no safety, just plenty of pressure on the trigger. Fifteen rounds in the gun and fifteen in the spare mag. If you use all of them up and someone's still shooting at us then we're pretty much fucked anyway. You two," he indicated Annie and Curtis, "stay here until we get to the DI and I wave you in."

He turned back to Murray, "Ready?"

Murray nodded, placing his left hand on Knight's shoulder and pointing the gun towards the back of the cottage, moving it from window to window as they went forwards to where Lake lay in front of the sheds. As much as Annie wanted to run in, she knew better than to put all four of them at risk of a shooter from the cottage. She watched as Knight knelt beside Lake then looked over his should back at her, shaking his head. She couldn't wait any longer and ran towards them, trying to keep low and make herself as small a target as she could, but at the same time knowing any half-decent shot could take them all out with ease. Curtis stayed with her on the left, using his own body as a shield between Annie and the cottage.

As soon as she got to Lake, she knew there was no chance of him surviving his injuries. The explosion had taken his right leg almost up to the top of the thigh, the tattered remains a mess of blood and bone. His left was mangled and twisted at an impossible angle, shrapnel injuries covered his body and his suit was shredded.

Knight was trying desperately to fix a compression bandage to Lake's right thigh, but she could see it was pointless, with the blood soaking the cotton bandage and running over Knight's hands as he tried to apply pressure. He turned to her, "He's bleeding out from his femoral. He should be dead by rights already. God knows what internal injuries he's got as well. Even if we got here straight away with an ambulance, he wouldn't make it."

Annie knelt with difficulty beside Lake's head. His eyes were open but fixed and glazed as they faced up at the dark skies. His breathing was coming in shallow rasps, blood running freely from his mouth in dark streams.

She took his hand in her own, "Ged, it's Annie. We're with you."

Whether he could hear her or not, she didn't care. She just wanted him to know he wasn't alone as he died here, in a shitty garden behind a shitty cottage. His body hitched once and then was still, a slow breath escaping, and then nothing. She closed his eyes and Murray took off his fluorescent jacket and laid it across Lake's body.

Curtis shouted, jarring the others around the body, "She's in here. It's the Super." He had gone to the side of the building as the others had tended to Lake and was now standing looking into a window. Using his baton, he smashed the glass that remained in the pane. He didn't wait for a response and climbed in, dropping out of sight. Annie got up, stumbling slightly, and ran to the window Curtis had disappeared into. He was already over by Clarke, using a small knife to cut the cables from her torn wrists and helping her up from the bed back to the window.

He looked out at Annie, "Best go out the way I came in sarge, least we know it's safe."

He had a point, his still being alive being the assurance to his comment. Leave the rest of the cottage to be checked later. Annie was as sure as she could be that it was now empty. If there had been anyone inside, they'd had more than ample opportunity to fire on any of them while they had been trying to help Lake.

Clarke was standing the other side of the window, dazed and confused.

"C'mon Ma'am, out ya go." Curtis was doing his best to urge Clarke to move, and he threw his jacket over the bottom of the window to cover the shards of glass still in the frame so she could scramble out, falling onto the weeds outside. Annie helped her up as Curtis climbed back through, putting an arm around Clarke to support her. Annie stepped in front to shield Clarke's view of Lake but was too slow, the look of horror on the Superintendent's face followed swiftly by her collapse again to the floor, pulling the PC down with her.

"Murray, help get her to the car, we need to get her away from here now." The sergeant had already handed the gun back to Knight and run over, helping Curtis get Clarke up and moving her away from the cottage, taking the same path they had used to enter.

Annie slumped back against the wall. She could see Knight on his radio, and no doubt there would be some fallout over their actions. They'd managed to get Clarke back against the odds but, in the process, another police officer was dead. They'd been played the whole time. Clarke was just the decoy to lure Lake there after all. If he'd gone through the window, he would still be alive.

She was looking back when she saw the camera on the front of the shed, pointing at the remains of the back door. Someone had watched. The whole thing had been watched.

CHAPTER 75

They had all pulled back to the cars, with the exception of Knight, who remained at the rear behind the garage, and Rush, still covering the front of the cottage. Curtis and Murray took Clarke away on blues, heading to the Conquest Hospital, not bothering to wait for an ambulance.

Annie stood alone in the lane. The rain had started again, a steady downpour, and she was getting soaked. She pulled her coat tightly around her, hearing sirens echoing in the distance as they headed towards her.

Minutes passed and a marked car pulled up at speed a short way behind where she was standing. She turned, walking back to it as Cornish stepped out from the passenger seat. "I won't bother asking what you were thinking. I'd like to think I'd have done the same in your position but I'm not so sure." He looked haunted, his face as grey as the clouds above.

"What a waste of life." She struggled to keep the anger and sadness running through her under control. "He didn't have a chance."

She'd been updated by Tony over the phone that Lake's murder had been uploaded to various sites and was also in the media's possession. She hoped at least the latter had the decency not to run any of it.

"Come back to the station; there's no point in standing around here. The bomb squad will have to clear the rest of the place before we send in forensics and search teams and that's going to take a few hours." Cornish put his arm out but Annie walked past, getting into the back of the car he'd just exited, closing the door behind her.

They drove back in silence, broken only by Cornish occasionally taking and making calls. When they arrived back at Hastings, the press parted at the rear gates to allow the car in without the usual thrust of cameras and mikes towards it. The station was sombre, officers in tears in places, as Annie walked to the Superintendent's office with the DCI.

She drank a coffee as Cornish made more calls, speaking to the Chief and getting updates. She told him what had happened, how Clarke had been the decoy all along to draw Lake to the address, the camera covering all that had happened. She had nothing left in her. Whoever had done it was gone in the wind. Four people dead and no closer to finding out who was responsible than they had been on day one.

Cornish told her that he'd heard from the officers at the hospital. Clarke wasn't hurt other than the injuries to her wrists and whatever drugs that had been injected into her during her time at the cottage. He had two detectives with her to follow up on what she'd told Murray and Curtis on the way to the hospital. All she could say about her attacker was he used the name Janus, give a physical description, and that it all seemed to revolve around an enterprise to provide online murders for those prepared to pay the price to watch.

Annie sat, shaking her head in disbelief. They hadn't been able to find a motive because there was no motive. Innocent people killed just so that a person with a large enough bank balance could live out their fantasies vicariously over the web. They would try to break down and decode the laptop she had seen on the table in the room where Clarke had been held. It would have been wiped, she imagined, but they would try anyway. Lake's body would be recovered back to the mortuary, his ex-wife having been found and told what had occurred. Was that it then? Was it over?

CHAPTER 76

Annie sat alone in Lake's office looking at his desk. Tony had been in to check on her, asking her to stay with his family for a few days once they had finished at Hastings and moved back to the MIT office to continue the investigation in the days and weeks to come. She declined, of course. All she wanted was to get Bella, go home, and shut the door on the world. Nothing could have prepared any of them for what had happened in the few short days since the first body had been found at Glyne Gap. The repercussions would be felt across the force for years to come, and the murders would be trawled over by armchair sleuths on internet sites and dramatic reconstructions on the television, the killer only gaining greater notoriety as the years passed.

She looked at the time on her phone: 6.10 p.m. The bonfire festivities would be starting in earnest around the county in less than an hour. It had stopped raining at last, meaning the crowds would be turning out in their droves. She wished she had a change of clothes; the ones she was wearing stank of smoke and damp.

Cornish had told her to go home. There was nothing else she could do for the night. They had cleared the cottage, finding another charge set just inside the front door, should anyone have tried to enter that way. The search teams would go in on Friday morning after CSI finished their examination, now that it had been considered safe to do so by the army. She had low expectations they would find anything useful; the male calling himself Janus had been too careful so far.

'Ride of the Valkyries' began to play on her phone and she answered the call without bothering to check the number, "Hello."

"Hello Annie. Had a bad day?" The voice on the end of the line had an electronic quality, similar to what she had heard used by Stephen Hawking on documentaries. She knew instantly who it was.

"Janus?"

"Apologies for DI Lake. It wasn't personal." The voice was flat, no emotion coming from it.

Annie gripped the phone tightly, "Why are you ringing me? Is it fun for you?"

"No Annie, as I told you and told Superintendent Clarke repeatedly, it's business. My only regret in all this is that we never got the chance to meet. Such a shame."

"We can resolve that whenever you want, you piece of chicken shit. You sit behind a screen playing your games with people's lives, all the work being caried out

by someone else so you don't get your hands dirty."
She wanted him in the office with her, with her hands
around his throat, taking the life from his body the way
he had taken Lake's.

"I think you'll find that the late DI Lake was all my
own work. I wanted that at least to be more personal,
so we had that between the two of us going forwards.
If you are intent on meeting me though, that can be
arranged. Take a look in your coat pocket, there's a
special invite for you."

The line went dead, and Annie sat staring at the
phone. What did he mean, check her coat? She picked it
up from the floor beside her where she'd dropped it. The
waxed jacket was still dripping, and she began going
through the pockets. She stopped as her fingers touched
a slip of paper in the top left pocket. She withdrew her
hand, pulled on a latex glove and then removed the
paper, still dry, and unfolded it on a fresh sheet of A4
paper on the desk.

There was a single sentence printed on the paper;
"FIND THE 200 YEAR OLD GUY". What the hell was that
supposed to mean? It had to be related to Guy Fawkes.
There wasn't some male double-centenarian around
that Annie was aware of. She lifted the screen on her
laptop and typed 'world's oldest Guy Fawkes' into the
search engine. Top of the page that came back was an
article on the 'Battel Bonfire Boyes'. She clicked on the
link, puzzled by the spelling. The page that came up

was from the Battle Bonfire Society and talked about their pride in having the world's oldest effigy to Guy Fawkes. The head, which unlike the body was never burnt, apparently dated back as far as 1795. Was Janus saying he intended to be in Battle, after all that had happened? There was no rationale for that. *He should be well away by now? Why leave himself open to the risk of being found by going to Battle tonight?*

She called Cornish and he immediately came to the office, by which time Annie had bagged the note and made several photocopies. Cornish picked up one of the copies then looked at the information on her screen, "Why? What's in it for this Janus to be in Battle this evening? He's killed a police officer, we have Clarke back safe. What purpose could he have for still being local? He knows we've got everyone available searching for him?"

"He still wants to show us he's smarter than us. You only have to look on the internet to see how many people will be in Battle tonight. Even if he is there, we have no idea what he might look like and he can just stand in the crowds and laugh at us. He'll take a selfie and upload it to the media to have a final dig at how crap we are."

Annie was racking her brain to think of some advantage they might gain, some way to find Janus among the crowds. Facial recognition was a non-starter. They had no cameras with that capability in the town and they didn't have a photo of Janus to compare it with anyway. "He wants me there, for whatever reason. Otherwise, he'd have just sent this to one of the news outlets."

"If you think I'm going to lose two of my team to this fucker in one day then you are sadly mistaken, DS Bryce." There was no doubting the passion behind Cornish's comment.

Annie tried another approach, "There will be hundreds of officers in Battle tonight. I'll take someone with me. He won't be able to grab me off the street, will he? We can put out staff in plain clothes, get extra into the CCTV room to monitor the cameras. It's the only chance we have to find him. You must see that?"

Cornish stood, staring her in the face. "This won't happen without the Chief's sign-off. You know that, right?"

He was in, and if the Chief agreed, she might at last get face to face with Janus, and maybe hand out some punishment of her own.

CHAPTER 77

The crowds were ten deep along the Battle High Street footpaths, spilling in and out of the pubs waving plastic cups of beer and wine. The roads through the town had been closed to traffic earlier to prepare for the parade, and the main procession was due to start at 7.45 p.m., with a flare signalling the departure. They would head along the High Street and down towards the station before turning and heading back along the same route and into the Abbey Gatehouse, with the abbey traditionally involved every year. The marchers would then return to the green in front of the abbey, where the bonfire would be set alight and the firework display begun.

Annie stood at the entrance to the abbey grounds, looking out at the masses in front of her. Everywhere she turned there were police officers in fluorescent jackets, body-worn cameras clipped to the fronts as they walked among the crowd in pairs. Police Support Unit vans full of officers kitted out in public order equipment were parked in Mount Street to the north and Powdermill

Lane to the south, ready for deployment. Additional police were sequestered at the small police station opposite Market Road. Cornish had used one of the offices there to set himself up with the PSU commander, so he was nearby should Janus be located. It felt to Annie as if half the force were in Battle and she was worried this would spook Janus and convince him to alter his plans. He had been so careful until then. Why put himself at any risk when he didn't need to?

Cornish had arranged for one of the TSU guys to have a drone ready to go in the air at a moment's notice. He was sat in the abbey car park, the drone in a cordoned-off area beside him. *Much use that'll be*, thought Annie, *there is no way it will find anyone in all of the thousands in town for the celebrations*. It may come into its own though if they had to chase across the abbey grounds at the rear. They were closed to the public and so there shouldn't have been any people at the back. She pulled the collar up on her coat, her hair now plastered to her head. The temperature had dropped throughout the day but a steady, misty rain for the last hour had done nothing to dampen the spirits of the revellers. The festivities would go ahead regardless. Checking her watch, she saw it was fast approaching the time for the parade to begin, with marshals trying to clear the main procession route along the road and taking their places every few feet apart.

She shifted her weight onto her left leg, the stump on her right sore and aching where she had barely been able to remove the prosthetic in the last thirty-six hours. There were kids running up and down waving sparklers, trying to make patterns or write their names in the cold air, parents looking on anxiously ready to jump in and grab their offspring before they shoved the white hot stick in their hand into another child's face. Everywhere, people were enjoying themselves, blissfully unaware of what might take place.

The Chief had called a media briefing at headquarters for 8 p.m., that way ensuring that most of the mainstream news teams would be out of the way in Lewes and not sitting around Hastings. This had been Tony's idea, with Cornish jumping on the suggestion. There would be a photographer from the local rag there to record the evening's events, but that was standard. What had gone in their favour was that there was always a large police presence. Shipping in a few more PSUs to sit just outside the town and be available would go unnoticed, and similarly the plain clothes teams mingling with the crowds. The time of year and weather helped, with the teams wearing assorted beanie hats to cover their earpieces and only the clear, coiled wire perhaps giving the game away if you looked closely as it disappeared beneath the collar.

The Chief would be giving the bare details around Lake's death, trying a positive spin around Clarke having been safely recovered. It was the only good news they'd had to give in days. She was still in hospital for further observations until they knew what had been pumped into her system. Annie had managed to speak briefly to her on the phone of one of the officers guarding her room. She wanted Clarke to know what Lake had said about their relationship and that the details would stay with her. There was no need for it to become public knowledge; it wouldn't help Lake or Clarke and made no real difference. Clarke sounded grateful, thanking her. It was a small gesture, but she could grieve for Lake privately in the days ahead.

A flare went off with a loud bang, and Annie panicked, looking around her, expecting to see people being thrown from an explosion. It was only the maroon signalling the parade was starting at the other end of the town. Cheers rang out along the road ahead of her as groups jostled to get a better position. There was a pair of officers to the right of Annie, chatting happily with members of the public, neither seemingly taking any notice of anything else. Cornish had decided to keep the details to a small core of officers deployed specifically for the purpose of looking for Janus. The rest of those in the town were on duty solely for the bonfire celebrations, and she tried to excuse the pair next to her. They were blissfully unaware of what else was going on, doing their best to portray the community side of the police, and a friendly approach to the public in general. Those hunting for Janus were on a separate channel on the radios, with their own operator in the control room.

As the parade headed along the High Street, the crowds pressed closer to the road, marshals vainly attempting to hold them in check as the marchers came into view carrying their blazing torches above them. The Guy Fawkes, over ten feet tall this year, was drawn along in the middle of the group as they passed the, as yet, unlit bonfire on the green beside the abbey for the first time. Marshals let families cross the road as soon as the procession had passed so they could now congregate closer to the bonfire, waiting for the return of the marchers.

Annie felt her phone vibrate in her pocket and grabbed it. She opened the message from the withheld number: a photo with the words 'FIND ME' printed across it. She used two fingers and enlarged the image, not recognising what she was looking at. The photo showed the ruins of an old stone building and she called to the two officers nearby, "Either of you two local?"

One shook her head, but her male colleague headed towards Annie, "Yeah, I am. Work out of the nick over here."

The officer was bundled up against the weather, a thick scarf around his neck and his peaked cap pulled down and black gloves on his hands.

"Any idea where this is?" Annie handed him the phone and he took off a glove to look at the image.

He turned his face towards her, a puzzled look on it, "It's the dormitory remains beside the walled garden in there." He indicated behind him towards the abbey with his thumb.

Annie started to run towards the gatehouse entrance, open for the evening to allow the procession to enter. "You two, with me, and switch on your body cams."

She took her phone back, thrusting it into her coat pocket. "Get on the radio and let control know I think the suspect for DI Lake's murder is in the grounds of the abbey. Use Channel 3. And tell them to let DCI Cornish know. I want the drone in the air overhead now."

She was thinking rapidly: get the PSU teams to move in from Powdermill Lane and head up towards the abbey, cutting off any escape that way into the woods. She heard the male officer she'd spoken to relaying all her commands as the second constable trailed in their wake, the male PC barking out her orders into his radio and pausing for the response. She hoped he was getting the right answers back as she held up her warrant card to the volunteer at the gatehouse and continued straight through, She turned to the male constable, "Where's the ruins?"

The local officer was at her side and pointed straight ahead as they made their way through the abbey into the grounds. It was quieter there, with the noise from the crowd slightly distant as the trio made their way along the gravel footpath. Annie held up a hand, trying to get her bearings, and remembering the image she'd been sent.

"It was taken from over there." The male officer was pointing through the ruins towards the side. "It goes off at a right angle by the walled garden."

They made their way into the ruins, moving slowly, eyes adjusting to the darkness away from the bright lights of the High Street. Annie took her phone out to look again at the photo and stopped, momentarily confused, as she tried to understand out why the mobile wasn't working, the screen dark and unresponsive.

A choking sound behind her made Annie turn and she saw the female constable stagger back to the wall, a hand clutching at her throat as blood began to pour down the front of her fluorescent jacket, a shocked look on her face. As Annie started to move to help, the male officer kicked out at her leg, tripping her onto the floor, and she felt something metal touch the skin at the back of her neck before an electric shock surged through her body, making it spasm then go rigid. Her teeth ground together and Annie felt her arms pulled down to her sides as she was rolled over onto her back.

Janus, it could only be him, stood over her, his legs straddling her as he knelt down on her stomach, his knees across her elbows. "Hello Annie. So good to meet in person at last."

She tried to move, to throw him off, but he used his weight to hold her down. With her arms pinned beside her, she could do little except try to arch her back to buck him off, but stopped as he brought the straight razor down toward her face, the yellow of his fluorescent top shining off the blade, the red light on his bodycam flashing to show it was recording.

"After all that's happened, you still ran off into the dark with people you didn't know. I knew you would, so eager to catch the bad man, but I had hoped for better from you. If you'd acted with your brain instead of your heart, then you could have arranged for all of the resources to be in place without moving from the front of the abbey, couldn't you?" His voice was calm but the tone wasdisappointed, almost as if he was scolding her for her behaviour.

Janus ran the steel of the blade gently down her left cheek, drawing a thin trail of blood which ran down her face. The blade was so sharp she barely felt it as it cut deeply through her skin.

He moved his face closer, the blade now pressed against her throat, preventing any movement. "I have to say, I wasn't expecting you to go rushing in to try and save Lake. That was very much against procedure. But, never mind, it changed nothing other than having you there to watch him die."

Annie glared up at the face above her, the thin wire-framed glasses and dark eyebrows on a handsome face.

He was fairly non-descript in the uniform; he could be any of the hundreds of officers in the area. She wouldn't give him the pleasure of asking how or why. Let him talk. The longer this continued, the greater the chance they would be found.

His next comments put paid to that hope instantly, "You really should have checked first who you were taking with. This radio's not even turned to the right channel. Oh, it's still on. If I'd switched it off then your control room might have wondered why and sent someone to check on the officer it belongs to. I couldn't have that, what with him now being in the boot of his own car. If you are putting officers on points then may I suggest double-crewing in future. That way, they're less likely to end up as a statistic."

Annie realised that all the conversations she'd heard the supposed officer making on the radio had never been transmitted. He was having a conversation with himself. The female constable now slumped dead against the stone wall wouldn't have been able to hear the other side or the response from the control room as he'd been on the other channel. No one was coming for her, not yet, not until they realised she was missing. Her phone, he must have switched it off before he handed it back to her. So stupid, ready to just take for granted that it was a police officer simply because they had a uniform on. There were so many officers deployed for the night, it was no surprise the pair she had taken with her wouldn't have known each other. Her arms were going numb with the weight of Janus pressing on them; she had to do something before she was completely helpless. Her fingers scrabbled against her trousers, trying to get to the contents of her pocket.

Janus was enjoying himself, "You know how I got Lake's number and yours? Check your phone, Annie. I've been listening into your conversations, had access to all of its contents for days now. Technology is a wonderful thing, isn't it, I personally couldn't get by ..."

He grunted in pain as his body arched, rolling off Annie and onto the gravel. Janus had dropped the blade and was clutching at his left leg, a pen now sticking out of his calf.

She rolled, grabbing for the cut-throat razor and slashing it down towards Janus, hoping to catch him, but he drew his legs in then kicked out with his right, his booted foot catching Annie on the forehead and snapping her head backwards, the blade flying out of her hand. She rolled on her front and tried to stand, her head spinning as her prosthetic foot slipped on the wet gravel and she fell forward again onto her hands. Blood and rain had run into her eyes, and she swiped it away with the back of one hand, the other searching the ground half-blindly for the blade. Her groping hand touched cold metal and she grabbed it quickly, cutting her fingers on the blade but grateful she had hold of it before Janus. She managed to stand, the world around her suddenly erupting with explosions as the firework display was set off. Rockets soared into the night sky, the bright, coloured flashes illuminating the whole abbey grounds and Annie saw her phone lying on the gravel, the screen smashed and useless, and any chance she had of calling for help lost.

She could hear the shouting from the crowds outside the abbey in the street as the fireworks soared and blazed above her. She was alone. Janus was nowhere to be seen.

CHAPTER 78

Janus made his way back through the woods, onto the footpath, and out to where he had left the police car off Powdermill Lane, backed into the field behind the wooden gate. His leg was throbbing from the puncture wound in his calf as he took the chain back off the gate and opened it before returning to the car. Even if it had been spotted empty, he had doubted it would have caused much concern; there was far too much happening to worry about an officer who had, most likely, gone into the woods for a piss.

He pulled slowly out of the gate, not bothering to close it behind him, turning left and then left again onto Lower Lake, that part of the road now opened with the procession back on the High Street. Janus then headed right, following Marley Lane all the way towards the A21, that way missing out the large police presence still at Sedlescombe. He would ditch the marked car very soon, part way up. It would be too obvious, a Sussex Police car on the M25. Additionally, as soon as they identified which car it was, they would be able to pinpoint its location. He had a contingency in place, as ever: another clean vehicle left for him to collect. They would find this one with its sad contents later, by which time he would be back in London and in his office. He would take a break for a couple of weeks. It had, after all, been a very busy time and maybe he would travel to Europe, use his other bases there for a while.

He checked his speed, keeping it within the limit. Just a standard patrol car going about its duty.

He wondered how Annie would deal with all that had happened. He was sorry he had mentioned her phone now she was going to be alive; he would have liked to have checked up on her, but they would have figured out eventually how he had managed to know so easily what they were doing. If he had managed to get into their headquarters and Annie's house, he imagined they would be checking every device they owned. He had already taken the sim out of the burner phone he'd used to send the image of the abbey ruins to Annie and snapped it. He would destroy the phone as well. If she hadn't been so keen to charge into the grounds and bothered to check where the image had come from, she would have found it was just a few feet from where she had been standing. He had relied on her instead being focused on trying to arrest him. Sometimes people acted exactly as you expected them to. It was almost as predictable as the cheerleader home alone in a horror movie going to open the door and asking who was outside right before she was stabbed.

It was why he had to make his own life interesting; the world was such a dull place otherwise.

EPILOGUE

It had been over month since Lake's murder. A funeral had been held with full honours, and even the Home Secretary had attended, but that was more down to the media being present than for any other reason. Annie had gone with Clarke, standing several rows back from Lake's family. There was talk of the George Cross being presented to his ex-wife, not that it would bring any consolation to his children.

Every time Annie caught her reflection in a mirror she would remember Lake; she now had a matching scar on the left side of her face running down her cheek. Neater than his had been, a slim white line, and a constant reminder of Janus, as if she needed one.

The car he'd used to leave Battle had been located within hours, parked in a lay-by on the A21 to the north of Whatlington, the dead officer bundled into the boot, discarded as insignificant. Their family simply another destroyed by Janus. Annie had gone to that funeral as well as the young female constable who had gone with her and Janus into the abbey grounds. She had no words when she saw the girl's parents; it was her fault after all that their daughter was dead. If she'd waited, made sure to get the area cordoned off and brought the teams in methodically, the girl would still be alive. But she had known better, wanting to get to the person responsible for killing Lake only hours before and believing she was good enough to do it on her own, making the same fatal error he had.

They had suspended her immediately while an inquiry was conducted into the events that had led to three members of the public and three serving police officers being murdered in quick succession. The footage from the body-worn camera of the female officer killed in the abbey grounds would be scrutinised in detail to see if Annie's actions warranted any formal sanction.

Cornish had temporarily been put into a back office role at headquarters, but at least he was still at work. Annie spent her days at home, taking Bella for her daily walks and waiting for the outcome of the investigation into her actions. Tony would call in frequently, and she had relented to his constant requests and had dinner with his family the previous weekend. He'd told Annie that Livingston had been allowed to take early retirement on a full ACC pension. It must be nice to be looked after by your friends instead of getting the sack. She wondered how long the Chief would be before he followed him, the PCC having already intimated, if rumours were to be believed, that his contract was not going to be up for renewal the following year. Maybe the change of senior personnel would be good for the force, with new faces coming in from outside.

Annie kept in touch with Clarke through a call at least once a week. Jess had been given a period of sick leave but had gone back to work after only two weeks, the emptiness of her home matching the emptiness of her life. She had been told she would be getting a move to headquarters, taking on the role of Force Diversity Lead. Or, as she said bitterly to Annie, "Putting the dark-skinned woman up to show how advanced Sussex Police is in promoting minorities." It didn't matter to her; she couldn't stay in Hastings any longer and had already put her house up for sale.

Annie pulled on her coat and whistled, and Bella ambled through to the kitchen with her tail wagging enthusiastically.

"Come on you, let's get some fresh air." The sun was shining and it was a crisp December morning, the frost sparkling on the ground as she stepped outside and clipped the lead on the Labrador.

They headed out and along Beacon Road, turning into the fields where she unfastened the dog's lead from the collar. Bella wandered away, sniffing and then padding after Annie as she put on her headphones and began listening to a podcast by Louis Theroux on her phone.

Far above, whirring quietly, a drone flew unobserved.

ACKNOWLEDGEMENTS

This book is a work of fiction, as are all of the characters and events contained within it. I would like to thank the many colleagues I have worked with during my police career. Some of you, if you end up reading a copy of this book, may even recognise mannerisms and quirks of people you know. The dark sense of humour required to deal with some of the worst crimes that one person can do to another is often portrayed in police dramas. It doesn't mean that officers aren't taking their job seriously, it's just a coping mechanism to get through the trauma that they have to see and deal with.

It has taken me a long time and many attempts to put together my first novel. I had been encouraged by script writers and other novelists, who I have advised on policing matters, to put some of my own experiences down into a book. The problem with that, is each investigation relates to real people who have had their lives affected in one way or another, sometimes by terrible tragedy. Hence why I'm sticking with fiction,.

I am grateful to Lee Dickinson, Chief Editor at Bookediting.co.uk, for clearing up the many grammatical errors contained in my original draft and correcting my 'police speak'. Your help and advice have been tremendous. To Ruth Dugdall, thank you for your tips and suggestions, to gain help from an internationally published author with your pedigree is incredible.

To my wife, who read the manuscript before I sent it to anyone else, it's better for all of the things in this book to come from my mind, dark as it apparently is. Thank you for all your encouragement and support.

If you have taken the time to buy, borrow or otherwise obtain a copy of this book and have read and enjoyed it, thank you. Annie Bryce will be returning, I have invested too much in her to allow her to disappear to a desk job.

Finally, to all those detectives out there working long hours, missing birthdays, anniversaries and time with your families, remember that you do the job for a simple reason – to lock up the bad people and protect the rest.

Darren Bruce
June 2022

ABOUT THE AUTHOR

Darren Bruce is a retired Detective Sergeant with most of his career spent working on major crime and murder investigations in Essex and Suffolk. He has also been an advisor for script writers and authors. The Skinned Man is his debut novel. He lives in Suffolk.

You can follow Darren on Twitter *@darrenbruce55* or visit his website at *www.darrenbruce.co.uk*

Printed by Amazon Italia Logistica S.r.l.
Torrazza Piemonte (TO), Italy